THE
ACCELERATI

TRILOGY
BOOK 1

TESLA'S ATTIC

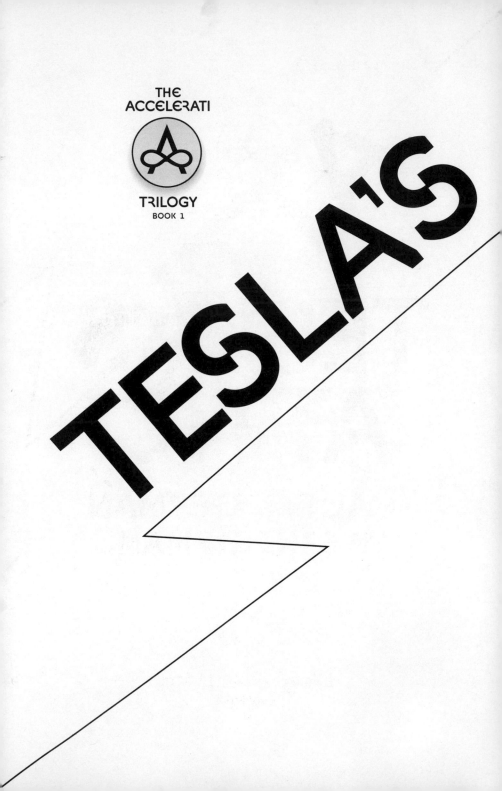

THE
ACCELERATI

TRILOGY
BOOK 1

TESLA'S

NEAL SHUSTERMAN
AND ERIC ELFMAN

𝒟ısɴᴇᴘ • HYPERION BOOKS
NEW YORK

Printed in the United States of America
10 9 8 7 6 5 4 3 2 1
G475-5664-5-13335

Library of Congress Cataloging-in-Publication Data
Shusterman, Neal.
  Tesla's attic/by Neal Shusterman and Eric Elfman.—First edition.
      pages cm.—(Accelerati trilogy; book 1)
  Summary: "With a plot combining science and the supernatural, four kids are
caught up in a dangerous plan concocted by the eccentric inventor, Nikola Tesla"—
Provided by publisher.
  ISBN 978-1-4231-4803-6
  [1. Inventions—Fiction. 2. Tesla, Nikola, 1856–1943—Fiction. 3. Colorado Springs
(Colo.)—Fiction. 4. Science fiction.] I. Elfman, Eric. II. Title.
  PZ7.S55987Te 2013
  [Fic]—dc23   2012039773

Reinforced binding

Visit www.disneyhyperionbooks.com

1 LIKE A HOLE IN THE HEAD

Nick was hit by a flying toaster. Or, to be more precise, a falling toaster. It was a chrome-plated antique made of such heavy metal that it left a dent in the wooden floor, but not before leaving a gash in Nick's forehead.

"Ouch!" was one of the tamer words Nick said as he fell off the rickety spring-loaded attic ladder, which retracted back into the ceiling like the landing gear of a spacecraft.

Danny, his younger brother, ran into the hallway and promptly shouted, "Dad! Nick got killed by the attic!"

There was certainly enough blood to suggest that he might have been killed, and although Nick was disturbed by the sight of his own blood, he was more worried about his father's reaction after all they'd just been through.

Their dad came running and quickly sized up the situation.

"It's okay, it's okay, it's okay," which is what he always said when things were clearly not okay. He took off his T-shirt and pressed it to the wound. He was sweaty from moving boxes into the house, and Nick suspected that this was not particularly hygienic, but when your head is gushing, you don't argue.

"Danny, get in the car," their father ordered, and, still strong from his old baseball days, he picked Nick up and carried him down the stairs.

"Dad, I can walk. It's my head, not my feet." Nick had just

turned fourteen, and he could not remember the last time he'd been carried by his father.

As they burst out of the warped and peeling front door of their new home, Nick had a horrible image of all the kids in the neighborhood watching this little domestic drama with mild amusement.

Great, Nick thought. *Just how I want to be introduced to the neighbors.*

Their car was still packed with most of what was left of their belongings, all still smelling faintly of smoke—a constant reminder of what was propelling them across the country. The car had broken down twice on their way to Colorado Springs, and Nick wondered if it would give out on them again between here and the emergency room.

"Just keep pressure on the wound," his dad said as he started the car and backed out, crushing one box or another in the driveway. With the shirt now as wet with blood as it was with sweat, they sped off into a neighborhood they didn't know, in search of a hospital they had no clue how to find.

If a fortune-teller had told Nick two months ago that he'd be leaving Tampa, Florida, and moving to Colorado Springs, he would have demanded his money back. There was simply no way. His mom was a well-respected dentist, and his dad, well, he worked regularly enough, and everyone knew and liked him. As far as Nick could see, their lives were built on some pretty solid ground.

Fires, however, have a way of consuming even the most well-built families.

Finding a hospital on your first day in a neighborhood poses its own set of problems, and GPS is nonexistent when your cell-phone service has been turned off because your father forgot to pay the bill. Nick suspected he would either heal or bleed out before they got there, because even in an emergency, his father was not a man who would ask for directions.

When they finally found it, Colorado Springs Memorial was no different from any other hospital. The emergency room was full of various coughs, fractures, and bloody makeshift bandages, all swimming in an air of impatience and irritation.

For the most part, Nick's bleeding had stopped, but he kept pressure on his wound. Beside him, Danny played a handheld video game while their father filled out forms and then tried to convince the Empress of Admissions that their insurance was good in Colorado. Nick figured it was like negotiating with terrorists.

Shortly before they took Nick in to get stitches, Danny, without looking up from his game, said to him, "Are you gonna die, too?"

Nick almost said something mean back to him for asking such a stupid question, but then an unexpected wave of understanding hit him. Or perhaps it was a concussion.

"I'm gonna be fine," Nick said. "We're all gonna be fine."

Danny finally looked up at his brother. "Prove it."

Nick remained silent. In theory, they had moved here to start a fresh, shining new life. But even the most promising theories can be impossible to prove.

When you see a fire raging out of control, it's hard to believe it's nothing more than a simple chemical reaction: potential energy released in the form of light and heat. It seems alive, with a soul as dark as the flames are bright. Watch it long enough and you can truly come to feel that its raging destruction is motivated by fury and a cruel desire to cause pain.

3

The blaze that had consumed Nick Slate's home and changed his life was that kind of fire, burning so hot and so fast that the house was reduced to cinders in a matter of minutes.

It seemed they all woke up at once, his father racing to Danny's room, his mother to Nick's. They bounded down the stairs, the smoke already so thick it was impossible to see.

Nick held his breath and got low, knowing his house well enough to be sure of what to do: make a right turn at the bottom of the stairs, go straight for five yards, then turn left and out the front door.

But time and space are very different when you're in a panic.

Nick bumped into a wall, lost his sense of direction, and took a gasping breath of black smoke. Immediately he began to cough and grow dizzy.

"Keep going, Nick!" he heard his mom say. "Don't stop!"

Then something in the kitchen exploded, sending a shock wave down the hallway and blowing the front door off its hinges. Through the smoke and flames Nick saw a smoldering portal into the night and he leaped for it, escaping onto their front lawn, where he joined his father and brother.

His mother had been right behind him.

But when he turned, she was gone, and there was nothing there but the burning house.

"Mom!" Nick shouted.

His father pushed past him and ran back to the door.

In his heart of hearts, Nick still believed that his father was the hero he had once been. He believed his dad would race into the flames and bring his wife out in his arms like the old photo of him carrying his new bride over the threshold.

But even before his dad got to the house, a second explosion threw him backward and collapsed the porch, blocking any entry into the house. The three were left standing there, stunned beyond wailing, watching their life crumble in on itself, taking Nick's mother with it.

The toaster left Nick with four stitches, simple and quick. The emergency room doctor spent the whole time describing the really bad wounds he'd had to sew up in his career, as if Nick's little forehead gash was inadequate. Nick would have to come back when an alien burst out of his chest—now *that* would require some serious knitting.

"A scar's not necessarily a bad thing," Nick's dad said as they drove back to the fixer-upper they had inherited. "A scar shows that you've lived. Harry Potter has a scar on his forehead, and look at him."

"Dad, Harry Potter's fictional," Nick said.

"You're missing my point." And for the rest of the ride back, their father glorified scar tissue to the point that Danny was determined to get a scar, too.

They approached their overgrown driveway and the weathered Victorian house behind it. Nick looked at the upstairs windows staring like perpetually mournful eyes and he felt a wave of nausea that had nothing to do with his injury.

"Hey," said his dad. "We've been through a lot." Very softly, he brushed his thick fingers over the gauze taped to his son's forehead. "Why don't you pick whichever room you want for your bedroom."

The house they were moving into had been empty for years, but the furniture still smelled like Great-aunt Greta. Nick had never met Great-aunt Greta, but he could be certain what she smelled like.

It was their father's decision to move here. Nick could have raised a stink and insisted they stay in Tampa, and he knew that his father, as broken as he was from the tragedy, would have given in. But instead Nick had said, "Let's do it," taking on the role of his father's sounding board—a role that used to be his mother's. "It'll be an adventure."

So they took what little they had from the hotel room they'd been squatting in for the previous two months, and they set off for Colorado.

Their father resumed unloading boxes from the car, while Danny planted himself in front of the TV and changed the channel from one version of snow to another, refusing to believe there was no cable.

Upstairs, Nick found the offending toaster where it had fallen, and picked it up.

It was an old thing of curved chromium steel with spots of rust that had begun to chew away at the chrome. The base was made of a black material that wasn't quite rubber and wasn't quite plastic, and its two deep slots were filled with coils of wire descending into darkness. It seemed ridiculously heavy for an object of its size.

There was something else about the toaster, too, something that troubled Nick, but he couldn't figure out what it was. One thing for sure—it was an ancient relic that belonged exactly where it had come from.

So Nick reached up and once more pulled down the trapdoor that led to the attic. The wooden ladder unfolded smoothly, and he backed away in case anything else decided to fall. When all seemed clear, he climbed up with the toaster.

He found himself in a space much larger than he'd expected. Bare wooden beams, covered with cobwebs, stretched to a pyramid point high above his head.

He looked for a place to put the toaster down, and realized

there wasn't a place. That's why it had fallen. The attic was packed with old stuff that could only charitably be described as junk:

Furniture so moth-eaten there was little more left than springs. A bicycle rusted beyond repair. A bulky reel-to-reel tape recorder. An antique box camera. Some kind of old-fashioned pump vacuum cleaner. An electric mixer with odd, flat paddles. Plus other objects of questionable technology, the purpose of which Nick couldn't begin to guess.

He pictured the room with the junk cleared away, and he realized the attic could make a very livable space.

Danny poked his head through the trapdoor. "Bet there's lots of spiders."

"Only the man-eating ones," Nick replied.

"Ha-ha," Danny said, but he retreated at the prospect anyway.

As he looked around at this boneyard of uselessness, Nick Slate had a simple idea. An idea that would not only change the direction of his life, but the very course of human existence.

He would hold a garage sale.

2 EVERYTHING MUST GO

If you asked Caitlin Westfield why she bought that old tape recorder at the garage sale, she'd have tons of logical explanations:

1. It was a "found object" she could use for her art project, arranging the parts into a deconstructed assemblage.
2. It was a cool-looking piece of retro technology, probably worth something to a museum if she didn't smash it to bits.
3. The new kid in town, who was selling it, looked like he could use all the money he could get.

All of those reasons would be true, but none of them was the answer. In all honesty, Caitlin couldn't say why she felt so compelled to buy it, except that she was drawn to it in an uncanny way.

It all began with a green flyer.

If it had been any other color, Caitlin might not have stopped to read it, but bright green was her favorite shade. She often painted her nails the exact same green. She took it as coincidence, though she would eventually come to doubt the very concept of coincidence.

ANTIQUES, VINTAGE TOYS, FURNITURE, TONS OF COOL STUFF, the flyer read, and Caitlin's mind was already spinning. Her calling—although her parents and her boyfriend, Theo, would call it a "hobby"—was taking charming, rustic, and sometimes rusting objects from years gone by and smashing them with a sledgehammer.

The results she would glue in aesthetically challenging patterns on canvas, turning garbage into art. She called it *garbart*.

Her art teacher, of course, was the highest order of imbecile, and kept failing her because she couldn't draw a bowl of fruit.

But, man, could Caitlin *smash* that fruit bowl.

She was one of those rare girls who managed to strike a perfect balance between being wildly popular and wildly original. She was the only cheerleader in her school's history to have her father file a patent for her, because she had personally redesigned the pom-poms that her entire squad now used: a clever accumulation of shiny objects that caught the eye—both figuratively and, occasionally, literally.

While garage sales were the prime hunting ground for her *garbart*, she had a particular interest in *this* garage, because she recognized the address. The house was something of a local legend, a sprawling eyesore plopped into an otherwise conventional suburban neighborhood. Not quite a mansion, but bigger than most of the homes on the street. Caitlin imagined someone would eventually buy it and turn it into either a bed-and-breakfast or a funeral parlor.

At any rate, she was curious to see who had moved in.

Her plan had been to go with Theo, but as usual he texted *rl*. Which meant he was "running late."

She texted back *mut*, their standard code for "meet you there," though she knew Theo wouldn't bother to show. Especially if there was a game on. So she called to remind him that he had promised to join her.

"Well, it's like they say," Theo told her, "the best-laid plans of bison men often go away."

Caitlin chose to believe that his habitual mangling of common expressions was clever and intentional, because the alternative was too troubling to consider.

In the end, Theo had said he'd come "if he could," which meant he wouldn't, so she resolved not to miss his presence.

She was just getting ready to leave her house when the storm hit. After a change in barometric pressure that fogged all the windows of her house, the sky let forth with the kind of psychotic determination that made people build arks. Caitlin had to admit that as much as she cared about the sale and the house, she didn't care enough to weather the weather.

She was ready to settle in for popcorn and a movie when she felt a sudden change of heart and raced outside into the rain.

Nick stood helplessly looking at the junk spread out on the long driveway, now getting even more ruined than it already was by the sudden downpour.

"Don't just stand there!" his father shouted. "Let's get this stuff into the garage!"

Nick, his father, and brother hurried out into the rain, frantically trying to carry it all to safety, but who were they kidding? It had taken more than an hour to put it all out. There was no way the three of them could bring it all in.

"I don't get it," Nick said, darting back to the garage, his arms full of stuff. "I checked the weather report. It said partly cloudy. No rain in the entire state."

"Weather forecasts never get it right," his dad pointed out. "Remember back home?"

"That's Florida!" He felt a little pang, because even his dad still thought of Florida as home. "This is the Midwest. Rain isn't supposed to be crazy here."

"*Mid*west?" asked Danny. "I thought Colorado was the *West*."

"It's the Rockies," their dad explained. "More west than Midwest, less west than west West."

Danny nodded, like somehow that made perfect sense to him.

After two shuttle runs to the garage from the driveway, all three were drenched to the bone, and only a handful of items had been gathered.

"What's the use?" Nick said. "Even if we get it all into the garage, no one's going to come in this rain. We're screwed."

"Tell you what," Dad said. "You made a great effort. It's worth something." He reached into his wallet and handed Nick three twenties. "Sixty bucks. You probably wouldn't have made more than that anyway."

Nick got a peek inside his father's wallet. Those three bills were all he had in there.

"Keep it, Dad," he said, waving him off. "I'd probably just waste it on junk food anyway."

His dad held out the money hopefully for a moment more, then put it away.

"Well," he said, "at least let's appreciate Colorado rain." Then he opened up three sagging lawn chairs and set them up in the garage, looking out.

That could have been all there was to it, had the storm not had consequences completely unintended by those who had created it.

The storm could not exist without a substantial accumulation of storm clouds, which by their very nature block out a sizable amount of sunlight. Thus the garage was dim, even at nine o'clock in the morning. Such a dim space required light, but it was an old garage that had never had a ceiling light installed.

"I can't see my comic book!" Danny whined as they sat there.

"So go in the house," Nick told him.

"No!" Danny said. "I want to appreciate the rain, like Dad said."

Their father pointed to a back corner. "Why don't you plug *that* thing in?"

That thing was an old stage light, basically a single oversize lightbulb atop a rusty pole. It looked like a giant electric Q-tip. This was one of the items Nick had brought down from the attic with considerable effort, since the thing was so heavy and tall. They hadn't put it out with the rest of the stuff because the slope of the driveway made it lean at a dangerous angle.

Nick stood up and found an outlet, moved the lamp to the center of the garage, and plugged it in. He found a small knob just beneath the bulb and twisted it a quarter turn to the right. The oversize bulb lit up like a beacon and, for better or worse, began the process of changing the world.

Caitlin was deathly afraid of getting struck by lightning again.

Intellectually, she knew how low the chances were; she had removed both of her earrings, and the only metal on her person was her phone. Although it had an internal antenna, it was hardly the lightning rod that metallic pom-poms were.

No one faulted Caitlin for her astraphobia—fear of lightning—because it was earned. But it was a nuisance nonetheless.

Today she put that fear aside as she strode through the storm, because for some reason she couldn't put her green fingernail on, something was drawing her toward that garage sale. Getting there was more important than protecting herself from a heavenly strike.

As she neared the house, Caitlin had to admit she was impressed by the size of the old Victorian. But up close it was even more run down than it looked from the street. Cracked beams. A few broken windows and torn screens. Some of the gingerbread trim had rotted through or was missing altogether. The entire structure needed work. She wondered what kind of family would move into a house like this. How bad off would they have to be if this was the best they could do? Not to mention having to sell their old junk at a garage sale instead of hauling it all to the dump.

To her surprise, in spite of the downpour, she found she was not the first to arrive. About a dozen people already stood in the rain, some with umbrellas, some without, searching through the waterlogged items with great purpose, even if they had no idea what that purpose was.

Inside the garage was a most compelling light. It seemed to almost have gravity, pulling her, and apparently everyone else, down the driveway toward the garage sale.

As Caitlin pushed through the crowd to the picnic table set up in front of the garage, she passed two desperately uncool kids she recognized from school. One was a gloomy dude dressed all in black, named Vince, and the other was a stocky Hispanic kid whose name she couldn't recall. She gave each a courtesy wave and kept moving forward.

The family running the garage sale—or, more accurately, the teenager running it—simply didn't have enough hands to take all the money that was being thrust toward him. His little brother kept having to kneel down to pick up the fallen bills.

At the picnic table, an older gentleman hefted a large multi-faceted glass tube. He held it up to the lamp in the garage, watching as a prism at the core of the tube split the light into small rainbows.

"It's a genuine antique, probably worth a lot of money," said the kid running the garage sale.

"I'll give you forty dollars for it," said the man.

The new kid laughed. "I was gonna ask for twenty, but I'll take it."

The man handed over two bills and walked away, cradling the glass tube in his arms like a baby.

Caitlin watched as two women vied for the boy's attention— one buying what looked like an electric flour sifter, and another who wanted some kind of old-fashioned salon-style hair dryer. Both of them held out money simultaneously.

"You must be quite a salesman," Caitlin said to the kid after the two customers left with their purchases. "None of these things is worth what they're paying."

"I know," he whispered back to her. "I don't get it either." He handed the bills to his brother, who was organizing the money in an X-Men lunch box.

Caitlin figured he was about her age. The Tampa Bay baseball cap he wore revealed dark hair that was cropped short and only partially hid a small bandage on his forehead over his left eye. He had a nice tan, but his clothes were about three years behind the times. *Florida*, she thought, with a mental snort, and felt a bit sorry for him. The word *assemblage* went through her mind: a found object that needed bits and pieces of other things to make it into something new. Something better.

The kid went on: "I never figured this part of Colorado had so much money."

"It doesn't," Caitlin said.

She paused, waiting for the kid to overenthusiastically introduce himself, which was the way most boys reacted to her. When he didn't, she took the astonishing step of introducing herself first. "I'm Caitlin, by the way."

"I'm Nick." He spread his hands wide over the table. "You're a little late for the good stuff, but there are still some things here, and there are a couple of bigger pieces in the garage I can show you if you'd like. Have fun!"

"Thanks, I will," Caitlin said, vaguely disappointed in his response, and she looked over the collection of objects.

Vince, even gloomier than usual, walked up to the picnic table holding a black box that looked something like a car battery, yet not. Corrosion had eaten through the top surface, where wires, bent and frayed, were hooked loosely around electrodes.

"So what's this?" he asked Nick.

Nick examined it. "I think it's an old wet-cell battery. But it's dead."

Vince shrugged. "Everything dies," he pronounced. "Batteries are no exception. I'll take it."

"Um, okay," Nick said, handing it back.

"Vince, are you crazy?" Caitlin asked. "It's an old, dead battery."

"Thanks a lot," said Nick with a smile. "Killing a sale with the truth, now that hurts." Then he turned to Vince. "But she's right. It's not worth—"

"I'll give you ten bucks for it," Vince said, and Nick's brother opened up the lunch box like a waiting Venus flytrap.

"But it's not worth a penny," Nick protested.

"All right," Vince said. "Nine."

"I'll take three," Nick said. "And that's my final offer."

"You drive a hard bargain." Vince dropped three singles into the cash-stuffed lunch box.

"I don't think that's the way it's supposed to work," Caitlin said drily, after Vince left with the wet cell.

Nick turned to Caitlin, the look on his face almost one of

suspicion. "All these people coming in the storm, giving me all this money. It's like there's a conspiracy."

"That's crazy," said Caitlin. Then, as Nick was distracted by another buyer—a nun with an antique vacuum cleaner—she couldn't deny a desperate feeling to find her own particular object.

She moved to the end of the picnic table and found herself next to the Hispanic kid from school, whose name was on the tip of her tongue, but not really. Marshall or Randall or something. He had some odd family issue that rumored its way through school last year, but she hadn't cared enough to pay attention.

"Hey, Caitlin," Marshall/Randall said. "You're not going to find much here that you'll like. It's all a bunch of old crap, you know, already picked over."

"Well, as it happens I'm looking for—"

"For something new, of course," Marshall/Randall interrupted.

"Something old, actually," Caitlin corrected. "Something—"

"Something trendy, huh? Nah, nothing trendy either," he went on, more than happy to finish her sentences. "It's all ancient *basura*. What would you expect at a garage sale, huh?"

"Mitchell, right?" Caitlin said, his name suddenly coming back to her.

"Just Mitch."

She wanted to ask him if he'd felt drawn there, too, but all she managed was, "Why are you here?"

Mitch shifted uncomfortably under her gaze. "Just thought I'd, um, drop by. . . . Uh, excuse me."

Caitlin wasn't used to people leaving her in the middle of conversations. That was *her* M.O. There were usually more important or interesting places for her to be than stuck in boring conversations with borderline entities. So she was completely unprepared for Mitch to walk away from her and cross to the picnic table, where he apparently found his Object of Interest.

Even though the garage sale had at first appeared to be a bust, people began to arrive in droves just a few minutes after the storm had started. Nick never equated the illumination of the old stage light with the influx of customers. Why would he?

First he sold the killer toaster to their next-door neighbor, an elderly woman who probably came from the same era as the appliance. Then a girl with a pinched face and uneven pigtails bought the old box camera. Some guy sprang for what Nick guessed was an ancient television set. A woman bought the odd-paddled mixer, someone else bought the thing that looked like a cast-iron clothes dryer, and he even sold the antique sewing machine (or vegetable juicer).

His dad could barely carry the objects out to people's cars fast enough, and Danny had to graduate to a toolbox, because the lunch box was too small to hold all the money. Yet as he made sale after sale, Nick's thrill turned into bafflement, which turned into suspicion. Now he wondered what Caitlin had whispered to the pudgy kid. He wondered if they were talking about him behind his back. In fact, the kid was approaching him right now.

"Hi, I'm Mitch, Mitch Murló."

"Merlot?" asked Nick. "Like the wine?"

"No, Murló like Murphy and López smushed together, ground up, and pushed out the other end. My parents' idea— a half-Hispanic, half-Irish name that sounds French." Mitch looked around approvingly. "Nice garage sale you're running— so, you gonna start at Rocky Point Middle School, or are you older or younger and I'm just not guessing your age right?"

"Uh . . ." Nick had to take a moment to mentally diagram

Mitch's sentence. "Uh . . . yeah, no, you got it right, I'll be in eighth grade. I'll be starting—"

"On Monday?" Mitch interrupted. "Great! We should talk— I'll tell you which teachers to avoid, and where it's safe to sit without risking a beating."

"Thanks. Actually I—"

"Want to hear it now? Sure. First of all, there's Mrs. Kottswold. . . ."

Nick had already been assigned to classes, so any talk of avoiding teachers was moot. But apparently Mitch only needed himself to carry on a conversation. Nick endured another minute of school trivia before he could refocus the conversation on the garage sale. "Yeah, that's all good to know. So . . . what do you have there?"

"Oh, yeah, right." Mitch looked at the object in his hands, almost as if he were surprised to see it there, a little embarrassed by it, even. "It's a birthday gift for my little sister." He held up the disk-shaped metal device, with a movable arrow mounted in the center. It was possibly a toy—it looked like an early See 'n Say cast in steel. But instead of barn animals, it had geometric symbols engraved around the circle. An ivory ring was attached to a pull string. "This looks good," he said.

"Uh . . . right . . ." said Nick. "I'm sure your sister would love a weird piece of junk instead of something—"

"Something new in a box? You bet she would! She's not into the whole corporate America commercialization-of-birthdays thing." Mitch played with the string on the device. "Anyway, how much?"

Nick shrugged. "I was thinking of—"

"I only brought ten with me," Mitch said, pulling his wallet out of his back pocket. "But I can go home and get more."

"Okay, what's going on?" Nick demanded. "Did that girl Caitlin put you up to this? What are you all planning?"

"I don't know what you're talking about," Mitch said indignantly, holding out the ten.

Nick sighed and took the bill. "Fine. I hope your sister enjoys it."

As Caitlin wandered closer to the garage, she saw it. The perfect item.

An old reel-to-reel tape recorder. A big, bulky thing the size of a suitcase, complete with two plate-size spools of audiotape. In a flash of inspiration, she saw her entire *garbart* project. She'd pull the guts out of the machine and drape the wires and other electronic bits over and around the thing. Then she'd wrap the entire mess with the audiotape. She even had a title.

Media Frenzy.

She raced back to Nick, unable to control herself as she pulled bills from her purse. Even though Caitlin realized she was falling into the same trap as the others, she was powerless to stop it. She only wanted to spend ten, but she found herself holding out a twenty to Nick.

"How much do you want for that tape recorder?" she asked. "Is this enough? I have more."

Nick looked at the bill in her hand but wouldn't take it. He just shook his head. "It's junk! It's not worth anything. What's wrong with you?"

Caitlin felt tears—actual tears—building in her eyes. "I don't know! I don't know! Just take the money and let me have it! Because if you don't, I don't know what I'll do!"

Nick reached out to her in a kind of daze, but whether he intended to take her money or take her hand wasn't clear. Her last impression of him before he grabbed her was that he looked like a deer in headlights.

It turned out there was a reason for that.

The car, a Buick that had seen better days, wasn't speeding down the street intentionally. However, the man driving found himself in such an unexpected hurry to reach the garage sale he couldn't help himself. He barely noticed his car jumping the curb and, at the time, the tree in front of him felt like a minor inconvenience. With the rain beating down on his windshield and a pair of faulty wipers, he never even saw the two kids in his path. But he did notice the table of merchandise in front of the garage, illuminated by a certain light that could only be described as compelling.

Nick didn't have time to think, only to act. He rammed Caitlin, tackling her to the ground just as the car plowed into the tree. Had he hesitated a split second, they both would have been crushed by the car, but Nick's reflexes were just fast enough to save them. Now, as they lay together on the wet grass, Caitlin just stared at him.

"Excuse me, but did we almost just die?"

"Yeah, I think so." He helped her to her feet and they both stared at the car, its front end crumpled against the tree. Funny, but the moment *after* nearly dying felt as uneventful as the moment right *before* nearly dying. Nick figured the seriousness of the moment would hit him much later, when he actually had time to freak out about it.

Danny hurried up. "Did anybody die?" he asked. "Dad's in the bathroom, but if somebody died I'll get him out."

The driver forced his way past the air bags, got out of the car, and instead of looking at his vehicle, asked anyone who was listening, "Is this the garage sale? Is there anything left?" Then he went to the long table to pick through the dregs of the dregs of Nick's garbage, just like everyone else. All that was left were broken fragments of things that could not be identified when they were whole, much less now that they were in pieces. Yet people still sifted through them like prospectors panning for gold.

"These people are nuts!" Caitlin said, then added, "And I was just one of them!"

Apparently the sudden shock of nearly getting killed had jarred her out of the weird state she had been in—yet even now, Nick couldn't help but notice the way she was drawn back to that reel-to-reel recorder in the garage, and he followed her.

"I already paid you for this, right?" Caitlin asked, standing over the recorder, her hand on it almost possessively.

Drenched people kept arriving from the street. Many of them were not in rain gear or even carrying umbrellas. It was like they were drawn to the place like moths to a flame.

Or a bulb, Nick thought.

Nick turned to the oversize bulb on its stand, lighting up the garage and casting long shadows stretching out like spokes toward the mob examining the merchandise. There was something about that light. Not quite hypnotic, but soothing. Penetrating. Nick could feel it tugging at him like some sort of secret gravity. Was that crazy?

He reached over to the light, took the switch between his thumb and forefinger, and clicked it off.

The light died, its filament dimming to a faint orange glow before extinguishing entirely. And when he looked at the people scavenging the table, everyone took one last gander at the piece of broken junk in their hands and put it down.

"Well," someone said, "this was certainly a waste of time."

Everyone else seemed to agree, voicing thoughts from disappointment to disgust.

"I can't believe I missed the game for this."

"Look at my dress! Soaked!"

"They have some nerve calling this a garage sale."

"Did I just run my car into a tree?"

None of them seemed to remember that just an instant before they had been willing to shell out whatever money they had for whatever they could get.

Caitlin, coming up beside Nick, breathed a deep, shuddering breath. "I feel better now."

"I guess you don't really want that tape recorder, do you."

Caitlin looked down, a bit guiltily. "Actually, I still want it," she said, "just . . . not quite as much as before."

Nick nodded, reached into the box of cash, and pulled out a twenty. "Here," he said, handing it to her. "I made enough money anyway. You can have it for free."

Reluctantly, Caitlin took the bill, clearly disturbed by the whole experience. "Thanks," she said. "It's too big to walk home with. I'll come back with my mom later."

"Maybe," suggested Nick, "when you come over, you could stay for dinner."

But Caitlin gave him an awkward, apologetic grin. "Maybe I'll just get the tape recorder."

"Right," said Nick, trying to hide both his embarrassment and disappointment. "Well, thanks for stopping by."

And then she was gone, just like that, along with everyone else who no longer had any interest in the junk on the table. Last to go was the man who hit the tree, as there were pieces of his front bumper he had to throw into the trunk before struggling to drive off with a wilting air bag in his lap.

Well, at least Nick could console himself with an incredibly fat wallet, even if somehow it felt like the money wasn't really his. That it had been stolen by unintentional trickery.

"Wow," said his dad, coming out of the house to see the flotsam and jetsam spread out on the table. "That turned out well!"

"Yeah," said Nick, "surprisingly well."

"Then can we get something to eat?" Danny asked. "I'm starving."

"You two go—my treat," Nick said, handing his father a few bills from the toolbox. "Just bring me back something. I'll stay and clean up this mess."

As his dad and brother drove off, Nick brought the tall stage light into the house, then went back outside with a large trash bag. But before he began tossing the remaining junk, one last car pulled up the long driveway, a pearlescent-white SUV that seemed to be dry in spite of the rain. Some kind of optical illusion, Nick figured.

As a flash of lightning ripped across the sky, all four doors opened simultaneously. Four men stepped out, all tall and each dressed in a pastel color—cream, pale green, pale blue, lavender—as if they had been on their way to an Easter parade. In one smooth move that almost seemed choreographed, the four men opened umbrellas.

They walked up to the picnic table and stood around Nick, who tried not to feel, or at least not to show that he felt, intimidated.

"So sorry we're late," said the tallest of the four. "We only heard about this at the last minute."

One of the others held up a copy of the flyer and read aloud, "'Antiques, Vintage Toys, Furniture, Tons of Cool Stuff.'"

The tallest guy wore a vanilla-colored three-piece suit, while the others had on slacks and crisp shirts. Due to a trick of the light, perhaps, or the contrast between the pastel shades and the gloomy weather, their clothes almost seemed to be glowing.

"'Tons of cool stuff,'" the man in the vanilla suit repeated, then he flashed and held a cheery, soulless smile that creeped Nick out. "Sadly, I imagine no one showed up in this storm."

The other three men laughed at that, as though he had just cracked a joke that Nick didn't get.

"Maybe," the vanilla suit went on as he reached under his jacket and pulled out his wallet, "we can still make the day pay off for you."

"Actually . . ." Nick hesitated, enjoying this moment. "We sold practically everything."

The man's smile faltered and lost its genial quality, leaving just a faintly sour glint, and the other men stopped laughing.

"Yeah," Nick went on, "we had a great turnout in spite of the rain. Sorry."

The vanilla suit glanced at the other men and nodded at the picnic table. They fanned out, looking over the leftover detritus—mostly small personal items Nick had brought with him from Florida.

"Well, that's unfortunate," Mr. Vanilla Suit said, turning back to Nick. "Very unfortunate."

"For you," Nick clarified.

The man paused, then nodded. "Of course. For us. But you're a very lucky fellow." His creepy "friendly" smile returned. "Say, you didn't happen to get the names and addresses of the people you sold the items to, by chance?"

"At a garage sale? You gotta be kidding." As weird as Nick felt about this entire encounter, he had to laugh at that. Then he turned and saw the other men collecting the remains from the table, sweeping the small and broken items into boxes and bags they had produced.

"Hey," Nick said, raising his voice, "what are you doing?"

"Don't worry," said the vanilla suit, placing a fifty-dollar bill on the picnic table in front of him. "I'm sure this will more than cover it." Then he reached into his wallet and withdrew a business card that looked as slick as his suit. He placed it gently on top of the fifty. "But if anyone should happen to bring back anything you sold them, I would ask that you get in touch with me."

Nick shook his head. "No, uh, I don't really think . . ."

The man placed another fifty-dollar bill on top of the first, making a currency sandwich with the business card. "We'll make it worth your while. *Very* worth your while."

Before Nick could answer, the four men jumped back into the SUV with their boxes and bags. Through the windshield Nick saw Mr. Vanilla Suit angrily whip out a cell phone as the car sped in reverse down the driveway. Then its tires squealed on the asphalt as the driver shifted gears. The car raced up the street, its tinted windows hiding the men inside.

Nick looked at the two fifty-dollar bills on the table. Not much he could do about it now, he supposed, and he added the bills to the others in the toolbox.

"So much for having to clean up the garbage," he muttered as he crumbled the business card into a small ball and dropped it in the empty trash bag.

3 ALL SALES ARE VINYL

*F*lickering light. A door bursts open. Flames. Smoke. Words lost in the roar, the crackling, the burning—Nick shouts to his mom—she was just behind him a split second ago—but a second can split in a million different directions. . . .

Nick woke from the dream into dim morning light coming from a small frosted window in the far wall of his attic room. High above, the four triangular planes of the roof joined together in a pyramidal skylight, but the glass had been covered with black paint. The only way he knew it was a skylight at all was because of the small spots where the paint had peeled away. At even the brightest times of day, the attic lingered in twilight.

With all the junk gone, the attic was pretty bare. It would take a lot of work to make this room feel homey. Nick's bed and a small desk—all that his dad could afford to buy him right now—appeared small and lonely in the otherwise empty attic space. Nick figured he would soon fill the room with furniture, a wide-screen TV for sure, and maybe a pinball machine or a pool table.

Yeah, he thought, *dream on.* None of those things would fit through the attic opening anyway, even if they could afford them.

Nick pulled himself out of bed with a yawn and a scratch, and tripped over his shoes and dirty clothes. He pulled the handle that released the rickety attic ladder and clambered down to the second-floor hallway, then made his way to the main stairs and down to the kitchen.

At the table, his brother was scarfing down cereal, studiously reading the back of the box. His father, still in his flannel bathrobe, was standing at the open back door.

Just outside stood the elderly woman from next door, wearing a home-knit sweater that said I LOVE MY PUG, and her pug, who wore a matching sweater that said I LOVE MY OWNER.

"You should be ashamed of yourself," the woman was saying to Nick's father. "A person could get hurt."

Under her arm, like a metallic football, she held a scuffed chrome object. It was the dreaded toaster. Something Nick hoped he'd never see again.

"Uh," said his dad, trying to gather his uncaffeinated brain, "like the sign said, all sales are vinyl, are viral—um, final."

"I'll take care of this, Dad," Nick said, moving toward the back door.

His dad didn't argue. He just went looking in cabinets for coffee, not realizing he hadn't bought any yet.

"Is there a problem with your purchase, ma'am?" Nick asked.

"Don't try to sweet-talk me," she snapped. "You salespeople are all alike."

"Salespeople?" Nick held up his hands. "I'm a kid."

"Bait and switch and leave the customer high and dry without so much as a how-do-you-do," she went on.

Nick had no idea what any of that meant, but her voice was too annoying for this early in the morning to argue with.

"Fine," he said. "I'll take it back. How much do I owe you?"

"Twenty dollars."

"She paid five," said Danny from the depths of his cereal bowl. "I remember."

"Five for the toaster, the rest for damages," the woman snapped. "And you'll be lucky if I don't sue."

Nick reached into his pocket and found five crumpled singles. He handed them to the woman. "Here's five for the toaster. If you want more, consult my lawyer," and he pointed to Danny.

The woman snatched the bills begrudgingly and thrust the toaster into Nick's hands.

"So what's wrong with it?" he asked. "Did it burn the toast?"

The woman barked out a laugh. "Try it yourself," she said, giving him a denture-cream snarl. "I'm sure it'll make your family breakfast very special."

Once she was gone, Nick plunked the toaster on the counter. It wobbled a little on its uneven feet.

Should I do this? he wondered, staring at it. *Probably not.*

"You gonna make toast?" asked Danny. "Because I found some jam in the pantry. It's green."

"That's not jam, it's mint jelly," Nick told him.

"Then how come it says 'Strawberry'?"

"Hmm," said Nick. "Maybe let's not eat it." He examined the toaster, running his hands over the chrome. Now that he looked closely, he could see it had unexpected grooves and indentations that had nothing to do with making toast. They weren't dents either. They appeared to be part of the design.

On the bottom, engraved in spidery cursive script, was the phrase *Property of NT.* He wondered if it had been there before, and realized that he didn't care. Then Nick noticed one more thing.

"There's no plug," he said.

"Maybe it runs on batteries?" Danny suggested.

"Hmm . . . maybe." Nick got two pieces of white bread, put them in the slots, and lowered the hard black lever. The moment the bread was in, the toaster began to hum, and the coils inside began to glow.

"It looks like it's working," Nick said, wondering what the old woman's problem was. "I guess it does run on batteries."

In a moment the hum grew from a faint buzz into a swarm of bees, into the roar of a jet engine. The bulbs in the light fixture above him shattered as an arc of bright blue light burst from the toaster, knocking Nick against the opposite wall. Then the blue light was gone, and the toaster fell silent.

"Dad!" yelled Danny. "The toaster killed Nick again."

Nick's father, whose coffee expedition had taken him to the far corners of the house, came running back into the kitchen.

"What's the matter?" he asked. "What happened to all the lights?"

"I think the toaster has a short circuit or something," Nick said, shaking his head to clear it.

"Great. I'll see if I can find a fuse box after I take you both to school."

Nick stood up, checking his chest for a big gaping electrical burn hole, but there was nothing. Whatever that energy surge was, it wasn't lethal. It didn't even hurt.

Just then the toaster went *ding* and the toast popped up, incinerated into thin strips of smoking charcoal.

4 HEISENBERG/PRINCIPAL

If there is ever a time when you do not want to stand out in any way, shape, or form, it's your first day in a brand-new middle school.

It would have been bad enough for Nick if he had started on the first day of the school year like everyone else, but to begin in April made him an unknown quantity, a mysterious interloper from some exotic foreign state. The girls would already be wary, the guys already suspicious, and everyone would hate the sports teams he now had to root for in secret. How anyone survived a move to a new middle school was beyond Nick.

He chose his clothes carefully that morning. Nondescript jeans with no designer label—just in case that particular designer was out of favor here. A simple beige T-shirt that would go well with any color someone around him might be wearing. He even ditched his Tampa Bay Rays baseball cap that first day. His plan was to dive into the shark-infested waters of this school without so much as the slightest splash.

Unfortunately for Nick, Mitch was all about cannonballs.

Nick had just entered the school when, from way down at the far end of the hall, louder than every other conversation, he heard, "Hey, Nick, over here, it's me, Mitch! Hey, everyone, that's Nick—he's the NEW kid!"

All eyes turned to Nick with that singular gaze of eighth-grade judgment, the unspoken "not one of us" gaze that has sent many a teacher into prolonged therapy.

"Your name's Nick?" somebody said. "We've already got too many Nicks."

"He's cute," he heard one girl say.

"No, he's not," he heard another say.

Suddenly the hallway felt like a gauntlet he had to pass through, and the first-period bell hadn't even rung.

He saw a few familiar faces:

There was Caitlin, wrapped in the octopus-like arm of a guy who seemed too tall to be an eighth grader. As Nick passed by, she offered him the same slim, awkward grin she had left him with at the garage sale. She had come back to pick up the tape recorder from his father while Nick was in the shower that night. He knew she couldn't have planned it that way, although it felt like she had.

There was the girl with the pigtails who had also been at the garage sale. She now looked him over like a piece of meat that she was considering buying at the market. He couldn't remember if she ever told him her name.

There was Vince, who greeted him in a Lurch-like monotone, saying, "Welcome to the most pathetic school on this or any other planet."

And, of course, at the end of the hall, there was Mitch, who might as well have been printing out "Kick Me" signs to paste all over Nick's body with every word that he said.

"Dude, I've been waiting for you," Mitch told him. Then he turned to an uninterested kid beside him. "Hey, have you met the new guy?"

Nick grabbed Mitch by the arm and walked him away from the crowd. "You already asked everybody that. Please don't ask again."

"Sorry," Mitch said. "I was just trying to help. I know how hard it is to move into a new school." Then he turned to a jock passing by. "Nick's from Tampa. Probably roots for the Buccaneers, huh?"

Which coaxed forth a "They suck!" from somewhere behind Nick, making his journey to the dark side complete.

The jock, meanwhile, walked by without a word, bumping Nick with almost enough force to knock the books out of his hands. Whether it was intentional or the jock was simply a klutz, Nick couldn't say, but the force of the impact was enough to throw him back against the lockers and rattle his skull.

Mitch didn't notice. "Listen," he said as the first bell rang, "there's something I have to show you."

"Maybe another time, okay?" Nick shook his head to clear it, and he tried to move on to his first class in the now-hellish school, but Mitch clung to him like a barnacle.

"It's the thing I got at the garage sale. There's something weird about it."

Nick thought about Toaster Woman and took a deep breath. "I never said it worked when you bought it. All sales are—"

"Final, I know," Mitch said, shaking his head. "But I don't want to return it. You just gotta see what it does." He reached into his pack and struggled to pull the device out. By this time the hallway was nearly empty. "I was messing around with it last night," he said, "you know, before gift wrapping it for my sister. Go on, pull the string."

If only to get rid of him, Nick grabbed the ivory ring, pulled the string out, and released it.

"Mitch," Nick began, "I really can't do this now, I have to—"

"—*check my pocket before it's too late,*" the machine said in a harsh, tinny voice.

"You hear that?" Mitch asked, excited. "Listen to the machine, man. Do what it says!"

But with the late bell about to ring, Nick had no patience for whatever joke Mitch was about to pull.

"I will not listen to a stupid machine." And he pushed past Mitch, hurrying to his class with mere seconds to spare.

He headed for the first seat he could find—an open desk toward the back. And as the classroom was still quieting down, he slipped into the seat, drawing no attention to himself whatsoever.

Back on track, he thought. Until the cell phone in his pocket, which he had forgotten to turn off, began to ring.

And once again all eyes turned to him.

"Whose cell phone is that?" the teacher demanded. "Hand it over."

And from somewhere in the room he heard someone say, "Ha-ha, the new kid's already got detention."

Cafeteria food is the same throughout the cosmos. It transcends both time and space as a universal constant. And although Nick longed for familiarity, this particular fact was not very comforting. By the time he found his way to the cafeteria, he was last in line.

"Move along, you get what you get, no substitutions, I'm in no mood today," said a lunch lady in the white, nurselike uniform of all cafeteria workers. She dished out meals with skillful speed, such that the line moved much more efficiently than it had at Nick's school back home.

No, Nick had to remind himself, *this is home now.*

"I hate it when Ms. Planck is in a bad mood," said the girl in front of Nick. "I always end up with something I have moral objections to eating."

It was the girl with the pigtails. This close he could see that her hair was parted with such precision and severity it appeared to be pulling her skull in half. Even so, her pigtails were slightly lopsided, like a picture you just can't get to hang straight on the wall.

"I'm Petula," she said, holding out her hand for Nick to shake. "That's *PETu*la like *spat*ula, not Pe*TOOL*a like pe*tun*ia."

"I'm Nick, like . . ." He decided not to finish that sentence.

"With or without a *k*?" Petula asked. "These things are important."

"With," Nick said.

Petula turned to see Ms. Planck dishing up her lunch.

"You get beef," Ms. Planck said. "We just ran out of fish. Don't complain to me, I don't do the purchasing."

"For dessert I'd like—" Petula began.

"You get what you get," said Ms. Planck, putting a dish of Jell-O on her tray.

Petula looked at Nick and pointed to the glob of red. "Told ya," she said, although Nick couldn't figure out what moral objection she could have to Jell-O. Nonetheless, she pushed it into the trash on her way out.

Seeing that Nick was last, Ms. Planck took a moment to breathe and wipe her forehead before she served him.

"You new, or is that just a new haircut that lets me see your face?"

"New," Nick told her. "You know, I don't think that girl cares for Jell-O."

"I know," Ms. Planck said. "Petula doesn't need dessert. She's already wired enough without sugar." She looked him over. "So have things changed, or does it still suck to be new?"

Nick smiled at her directness. "Pretty much, yeah."

34

She ladled a spoonful of beef something-or-other onto his plate, then gave him a second helping.

"Tell you what, because I'm in a good mood, I'll give you a few pointers."

"I thought you said you were in a bad mood."

"You weren't listening. I said *no* mood." She pointed toward the tables in the cafeteria. "Third table from the left? Cursed. Regardless of who sits there, it never ends well. No one's made the connection yet but me."

She pointed at another table. "Back row, second table in, people who think they're popular, but aren't. Sit with them, your head will swell until you can't fit through the door."

She pointed at another table. "Front row, center. Future CEOs of Fortune Five Hundred companies. Don't let their zits fool you."

Nick tried to absorb the information, and notice the faces and locations. "So, taking all that into consideration, where do I sit?" he asked.

"Doesn't matter. In my experience, the seat finds the child." And she spooned yet another blob of beef onto his plate. Then she leaned over the sneeze guard and whispered, "But if you really want to be accepted like no other new kid was accepted before, I'll tell you what you have to do."

Nick leaned in closer. "I'm listening."

"You see over there? The kid with the buzz cut?"

Nick saw her pointing to a large kid with his back to them, at a table with other large kids. It was a table for eight, but only four of them seemed to fit.

"Go over to him," Ms. Planck went on, "and dump your entire tray of food on him."

"What?!" Nick almost shouted.

"This is gold I'm giving you here, kid," Ms. Planck said. "Gold! And I don't do this for everyone."

Nick could only stare at her, opening and closing his mouth wordlessly. "But that guy is twice my size," he finally managed. "He'll kill me."

"Trust me on this one," Ms. Planck whispered. And there was something in her eyes that told Nick he could.

Slowly he walked into the cafeteria, and as he got closer to the table, he realized that this was the same muscle-bound kid who had pushed him aside like a freight train in the hallway that morning.

Nick swallowed hard. He felt the lunch that he hadn't even eaten yet wanting to come up. But he put his faith in the lunch lady, and as he passed the human freight train, he tilted his tray and dumped a massive triple serving of beef something-or-other, mashed potatoes, and Jell-O, not just on the kid's shirt, but on his head, on his shoulders, and into his lap.

"What the—? What the—?" the massive kid said.

"Oops. Sorry."

The kid stood up, a full head taller than Nick, his entire body quivering in fury, like a thermonuclear device ticking down to zero.

And finally Nick was convinced that Colorado Springs was trying to kill him. First, the falling toaster. Then the car careening in the rain, nearly pinning him and Caitlin to the tree. The electric shock this morning. And now this.

But then, from behind Nick, someone began to clap. Then someone else. And it built into applause from the entire cafeteria. As the freight train stood there, too angry to do anything but steam, everyone else began cheering.

The bell rang, and as people funneled out of the cafeteria, kids Nick didn't know came up to him and clapped him on the back.

"Hey, man, that was classic!"

"Heisenberg so deserved that."

"Yeah," someone else said. "I've wanted to do that for years but never had the guts."

Nick was practically carried out the doors by the throng. He looked back to see Ms. Planck behind the warming trays, folding her arms across her chest and smiling in triumph.

As the last period of the day was ending, Nick was called out of class to the office. He suspected it was about his stunt in the cafeteria, and was convinced of it when he saw his father sitting with the principal.

"It was an accident," Nick blurted. "I didn't mean it. And anyway, it wasn't my idea."

"Sit down, Nick," said the principal, whose name he didn't even know yet. "There appears to be a problem with your permanent record."

"What kind of problem?" Nick asked, afraid to sit down.

"The problem is that there isn't one."

"Excuse me?" said Nick's father.

"According to Tampa Heights Middle School," the principal said while glancing at his computer screen, "there is no student named Nicholas Slate. Not in that school, or the entire district. And although I found fifteen Nick Slates on SpaceBook, none of them are you."

"What?" said Nick. "I have a SpaceBook page. I exist."

The principal put up his hands. "All right. Let's all calm down now. There's no need to call the police."

Which, of course, made Nick's father do anything but calm down.

"So there's a glitch in your computer system. So?"

To that, the principal just laughed and laughed. "This is

Colorado Springs, home of NORAD. We don't have glitches."
Then he frowned.

"So what are you saying?" Nick's dad asked.

"Simply stating the obvious. That you and your sons are not who you claim to be."

"What—has Danny's record disappeared, too?"

"That question you'll have to take up with the elementary school."

The principal said little more, just continued to give them suspicious eyes and make veiled threats until his father finally stormed out to the car.

Nick went to get his books from his locker. School had been over for twenty minutes now, and the hallway was pretty much empty. Finally he let his frustrations fly and slammed his locker shut—to find someone standing there, filling the hallway, blocking any escape.

Heisenberg.

Nick knew, without any uncertainty whatsoever, that he was about to get the pounding of his life.

Heisenberg, his face fixed in a death frown, advanced on him. And before Nick could say a word, Heisenberg lifted him off the ground . . . and pulled him into a bear hug.

"Thank you," Heisenberg said. "They told me in my anger management class that I was going to be tested. They sent you, didn't they?"

Nick tried to answer, but the hug was so tight he couldn't breathe.

And with tears in his eyes, Heisenberg said, "Now I've passed the test. I've never been so happy."

Then he put Nick down and ran off to get some tissues.

5 TESTING, TESTING

Caitlin had avoided Nick the entire day. She had her reasons, which had little to do with Nick and everything to do with the object she'd bought at the garage sale.

The day before, Sunday, she had planned to spend the morning creating her work of art. She donned her smashing clothes and laid a tarp in the garage, with the poor, defenseless recorder in the center. She approached it, hefting the sledgehammer, wondering how many swings it would take to disfigure it just right.

But she had never used a reel-to-reel recorder before, and she had to admit it intrigued her. Was it possible the thing still worked?

She looked for a power cord and found it had none. But when she pressed PLAY, the spools rolled and tape fed across the playback head. Apparently the tape was blank.

She pressed STOP, plugged in the microphone, and hit RECORD.

"Testing, testing. This is Caitlin Westfield. Testing, testing."

Then she rewound it, watching the tape counter reverse to 000, and played it back.

"Testing, testing," said her voice through the woven speaker grille. *"This is Caitlin Westfield, and this is a waste of time."*

She almost didn't catch it, because to be honest she wasn't

really listening closely, and she really *had* been thinking what a waste of time this was.

"That's weird," she said, and immediately decided that she had misheard. She played it again. When she heard the same thing a second time, she concluded it must have been what she had originally said, because what other explanation was there, really?

Just to prove it to herself, she hit RECORD again.

"Testing, testing. I'm testing this stupid machine again so I can smash it and be done with it."

And her own voice on playback said, *"Testing, testing. I'm testing this stupid machine again so I don't freak out."*

Now Caitlin *was* freaking out.

If it was some sort of trick, there was no explanation for it. Her heart began to beat way too fast to be healthy. She hit RECORD again, and as the reels turned, she looked at the machine from every possible angle, to see if there was anything unusual about it whatsoever.

That's when her cell phone rang.

She pulled it out of her pocket and looked. It was Theo. Her boyfriend had a penchant for calling at the most inopportune times. She put the phone on speaker and set it down so she had both hands free to study the device.

"Hey, Caitlin, it's me."

"Hey."

"Wha'cha doing?"

"Art project."

"Oh. Because a bunch of us are going to the mall. Maybe we can see that new horror movie."

"I'd really like to, but I'm kind of busy," Caitlin told him. "Come over later?"

"Yeah, sure, we can hang out."

"Bye, Theo."

"Bye."

It was only after she hung up that she realized the machine was still recording.

She pressed STOP, looked at it for at least a full minute, refusing to believe she was thinking what she was thinking—and knew, if her thinking was correct, this was major.

Then she rewound the tape to 000 and pressed PLAY.

"Hey, Caitlin, it's me."

"Hey."

"Whatever you're doing isn't important, but I've got to ask, so tell me anyway."

"Art project—like you care about anything that matters to me."

"Oh. Because I don't want to be the only guy at the mall without a girl. We'll make out at the movies."

"That sounds awful. I've already checked out of this conversation, but you can come over later, because I might actually be that bored."

"Yeah, sure, maybe then we can make out."

"Bye, Theo."

"Hmm, I wonder what's for lunch."

Calmly, Caitlin turned the machine off, wrapped it in the tarp, then carried it out back and dropped the entire thing in the trash.

Then she went to her bedroom, closed the curtains, and hid beneath the covers.

The device remained in the trash for an entire ninety minutes before Caitlin took it out and hauled it up to her room. Any thoughts of smashing it were gone. She didn't know what this thing was, or why it could do the thing that it did. But there was no doubt about it—somehow this old recorder took the things you *said* and turned them into the things you were *thinking*.

Even more than that, the machine seemed to delve deeper, to the things you were *feeling*—and didn't even know you were feeling until it played them back.

To a girl like Caitlin, whose heart was wrapped in so many layers of disguise that she never knew exactly what she really felt, this machine was either her salvation, or her ruin.

On Monday, as Nick struggled to fit into the school, Caitlin struggled with the tiny chink that the reel-to-reel player had put in her armor. Her well-crafted social veneer only worked if she was convinced she truly was the person she presented.

She believed herself to be the kind of girl who didn't play games, who said what she meant in take-it-or-leave-it terms. But the impossible nature of that tape recorder hinted that there were parts of herself she didn't entirely know.

Caitlin had always been a fearless girl. But this frightened her.

Throughout the day, her thoughts kept gravitating to that new kid. Nick. The way the strange light had pulled her, and all the other people, to the garage sale.

Nick had valiantly saved her life. She tried to imagine Theo doing the same, but she couldn't. Not that Theo wasn't a decent guy, he just wasn't *that* kind of guy.

There was a heightened sense of something surrounding Nick Slate. The energy of the school seemed to change around him. He even humbled Heisenberg.

By the end of the day, it was her own interest in Nick that troubled her more than anything, so she resolved to take a healthy step away, and under no circumstances let him into her world.

Nick's world that afternoon had little to do with inexplicable garage-sale items and a lot to do with inexplicable math homework. In spite of Vince's claim that the school was pathetic, it was somewhat less pathetic than Nick's school in Tampa, because Colorado Springs eighth graders were way ahead in mathematics. Nick, in his attic room, was doing his best to get up to speed, because whether or not his principal believed it, he did in fact exist.

Danny, on the other hand, took his official nonexistence as a no-homework pass.

"It's not every day you get to be deleted," he said. "I'm gonna make the most of it."

Nick had to admit that, for someone who didn't exist, he had made an impression on his first day at Rocky Point Middle School. He had no idea how he would fare on his second day. Not only academically, but also socially. Caitlin came to mind—and her boyfriend. Theo was tall, mostly because of a long neck featuring an Adam's apple the size of Nick's fist. Nick, on the other hand, had not yet hit his growth spurt, which his father insisted was genetically inevitable.

"It's all about perception," his father had told him. "Think tall, and other people will think it, too."

Nick doubted that any kind of mind control would work on a girl like Caitlin.

When he took a break, he went downstairs and saw his brother in the front yard, waiting for their father to come home from a day of job hunting. Danny absently tossed a baseball in the air, only catching it about half the time.

Nick sighed. Danny had been born after their father's major league days, but they still loomed larger than life for him. Wayne Slate had been an excellent pitcher, but unfortunately he was better known by his nickname, "Whiffin' Wayne." He picked it up thanks to his less-than-stellar batting at away games against National League teams, when a pitcher couldn't take advantage of a designated hitter and had to bat for himself. His father wore the unwanted nickname much longer than his major league jersey. Nick was a pretty good pitcher in his own right, and batter as well. In fact, he was pretty much the star of his Little League team back in Tampa. But for Danny, an early talent in the sport had not presented itself.

Danny dropped the ball once more, and Nick decided his homework could wait. He went out the front door to join his brother.

"Hey, space case," he shouted, "you need two people to play catch."

Danny tossed the ball to his brother. "We need mitts," he told Nick. "Dad says his old one's in a box in the basement, but I don't want to use it. It'll smell like smoke."

Nick tossed the ball lightly, and Danny caught it. "Back up," Danny said, which Nick did. Even so, he had to stretch to catch the next throw. At least his brother had a good arm. Nick returned the ball underhand. This time Danny dropped it.

"It's the attitude," Danny said. "Colorado's got thin air. The ball does weird things."

"You mean altitude," Nick told him as Danny threw another pitch so wild that Nick had to leap to catch it. "Step into it when you throw," he said, tossing it back.

"I am."

"With your other foot."

"That feels funny."

"Stop arguing and do what I tell you."

"You're not Mom. You can't tell me what to do."

Nick held eye contact with Danny for a moment, then had to look away. His brother's stare felt like an accusation.

It was then that Nick caught sight of a familiar, pearlescent SUV, driving too slowly to be anything but menacing.

He had no idea what to think, but even if he had, the thought would have been knocked out of his head by the baseball that beaned him right on his stitches.

"Ow!" Nick turned to his little brother, who looked both horrified and satisfied at the same time. "Danny, that really hurt!"

"Sorry. I didn't mean to hit you in the same place as the toaster. I was just aiming for your head." Then he looked down. "I thought for sure you'd catch it. You catch everything."

Nick found he didn't have the heart to yell at him. And when he looked back at the street, the SUV was gone.

Their dad came home a few minutes later with take-out food and a few sketchy job leads. "When it comes to retired ballplayers," he told them, "people balk worse than a bush league pitcher." Back in Tampa he had been exceptional at "odd jobs," but apparently no jobs were odd enough here.

As they all headed toward the house, Nick saw a small white rectangle on the doorstep. After his dad and brother went inside, he bent down to pick it up. It was the business card of one Dr. Alan Jorgenson. And Nick could tell by the smoothed-out crinkles that it was the same business card he had thrown away at the garage sale.

6 OBJECTS OF INTEREST

The problem with having too many variables in any equation is that the number of possible solutions begins to seem endless. Although supercomputers can calculate things to the gazillionth decimal, it takes a leap of human intuition to boil pages of calculations down to something as simple as $E = mc^2$. The simpler the solution, the harder it is to arrive at.

Nick's garage sale had generated more variables than there were letters to define them, creating a smoke screen that hid the truth: that an elegant solution had already been worked out by a great scientific mind.

One such variable—a rather persistent one—showed up at Nick's house later that evening.

Mitch arrived at Nick's front door after dinner, carrying the clunky See 'n Say thing under his arm.

"Dude, you're my hero," he told Nick, breathing hard. Apparently he had pedaled here at full speed. "That thing with Heisenberg will live on in legend long after we mere mortals are dead."

"Thanks," Nick said, and he couldn't help but smile. All things considered, Mitch might not be such a bad friend, once you got past the nuisance factor. And so far, he'd been the only one to make an effort. That had to count for something.

"Hey," Nick said, "I was just about to—"

"Get something to drink? Can I have something, too?"

And although that wasn't what Nick was going to say, it worked. "Sure. Come on."

As they headed into the kitchen, Nick silently counted how many seconds Mitch could stay quiet. He maxed out at seven.

"So, this thing," Mitch said, giving the See 'n Say a little shake. "I'm telling you, Nick, it's not to be believed. I mean, what it told you at school was useful, right?"

Nick shrugged. "I guess it could have been." He thought about his cell phone ringing, and wondered if he still had to serve detention if he didn't exist.

"I mean, it *knows* things." Mitch held it out to him. "Just pull the string."

Nick opened the refrigerator, where a bottle of apple juice sat on the rack. He took it out and unscrewed the top.

"C'mon, Nick, just pull the string."

With a sigh, Nick reached out, pulled the string, and let it go. "Fine, but I really think—"

And the machine said, *"—you shouldn't drink that."*

Now Nick looked at Mitch curiously, then looked at the juice he was about to swig.

He thought it was just unfiltered apple, but now that he looked at it, the color seemed a little off. He took a sniff and a rancid vinegary odor burned his nostrils. Dizzy, he set the bottle on the counter.

"Danny!" he called. "Did Dad buy this juice today?"

Danny poked his head into the kitchen and eyed the jar. "That? Nah, it's probably been sitting there for years. Dad thinks it's one of Great-aunt Greta's urine samples."

Nick nodded. "Thanks. That is all."

Feeling sick to his stomach for more reasons than one, Nick

took the See 'n Say-ish device from Mitch, who smiled the smile of absolute vindication.

"See? I told you," Mitch said. "This thing isn't a See 'n Say; it's more like a Shut Up 'n Listen."

Nick set the thing down on the table, held it in place with one hand while he pulled the string with the other, and said, "My father . . ."

And the machine said, ". . . *should play baseball again.*"

"Your dad was a baseball player?" Mitch asked.

Nick nodded. "A long time ago." He looked at the device. "How does it do that?"

"I don't know," Mitch said. "It was in *your* attic."

Then Nick thought about the toaster and how, without any direct electrical connection, it had blown out all the bulbs in the kitchen. Not to mention incinerating the toast.

What if these weren't the only two things that were beyond ordinary?

Nick looked at Mitch, who was still too pleased with himself and the device to see the larger implications. He lifted his baseball cap and scratched his head, as if it might stimulate his memory. Who had bought the various items at this garage sale? Besides Mitch, there were only two names he remembered. "Mitch, do you know where Vince and Caitlin live?"

Even though it was long after dark by the time they got to Vince's place, the house in its own way beamed perpetual daylight. It was overlit with way too many garden floodlights, all designed to make the house "pop." The home was blue with pink trim. Brightly colored flowers lined the path to the front door, and there were hummingbird feeders everywhere.

"*This* is Vince's house?" Nick asked. He couldn't even fit that dark, brooding kid in the same brain hemisphere as this house.

"I'm sure living here makes him feel miserable," Mitch said.

Which, Nick realized, was what Vince would want.

A doormat with a daisy pattern announced, WE'RE SO GLAD YOU'RE HERE. However, there were scorch marks on the edges, as though someone had tried to set it on fire.

Nick knocked, and the door was answered by a woman who was all sweetness and manic energy.

"Hi! How can I help you boys?"

"Uh, we're here to see Vince?" said Nick.

The woman couldn't be more overjoyed. No, really, she couldn't be.

"Well, isn't that wonderful? You know, Vince doesn't have many visitors. I'm *so* glad you're here."

"Yes," said Nick, "the doormat already told us."

Vince's mother led them into the house and opened a door to stairs leading down to the basement. "Vince!" she called down. "Two of your little friends are here to see you."

And from down below came a voice sopping with discontent.

"Go away. You're trying to trick me again."

"No, not this time." Then she turned to Nick and Mitch. "Go on down. I know he'll be happy to see you."

Nick and Mitch descended the stairs into the basement. To call it "unfinished" would be a wistful hope. Two walls had been covered with wood paneling, now painted black. The other walls were the original, rough-hewn rock from which the lair (because what else could it be called, really?) had been carved. In the middle of the room sat a desk, a number of disorganized bookshelves, and an army cot. The only window, near the ceiling, was covered with a sheet. On news reports, when astonished neighbors said things like, "He was always so quiet and kept to himself," the next image would be this basement.

"Oh," said Vince, with supreme disappointment. "It's you."

"Cool place you got," Mitch told him, looking around. "What imaginative things you've done with dirt."

"Color gives me a headache. So what do you want? I've got stuff to do."

"We wanted to talk to you about what you bought at the garage sale," Nick said.

Now Vince became suspicious. "I bought it fair and square. You can't have it back."

Nick didn't argue the point. Not yet, anyway. "I just want to know if you've used it yet."

"Yes," said Vince.

"And when you used it, what did it do?"

Vince's suspicious look intensified. "How do you know it did anything?"

Nick gave Mitch a nod, and he took out the Shut Up 'n Listen and pulled the string. Mitch said, "If I were you, I'd—"

"—*avoid an untimely death*," the machine voice whirred.

And while Nick and Mitch were a little troubled by that, Vince only said, "It couldn't be avoided. Come on, I'll show you."

On his desk, next to a pile of dust-covered schoolbooks, was a murky fishbowl. A single goldfish floated lifelessly on the surface of the water. Its death was most certainly untimely.

Then Vince lifted a rag to reveal the old wet cell, looking just as crusty and toxic as when he bought it. He hesitated. "You're sure you want to see this?"

Nick nodded. He could see that whatever it did, Vince had been itching to talk about it—but other than his mother waltzing around upstairs with a feather duster, he had no one to talk to.

"Sashimi died a couple days ago."

"I'm sorry for your loss," said Mitch.

"No you're not. Don't lie about things like that. It's annoying." Vince stared morosely down at the bowl. "I was going to give him the traditional swirling blue funeral, but I didn't get around to it. Then yesterday I was messing around with the wet cell, right? And I dipped both electrodes into the bowl—"

Nick interrupted him. "Why would you dip two electrodes from a battery into a dead goldfish's bowl?"

"Why *wouldn't* you?" Vince asked, blinking, like it was a trick question. Then, rather than say any more, he went to the wet cell, grabbed both wires, and dipped them into the water.

There was a faint electrical hum, and in that instant Sashimi, who had been floating on his back, righted himself and began to swim around the murky bowl like he had nothing better to do.

"No way!" said Mitch, taking a step back.

"It's alive! *ALIVE!*" Vince said, contorting his hands like a mad scientist. Then he dropped his arms to his sides. "Sorry; I always wanted to say that."

Nick could only stare.

"Cool, huh?" Vince said, and folded his arms, proud of himself. "Bet no one else in town has an undead goldfish."

"I bet you're probably right," said Nick.

Nick reached over and carefully pulled the wires from the water. As soon as he did, Sashimi was a floater once more.

Nick stared at the wet cell, not wanting to believe what he had just seen. "Do you even *get* how not normal this is?"

"Yeah," said Vince, as though that were obvious. "But isn't it great? I knew there was something about that thing when I bought it. I could feel it. I just didn't know what it was."

"Like the way you felt drawn to the garage sale?" Nick suggested.

"Yeah, I guess," said Vince with a shrug, but then as he thought about it, the shrug became a nod of recognition. "Yeah—exactly like that!"

Nick had noticed how, at the garage sale, people seemed drawn to specific items. He hadn't thought much of it at the time. He didn't quite know what to make of it now.

Mitch picked up the wet cell and carried it over to the wall, where a shadow box contained a variety of dead bugs, including a large tarantula. He placed the twin electrodes on the spider's back, and the dead creature reared up on its hind legs and spat at him.

Vince yawned. "Knock yourself out, I already tried all those."

"So does it work on bigger things?" asked Nick.

"Hmm," said Vince, "hold that thought." And he trotted up the stairs. He came back a minute later with a raw chicken fresh out of the refrigerator, marinating in a glass bowl.

The three looked at each other, and Nick nodded. Vince touched the electrodes to the pink flesh.

The dead chicken's drumsticks began to pump up and down, and the featherless, naked wings began to flap frantically back and forth, spattering lemon-soy marinade all over them.

Nick and Mitch screamed, and Vince heaved a very satisfied sigh. "I've waited my whole life for that," he said. And then Vince did something he very rarely did: he smiled. "I was thinking of making it my science-fair project," he said. "I think I have a chance of winning, even if Heather North does 'Chemistry of the Cupcake' again."

"You can't bring this to the science fair. You can't let other people see it." Then Nick took a deep breath, knowing what he had to say, and how it would be received. "I'm sorry, Vince, but you can't keep it." He turned to Mitch. "And you can't keep yours either."

Both Vince and Mitch clutched their objects closer to them.

"These things—whatever they are—need to be in the hands of . . . the hands of . . ."

"The hands of who?" asked Vince. "The government? Some corporation? Our parents? Can you imagine my mother with this thing?"

Nick sighed. "I don't even want to try."

And then Mitch sheepishly said, "My dad would be able to figure out what to do."

Vince laughed at that. "Your dad? Are you kidding me? I wouldn't give a penny for your father's thoughts."

Mitch seemed to fold at Vince's words.

"All I'm saying," said Nick, "is that we aren't meant to use these things."

And Mitch said, "What if we are?"

They both turned to him. Mitch clutched the Shut Up 'n Listen a little bit tighter. "I don't know about you—but I feel like this thing was mine even before I ever saw it."

"Me, too," said Vince.

Nick pursed his lips, a bit irritated. "Why does everyone feel that but me?"

Mitch shrugged. "Maybe because you gave all the stuff away."

The two of them held their objects in white-knuckled grips that suggested Nick would get them back only when he pried them from their cold, dead fingers. Nick thought back to the garage sale. All those faces he didn't know, all those people desperately grabbing things and hauling them away. How many people had been drawn to his garage, and filled with a feeding frenzy? All that stuff, that "junk," was scattered now throughout the neighborhood.

"What if *all* the stuff from the attic has bizarre properties?" Nick said. "And what if some of it is dangerous?"

"Well," Vince replied, "part of 'all sales are final' means it's not your problem anymore, right?"

While Vince had no trouble playing the "somebody else's problem" card, Nick just couldn't do it. Especially considering that strange, pearlescent-white SUV, and the man in the gleaming vanilla suit and his cohorts. They must have known about the things from his attic. That's why they were there, and why they took the dregs of the sale—but the items they really wanted had been sold before they arrived. Nick instinctively knew that they should not be allowed to get their hands on those items. So maybe dispersing them through the town was the best way to hide them. . . . But if he didn't track the other objects down, he felt pretty certain the vanilla dude would.

"I'll tell you what," Nick said, realizing Vince and Mitch were the least of his troubles. "I'll let you keep them—temporarily— on one condition. You tell absolutely no one."

Vince quickly agreed. "Secrecy is a key element of my existence. But Mitch here is the emergency broadcast system."

Nick looked to Mitch, who was going a little bit red, probably because he knew Vince spoke the truth. "How about it, Mitch?" Nick asked. "Can you promise to keep it secret, and make the promise stick?"

Mitch's pained look became intense. His hands folded into fists as he steeled himself for the ordeal, then he said, "Make me swear. Make me swear on a Bible like they do in court. That's the only thing that will shut me up."

Nick wanted to roll his eyes, but he realized that Mitch was being completely sincere.

"Vince," Nick said, "do you have a Bible around here?"

Vince gave him a twisted grin. "Are you kidding? My mother has a whole collection. You want the one with Thomas Kinkade illustrations? Or the Smurf Bible?"

"How about one that looks intimidating."

Vince nodded. "I know just the one."

They went upstairs, and from a shelf filled with framed inspirational quotes and fake houseplants with unnaturally bright leaves, Vince pulled out a family Bible that must have gone back several generations. It had a worn, black leather cover with a Gothic, inlaid silver cross. The thing was about as intimidating as the Spanish Inquisition.

"Wow," said Mitch, a little shaken, "I wasn't expecting that."

Vince hefted the book. "I call it the Damnation Bible. On the various occasions it's been suggested I may be going to hell, this is what I imagined the gate would look like."

Mitch timidly laid his hand on the volume and solemnly swore to tell absolutely no one about the Shut Up 'n Listen under threat of fire and brimstone. Once the oath was made, he was visibly relieved.

"There," he said. "That'll do it."

"One more thing," said Nick. "I need both of you to help me find the other objects and get them back."

"You mean going door-to-door?" asked Mitch. "I'm not good at that. Last year I did this wrapping-paper sale for Boy Scouts, and somehow I ended up with more wrapping paper than I started with."

"Leave it to me," said Vince. "I have ways of finding things hidden in the shadows."

And so, with an understanding reached, Nick felt a little bit better about the situation.

"Do me a favor," Vince said. "If my mother accosts you between here and the front door, tell her I was friendly and social."

"Actually, you were," Mitch said.

Vince just glared at him. "Get out."

■ ■ ■

"We don't want her to freak," Nick told Mitch as they approached Caitlin's house. "Or to think this is a big deal—and having both of us at her front door might be overwhelming."

"But it *is* a big deal," Mitch protested. "And Caitlin Westfield can't be overwhelmed."

"Maybe not," Nick admitted, "but one person at her door is a visitor. Two people are a conspiracy. That's why you should wait here and let me talk to her."

In the end, Mitch agreed. Of course, Nick's real reason for leaving Mitch out of this particular equation was that he wanted the chance to talk to Caitlin alone.

While Mitch lurked in the shadows across the street, Nick rang Caitlin's doorbell. He paced back and forth on the oversize porch of her oversize house, wondering if she was currently being suffocated by an oversize Adam's apple. Finally the door opened. It was Caitlin, who was alone, but didn't look especially thrilled to see him.

"Hi," she said. "Nick, right?"

"Yeah. Sorry to come over without any warning or anything, but I really need to talk to you."

She crossed her arms. "About what?"

She wasn't making this easy, and Nick noticed she wasn't inviting him in.

"Some of the stuff at the garage sale," he said. "It might be . . . toxic. Yeah. And I just wanted to warn you. I'd be happy to give you your money back for that reel-to-reel tape recorder."

"Thanks for your concern, but you gave it to me for free. And besides, I'm very happy with it, toxic or not."

Nick knew he had to choose his words carefully so as not to arouse suspicion. "Well, can you at least tell me if it . . . works?"

"Sorry to disappoint you," said Caitlin, with an impatient flick of her head, "but it doesn't."

"Really?" Nick asked, blinking in surprise.

"You said yourself it was a piece of junk."

He *had* said that to her, but that was then, before he'd seen the toaster. And the Shut Up 'n Listen. And the wet cell.

"Can I at least try it out?" he asked.

"Too late," Caitlin said. "I smashed it for my art project."

That threw Nick for a loop. "You what?"

"With a sledgehammer. Into tiny pieces. Glued them to a big canvas. *Media Frenzy*, I call it. So whatever it is you're worried about, you don't have to worry."

Nick stood there for a minute at a complete loss for words. "Oh," he finally managed, "well, if you smashed it—"

"I did. Is there anything else you wanted?"

"No, that's it."

"Well, then. Bye."

And she closed the door, not quite slamming it in his face, but hard enough to make it clear that the good-bye really did mean good-bye.

Inside, Caitlin leaned against the door, trying to hold back tears. She listened until she heard the front gate open and close. Only then did she look out the window to make sure Nick was really gone.

She went up to her bedroom and closed the door. Then she went into her closet and closed that door, too. Sitting hidden beneath hanging blouses and dresses, she turned on the reel-to-reel recorder and opened her diary.

While diaries are supposed to hold one's deepest, most personal musings, Caitlin was savvy enough to know that they often turn up as damning evidence in court, or embarrassing tidbits in celebrity exposés. As she had every intention of being famous for something one day, she was not about to feed the fires of public scrutiny by writing anything "deep" in her diary. Mostly it was a journal of the day's activities, and the things other people in her life would be pleased to read about themselves if they ever got their hands on it. There had been times when Caitlin actually wanted to write something genuine, but she found that she didn't know where to begin. It frustrated her so much that she had given up trying.

Now, as she opened the diary, she chose a particularly ordinary passage that she didn't even remember writing, hit RECORD on the machine, and read it aloud.

> Dear Diary,
> Today in debate team I argued in favor of electric cars,
> and I blew the other side away. I was pretty confident
> about my talking points, so I knew it would go over really
> well. People congratulated me—it made me feel great.
> Like maybe my debating skills could get me somewhere.
> Or my art. People love my smashed-objects collections, and
> my parents are happy with all my grades. They even like
> my friends, which parents never do. My mom and dad are
> cool. Mom's very Zen, spending quiet time in the garden,
> and Dad works hard to keep food on the table. Theo came
> over for dinner tonight. It's funny, he's always so awkward
> with my parents, but that's part of his charm. I can see
> us staying together. There are a lot of bright things in my
> future, but now I must get back to creating yet another
> work of art!

Caitlin shut her diary, pressed STOP on the recorder, and rewound the tape to the point where she started. Then, holding her breath, she moved her finger to the button marked PLAY and touched it lightly. Part of her didn't want to press it—she felt as if she were on a cliff, about to jump into her own depths, where she feared she could drown. But in the end, she closed her eyes, leaned forward, and pushed the button all the way down.

Dear Diary,
Today in debate team I argued in favor of electric cars,
and the scary thing is, even though I might have sounded
confident, I didn't feel like I knew what I was doing. If people
ever find out how insecure I really am, I'll just shrivel up and
die. I don't just smash things for the sake of art. I do it because
I'm angry, but I don't know what I'm angry about, and that
just makes me angrier. My parents don't see any of this. They
see how good my grades are, they see how many friends I
have, and they think nothing's wrong. Just like the way they
pretend that nothing's wrong with them. But I know how
depressed Mom gets, and how Dad buries himself in his work
to avoid thinking about anything else. Then there's Theo, who
came over for dinner tonight again, uninvited. I know it's
not like I'm going to marry him or anything—I doubt our
relationship will even make it to high school—but there'll be
another Theo, and then another. Someday, if I'm not careful,
I'll be stuck marrying a Theo. And that just makes me want
to smash something else.

Caitlin turned off the machine. This horrible, wonderful machine that could dig into her very soul, and put into words the things she couldn't. The things she protected herself from with such subconscious force that it exhausted her. But to hear these things out loud—it both condemned her and freed her.

She broke down into sobs. She knew it was all true. Yet, some-how, hearing herself speak the truth made it seem less powerful. Maybe she didn't have to be afraid of it. And maybe someday, if she listened to her heart played back enough, she'd truly know herself.

7 'NUFF SAID

While Caitlin's interest in Nick was, at this moment in time, lukewarm, Petula Grabowski-Jones's interest in him was red-hot.

To say that Petula had a specific crush on Nick wouldn't be entirely accurate. Petula loved anything new, be it technology or people.

When it came to photography, however, she was very old school, and she enjoyed using her father's classic 35mm Nikon just as much as her digital camera. "The best results are worth waiting for," she always said—when referring to photography, but not to people. With people, she wanted instant results.

As for the old box camera she had picked up at the garage sale, it was classic old school. In fact, it was beyond old school. More like preschool.

She experimented with it, taking a picture of her father while he was leaning against the wall of the family room, talking on his cell phone and scratching his armpit. Petula preferred candids. They were infinitely more truthful and embarrassing. She developed the large negative in her tiny closet/darkroom, which, while barely adequate, did the job.

The negative came out almost completely black, which she thought meant the camera was broken, but she decided to make a print from the negative anyway. As the nearly all-white positive image appeared in the tray of developing solution, Petula saw that the photo wasn't blank at all. She had, in fact, taken a perfect photo of the family room wall, without her father in it.

For a brief moment she entertained the exciting idea that her father was a vampire who would not appear in a picture, but, alas, he was far too lackluster for that. No, the solution had to be something else. She picked up the camera and looked at it from every side, finding *Property of NT* engraved in tiny letters on the bottom.

She filed this information in the area of her brain reserved for things that required further investigation.

The next day in school, Petula continued her observational study of Nick Slate. Others might call it stalking. Nick was performing his own observational study of Caitlin, who was traipsing around the school with a garage-sale device as well.

Petula cornered Nick at his locker between classes. "You know she has a boyfriend."

"I don't know what you're talking about."

"Come on, you've been staring at her like she's a filet mignon sizzling on the grill. Why set yourself up for disappointment?"

Nick slammed his locker. "I don't even know you, Petula. Why are you trying to give me advice?"

"I provide it as a public service," she said, secretly thrilled that he remembered her name, and that he pronounced it correctly.

"Well, if I wanted your opinion, I'd ask for it."

"No, you wouldn't. You're like the other boys—too hormonal to see what's right in front of your face."

"Well," Nick said, "what's in front of my face right now will make me late for class if it doesn't get out of my face."

"Suit yourself."

This was going better than most of Petula's other encounters with boys, and she held high hopes that they might have a future together.

"Once you come to your senses, check back with me," she said. "My calendar's pretty full, but I might be available for a date this weekend."

"Sorry, Petula, but I got over pigtails in fourth grade."

That made her gasp. No one, absolutely no one, insulted Petula's piggies. They were her signature look. It wasn't a hairstyle, it was a lifestyle. She'd spent years training her scalp to grow hair in the optimum directions for the perfect part down the middle. It wasn't her fault that more hair grew on the left side of her head than the right. She'd always considered her hair's mildly lopsided nature a charming bit of uniqueness.

"Since you're new here, I'll forget you just said that."

He shrugged, striding off to class. As she watched him go, she determined then and there that Nick Slate would come to appreciate the glory that was Petula Grabowski-Jones. Even if it killed him.

Caitlin had arrived early that Tuesday morning, a woman on a mission. With Theo toting the rather heavy recorder, she wandered the halls, selecting friends and teachers much less randomly than it appeared.

"Hi, I'm doing a multimedia art project, and your answers might be included," she told people, thrusting the microphone in their faces and then asking questions like:

"Tell me, Mrs. Applebaum, how do you feel about our principal?" and "So, Ashley, who's your closest friend? And why?" and "Drew, as the football team's star running back, what do you think of our quarterback? Can he really take us all the way?"

Not that Caitlin was going to publicize any of the answers, but she had an inquiring mind and wanted to know.

"Caitlin, this thing is heavy. Can I put it down?" Theo asked, after about five minutes.

"Don't be a wuss, Theo. It's not that heavy for a strong guy like you."

Which, she knew, the machine would no doubt translate as, *"If I flatter you, you'll do anything I ask."*

During lunch she continued her "random" interviews. That's when Nick stormed up to her.

"I've been watching you use that thing all day. You said you shattered it."

"Sorry, I lied."

"We need to talk about this," Nick said.

"Who's this guy?" Theo asked. "What do you need to talk to her about?"

"Don't worry, Theo, it's nothing important."

Then Theo smiled. "Oh, you're the guy who gave Heisenberg the beef dip. That was great!"

"Nick," Caitlin said, "I really don't have time right now. Would you like to answer a few questions, though?" She held the microphone closer to his face.

"The only thing I want to know," Nick said, steely, "is if that tape recorder has done anything weird."

"Exactly what are you accusing me of?"

Nick took a step back. "Accusing you? It's just a question."

"Are you harassing her?" asked Theo, who believed himself part of the conversation. "Because we have a zero-tolerance policy for harassment. I'm on the student council and missed out on being student body president by only three votes, which gives me a lot of clout. One word to the principal and you could be suspended."

Nick shook his head. "You have to exist to be suspended."

That comment put Theo in a feedback loop, which kept him quiet for a while.

"There's nothing to worry about, Nick. I'm just making some recordings for my project."

"Well, if there's anything unusual about that machine, you have to tell me. It's important."

"Fine," said Caitlin. "If I notice anything strange, you'll be the first to know."

"Second," said Theo. "Caitlin tells me strange things first."

From across the cafeteria Petula watched this exchange, and although she couldn't hear the gist of the conversation, it didn't matter. All that mattered was that Nick was continuing to devote all of his attention to a girl more popular than she was.

Never mind that Theo was carrying her heavy object. Never mind that Caitlin seemed to be brushing Nick off like so much dandruff.

All that mattered was that Petula was not going to let this go.

She observed Caitlin continuing to do man-in-the-cafeteria interviews during lunch. After lunch she watched as Caitlin tried unsuccessfully to fit the bulky recorder in her locker and then had Theo deposit it in the art room. There was no art class that period, so after the late bell had rung, rather than going to class, Petula slipped into the room. Caitlin had taken the microphone with her, but that didn't mean Petula couldn't listen to the things the machine had recorded. She rewound it and pressed PLAY.

The questions Caitlin asked all seemed to be very, very personal—and what surprised Petula was that people gave extremely candid responses. Mrs. Applebaum thought their principal was "a silver fox," whatever that was, and the school's star running back had a secret crush on the quarterback. Nothing she heard particularly interested Petula—until she got to a certain conversation.

Petula didn't consider herself a scheming person. She preferred to think of it as "interpersonal engineering." It was all about spin. Be that as it may, a magnificent idea came to her as she listened to that conversation and then recorded it on her phone. She had to smile. This was going to be a very good day!

Hell breaks loose in a variety of ways. Just like the varied splatter patterns when certain things hit the fan. On this particular day, the event in question came down at precisely two nineteen. It was seventh period, the last period of the day. Nick was struggling to keep up in a world history class that he could swear was about a different world than the one he had been learning about in Florida. The teacher, Mr. Brown, was somewhere between Sumeria and Phoenicia when the school's loudspeaker came on, blasting at high volume into every classroom. Everyone expected some announcement about buses, or sports-practice cancellations, but instead, a conversation between three people played for everyone to hear.

"I've been building up the nerve to talk to you all day. You said you shattered that recorder."

Nick immediately recognized his own voice and the conversation. But wait a second—had he actually said that out loud?

"I lied, but I had a very good reason, which I'm not going to tell you," he heard Caitlin say. That had not been a part of the conversation either.

"How can you be so pretty and so frustrating at the same time?"

Nick felt himself going red. Now he knew something was really, really wrong. He looked over to Caitlin, who was in his history class, and she glanced at Nick with the kind of panic reserved for random locker checks or an approaching tsunami.

"*Uh-oh, is my territory being threatened?*" he heard Theo ask. "*Quick, act intimidating.*"

To which Caitlin responded, "*Ugh! Theo, do you have to get involved? Just check out and think about lunch or something.*"

A few people around the room chuckled. Mercifully, Theo was not in this class with them—but no doubt, wherever he was, he was hearing this, too.

"*Oh, you're the guy who gave Heisenberg the beef dip,*" Theo said. "*I'm glad it wasn't me—I would have peed my pants!*"

More laughter around the room. Now Caitlin just stared forward, as if she were watching it all unfold on the room's SMART Board.

And then it got juicy.

"*Nick,*" Caitlin said, "*you're really cute, but you keep giving me grief. Hey, I've got an idea! Why don't you answer a few questions so I know if you like me as much as I might eventually like you?*"

"*All I want to know,*" Nick heard himself say, "*is if that tape recorder has done anything weird.*" Which is exactly what he *had* said, and exactly what he had been thinking. Caitlin's response, however, was very different.

"*Quiet! Do you want my so-called friends to find out what I'm up to?*"

That had been the moment when Nick had realized Caitlin was being defensive. Sure enough, he heard himself say, "*Wow, something's wrong. She's really defensive.*"

"*Hey! Hello! I'm still here!*" Theo then shouted. "*I know big words like 'harassment' and 'tolerance.' I'll run to the principal if you both keep ignoring me!*"

To which Nick responded, "*The principal's a moron.*"

Now Nick put his head in his hands, wondering if it was possible for this to get any worse.

Across the room Caitlin seemed frozen in time and space as she heard herself say, *"I'm uncovering people's secrets to feel better about myself. It's not hurting anybody, so leave me alone."*

"Caitlin, you have no idea how much trouble we might all be in, but you'll probably just say something vague and dismissive to make me go away."

"Fine," said Caitlin. *"I'll do my usual trick of saying something vague and dismissive, to make you go away."*

And it was all wrapped up by Theo, who said, *"I wonder what's for lunch?"*

Mr. Brown attempted to continue his lesson, but who was he kidding? The history class was history. About ten seconds after the broadcast ended, Caitlin bolted out of the classroom, a hurricane of emotional distress. Nick now knew what her garage-sale purchase did—and although he was embarrassed, it was nothing compared to Caitlin's humiliation. People were already congratulating Nick, and giving him condolences for openly calling the principal a moron. It further immortalized him at the school, but it really wasn't the kind of notoriety he needed on his second day.

When school let out, the buzz in the hallways was all about Caitlin. "Can you believe her?" Nick heard people say. "Calling us her 'so-called friends'? Trying to get dirt to use against us?"

Nick was pretty sure Caitlin hadn't said anything about using it against them—and since the machine stripped away any and all lies, he was sure she had no plans to do so—but that didn't stop people from inserting things between the lines.

Theo was in the hallway doing his own damage control—trash-talking Caitlin with the hope of deflecting his own embarrassment. Still, kids asked him what other big words he knew.

"How about periorbital hematoma?" became Theo's standard response, accompanied by a raised fist. It was the technical term for a black eye. Nick had to give him kudos for anticipating the question and Googling the perfect answer before class let out.

Nick survived the afternoon exodus without being collared by the principal and went straight to Caitlin's house.

Her mother came to the door looking distraught, but she was only a fraction as upset as Caitlin probably was.

"She's had a bad day," her mother said. "Are you in any of her classes? Could you maybe tell me what happened?"

Nick thought it best just to give her a clueless shrug.

Caitlin's room was easy to find. It was the one with the sign that said CAITLIN'S ROOM made out of broken pieces of found objects. He knocked on the door so quietly it couldn't be heard, so he knocked again.

He heard Caitlin moan. "Go away."

"Caitlin, it's me. Nick."

"In that case, go away even faster."

He had never walked into a girl's room uninvited before. In fact, he'd never walked into a girl's room at all. When he turned the knob it was unlocked, which meant that deep down Caitlin wanted someone to come in.

The curtains were drawn and the lights were off. In the dimness it looked like there was a headless woman on the bed. But it was just that Caitlin's face was under a pillow.

"What part of 'go away' don't you understand?" she asked, her voice muffled by the pillow. "Unless you have information about who played that tape, I don't want you in my room."

But since she didn't throw anything at him, Nick stayed, sitting down at the desk chair. "Sorry," he said. "I have no idea."

He sat there saying nothing more, feeling horribly awkward, waiting for her to speak again.

"You could have warned me about the recorder," she said.

"I did," Nick pointed out. "Remember?"

"I mean when you sold it to me."

"I didn't know any more about the junk in my attic than you did, so don't blame me."

Finally Caitlin tossed off the pillow and stared at the ceiling. "Why couldn't I have just sprouted wings and flown?"

"Excuse me?"

"I mean, if something impossible had to happen to me, why couldn't it have been something impossible but great, instead of something that would ruin my life?" She sat up.

Now that Nick's eyes had adjusted to the dim light, he could see how red her eyes were from crying. "Don't say that," he said softly. "It'll be okay."

Finally she looked at him with a scowl, all of her misery, all of her frustration finding a target.

"What do you know about it? You couldn't possibly know what it feels like to have your life shred to bits in one stupid instant."

Nick took a deep breath. "I think I do." Then he told her things he hadn't spoken of since the day his own life had been shredded to bits.

"We moved here because our house burned down. It happened in the middle of the night. My dad, my brother, and I got out. But my mom died in the fire. And the thing is . . ."

This was the hard part. He had to close his eyes to say it.

". . . I think it was my fault."

Then Nick couldn't hold it in anymore. He burst into tears. "I know it was my fault."

Nick realized any chance he had with Caitlin was now gone.

What girl would be interested in a guy who barges into her bedroom only to burst into tears? If she hadn't thought he was pathetic before, she most certainly did now.

He did his best to wipe his eyes, and when he looked up, he saw she was crying, too.

"I am such an idiot," she said.

"Nah," Nick said. "I'm the idiot."

Caitlin thought for a moment. "I have friends who lost their homes in the wildfires a few years back. . . ."

Nick remembered hearing about the Colorado Springs fires. If nothing else, he had moved to a sympathetic town.

"I was in a fire once," Caitlin offered.

"What happened?"

"My Easy-Bake Oven had a short circuit."

"Was it bad?"

"Terrible," Caitlin said. "I lost my brownies." She said it with such a straight face that Nick unexpectedly found himself bursting out into laughter. She joined him. And before long their tears, while not forgotten, were at least behind them.

"Okay," Caitlin said, "so what happened today isn't the end of the world. But how am I supposed to go back to school after the things everybody heard?"

"Here's what I think will happen," Nick told her. "For a while, everyone will go nuts with it. Some of your friends will shun you. People who didn't really like you to begin with will hate you even more."

"And this is helping how?" Caitlin asked.

Nick held up his hand. "But your true friends will get it. They'll stick by you. And then after a while—a week, a month—"

"Ten years?" Caitlin suggested.

"Maybe. What happened to you is kind of like a fire, in a way. I saw this thing once on TV. They said wildfires have to

71

happen every so often. Brush gets too thick, trees get too dense. You have a hot day and *whoosh!* But the healthy trees survive. In fact, there are some seeds that won't even grow until they burn first." Nick shrugged. "So have you lost some friends today? Maybe, but they weren't real friends. They were just brush. And the ones who stick by you, the ones who get it? They're the healthy trees."

Caitlin thought about it and smiled. "I think you're a pretty healthy tree."

"Yeah," said Nick, "a weeping willow."

"At least you're still *poplar*," Caitlin answered, and they both groaned, then laughed again.

Nick looked over at the tape recorder, sitting in the corner of her room. He imagined her running all the way home with it in her arms, a burden too heavy to bear, and yet she bore it.

"So you really think I'm cute, huh?"

"What?"

"That's what you said."

"No," Caitlin corrected, "that's what I *didn't* say. And if you don't want me to find a lumberjack to hack you into sawdust, you'll leave it alone."

Nick grinned. "All you had to do was ax."

Caitlin's ensuing loud "Ouch!" brought her mother to the door. "Is everything okay in here?"

"Everything's fine," Caitlin said. "I may vomit, but we're fine."

"Should I get the Pepto-Bismol?"

"Figurative vomit, Mom. God, sometimes you're so literal."

Nick prepared to take the recorder, but Caitlin stopped him.

"One thing first." Then she rewound the tape to the beginning, hit RECORD, and they sat there in silence as the machine erased everything she had recorded.

And sitting there with her in absolute silence, Nick didn't feel awkward at all.

Nick carried the recorder home. He thought about putting it in the garage, but he worried that Danny, or even his father, might fiddle with it. In the end, it went back up in the attic along with the toaster and the stage light that had somehow made his garage sale such an overwhelming success. Three unusual decorations in his new bedroom, all three of which he was afraid to use.

As for the Shut Up 'n Listen and the reanimating wet-cell battery—he would have to count on Vince and Mitch to keep their word, and keep the things to themselves. Besides, he wasn't as worried about what was known as about what was unknown. All those other objects that were out there. The TV, and the vacuum cleaner, and who knew what else.

There was no way to know whether or not the new owners had discovered the peculiar traits of their purchases, or what those traits might be . . . and more important, *why* these objects did what they did. Nick wished there was a way to shed light on his situation, but it remained as dim as the attic bedroom, where no amount of incandescent light could chase away the shadows.

Nick looked up at the pyramidal panes of glass where the roof came to a point above him, and the black paint that kept out the light of day. Well, maybe the purpose of his garage-sale items was obscured in darkness, but his room didn't have to be. At least he could do something about that.

Nick went down to the garage and got a folding ladder he'd seen there, grabbed a paint scraper from the old tool cabinet, and brought them both back to the attic. He climbed up to the skylight and began scraping off the paint.

Peering through the patch of glass he had just scraped clean, he saw his father throwing a ball with Danny. It looked like Danny was using their dad's old mitt and was doing pretty well. It made Nick feel good to see them sharing a simple, happy moment together, and he dared to allow himself to think that everything could be good again. Maybe not perfect, but at least okay.

As he continued to clear paint from the windows, letting light into the attic, he noticed something wedged into the frame holding the pyramidal panes of glass together, and he pulled it out. It was the business card of Dr. Alan Jorgenson.

8 ALTERNATIVE GENIUS

Nick's situation at school was leveling out in spite of everything. The guidance counselor had put him on a reasonable plan to get on track academically, and he had even intervened on Nick's behalf with the principal, whom Nick had taken to secretly calling "Principal Who" because he had not yet learned the man's actual name. As it turns out, the principal's last name was Watt.

"I'll have you know that your records have finally arrived from Denmark," Principal Watt told him. Indeed, the same computer glitch that had lost him and his brother like luggage now insisted that they had transferred from the Danske Akademi of Copenhagen. "We realize this is a technical error," Principal Watt admitted, "but we'll go with it." Apparently, having a new international student made the school look good.

During the busy school day, when everything felt so straightforward and ordinary, it was easy to temporarily forget about the extraordinary things from his attic, now spread around Colorado Springs and maybe even beyond.

Caitlin and Vince would both slyly nod to him in the hall, as if the three were part of some secret society. Mitch was not as subtle, offering theory after theory, sometimes loud enough for other people to hear. The only saving grace was that this was middle school and nobody cared.

"They're relics from an alien spacecraft," Mitch suggested. Or, "They were smuggled in from Atlantis before it sank." Nick's favorite of Mitch's theories was "We're all trapped in a dream and these objects were sent here to jolt us out of it."

Nick suspected that whatever the truth was, it was much more rational—but just as surreal.

Socially, Nick was still an unknown quantity to his classmates, but any sense of mutual threat was gone. He was free to exist on his own terms, even if, on paper, he was from Denmark.

Surprisingly, the one thing Nick thought would not be a problem was threatening him with grief—Little League. He assumed that he could just move right on to a Colorado Springs team, but baseball season had already started, the teams had been locked in, and games had already been played. At first he was stonewalled and told to come back next year, but his father's status as a former Tampa Bay Rays pitcher carried enough respect to get Nick a special tryout that Thursday.

"I have complete faith you'll show them how this game is played," his dad said before Nick headed off to school that morning, handing him a new baseball glove that he had purchased for the occasion, to replace the one lost in the fire.

At lunch that day, Nick made a point of being last in line again so he could spend some quality time with Ms. Planck.

"I just wanted to thank you," he told her as she served him lasagna that didn't look half bad. "Your tip about Heisenberg was gold, just like you said."

"I'm glad to see someone taking advantage of my knowledge, instead of just taking advantage," she said. "Anything else I can help with?"

Nick sighed. "Weird stuff you don't want to know about."

"Honey, I serve slop for a living—a pinch of weird stuff spices up an otherwise bland day."

Nick grinned. He imagined Ms. Planck was somewhat like a bartender in the movies, seeing people from all walks of life and having a unique perspective that she was happy to share with those who would listen.

"I had a garage sale this past weekend. Now I'm worried that I shouldn't have sold the things I did."

Ms. Planck considered it. "Well, it's like they say, if you love something, set it free."

"I didn't love any of the stuff."

"In that case, you're screwed." Then she laughed and scooped him up a nice serving of bread pudding. She looked at him fondly for a moment, then said, "I have no doubt that, one way or another, you'll fill the empty spaces left behind."

Across the cafeteria, Petula observed Nick having an extended verbal encounter with Ms. Planck. She timed it at precisely one minute and thirteen seconds. It thoroughly peeved her that all two of her conversations with Nick did not add up to this amount of time. What could he possibly have to talk about with the lunch lady?

When he left with his tray to sit down, Petula headed straight for Ms. Planck.

"Excuse me," she asked, "but—"

"Didn't you already get your lunch, Miss Grabowski-Jones?"

It threw her for a loop that Ms. Planck knew her last names. "Yes, but that's not why I'm here."

"Oh, then you must be volunteering to help clean the silverware."

"Nice try. I just wanted to know what you were talking about with Nick Slate."

"Have you considered that maybe it was a private conversation?"

Petula crossed her arms. "Have you considered that this is a *public* school?"

Ms. Planck began to remove the food from the warming trays. "Very good," she said. "You should take the Advanced Banter class when you get to high school. I suspect you'll do well."

Only for a moment did Petula entertain the idea that there might actually be such a class, and that she might, in fact, excel, but then she realized she was being mocked. She gave Ms. Planck her best withering glare, but Ms. Planck was not one to wither. She was what Petula's father would call "a handsome woman," which Petula took to mean a woman who was once beautiful but has now reached the age at which she grows facial hair.

Ms. Planck waved a ladle at her. "Oh, don't be such a sourpuss, Petula. If you must know, Nick was thanking me for giving him the lowdown on things around here, and sharing thoughts about his garage sale."

"Did he mention me?"

"Why would he do that?"

"I was at his garage sale."

"Well, dear," Ms. Planck said, "from what I understand, you weren't the only one." Then she took a moment to contemplate Petula. "You like the boy, hmm?"

"No!" said Petula.

"The proof is in the pudding," Ms. Planck said, and Petula reflexively looked down at the pudding in the tray, even though she knew that wasn't what Ms. Planck meant. "You're the one who played that awful conversation over the loudspeakers, aren't you?"

Petula's eyes went wide with shock.

"Oh, don't try to deny it—there isn't anyone else in this school obnoxious enough to do something like that. You thought it would push Nick away from Caitlin, but did it work?"

Petula shook her head.

"It was the wrong tactic, honey," Ms. Planck said. Then she leaned as close as she could to Petula and spoke quietly. "If it's your intent to make an impression," she offered, "it's best to have something he needs. Even if he doesn't know what it is."

Beef-O-Rama was a burger joint a few blocks from school that was trying painfully hard to be trendy but was one trend behind the times. Kind of like that teacher who uses last year's popular expressions, thereby becoming the very "epic fail" he just announced. People accepted the tackiness of Beef-O-Rama because they served decent burgers that hadn't killed anyone yet.

Nick and Mitch waited for the single overworked waitress to bring them menus, but Nick's mind wasn't on food. Nor was it on his upcoming baseball tryout. Once again his head was up his attic. Or, more accurately, on the things missing from it.

"Besides you, Vince, Caitlin, and my cranky neighbor, I don't know any of the people who bought stuff at the garage sale. This isn't just looking for a needle in a haystack—we don't even know where the haystack *is*!"

"I'm sure it will sort itself out," Mitch told him, signaling to the waitress again.

"How can you be so sure?"

Mitch lifted the Shut Up 'n Listen and pulled the string. "Nick's problem—"

And the machine said, *"—will sort itself out."*

Nick glared at the device as the last of the string sucked in and the arrow stopped spinning. "I really, really hate that thing."

"The point is you gotta live in the moment, dude, and stop worrying about those things you got no control over." Then he patted the device. "And enjoy the things you do!"

"Aren't you the least bit curious? I mean, what were all these things doing in my attic?" Nick took the Shut Up 'n Listen from Mitch and turned it over. There, on the bottom, was the same spidery inscription, *Property of NT*. "And who's NT anyway?"

Petula appeared suddenly, as if she had popped out of the woodwork. "Nikola Tesla, you idiot. Mind if I join you? Too bad if you do."

She shoved Mitch down the bench so she could sit right across from Nick, and she put a basket of fries on the table between them as a peace offering/bribe. "Here, share my fries." ·

"Nikola *who*?" Nick asked.

"Oh, yeah," said Mitch, "that inventor guy. They named the alternative school after him."

"Inventor guy?!" Petula stared at Mitch. "*Inventor guy?* He was just the greatest scientist of all time, that's all. He used to have a lab here."

Nick shrugged. "Never heard of him."

"Are you kidding me? He invented fluorescent lights—AC power—the wireless transmission of energy—and radio!"

"Ha!" said Nick. "You're wrong. The radio was Marconi."

Petula shook her head. "No—Marconi copied Tesla's patents. Tesla sued and won, but it was too late. Marconi got the Nobel Prize, and Tesla got zilch."

"So tell me, Miss Petupedia, why was all his crap in my attic?"

"Not quite sure. Further research is required."

"Wait, you've been researching this?" And then Nick realized. "The garage sale—you bought something, didn't you?"

Petula gave him an extremely wide grin. "Well, maybe if you hadn't been dragging your eyes all over Caitlin's wet T-shirt, you would have remembered me buying an old box camera."

Mitch, who had been quietly devouring all of Petula's fries, asked, "What does it do?"

"It takes pictures, you moron."

"So," said Nick, a little peeved, "I'm an idiot, and he's a moron—should I call the waitress over so you can insult her, too?"

"I use these words as terms of endearment." Then she reached into her purse and pulled out a slip of paper, which she handed to Nick. "If you want to know the deal with the camera, meet me at this address, Friday night at eight." As she got up to leave, she glanced over at Mitch, whose mouth had a lipstick-like ring of ketchup. "Come alone!" she told Nick.

"You realize we're making an exception allowing you to try out," the coach told Nick when he arrived at practice later that afternoon.

"I know. Thank you. I promise you won't be disappointed."

The coach was the first baseman's father, and the first baseman should have been playing soccer for all the times balls were rolling at his feet. But of course you couldn't tell the coach that, or you'd be warming the bench.

"I understand you're a pitcher like your father."

"For five years," Nick told him. "Before that it was T-ball."

"Right." Then the coach called to the team's current pitcher. "Hey, Theo, take a break and let this kid pitch for a while."

"Theo?" Sure enough, it was Caitlin's boyfriend on the mound. Nick grinned. Few things would be more satisfying than sending him to the bullpen.

Theo trotted off the field. "Great," he said to Nick. "Knock yourself out. Unless you want me to do it for you."

"All right, Nicky, let's see what you got," the coach barked.

"It's Nick," he said, wondering if correcting the coach earned you a space on the bench next to the player who said his kid sucked.

Nick jogged out to the pitcher's mound, the eyes of the team on him with mild curiosity.

The catcher took his position, a batter came up to the plate, and from the near-empty stands, Mitch shouted, "Hey, batter-batter-batter—swing!"

Nick wanted to tell him to shut up, but realized that saying anything would acknowledge that he actually knew Mitch. So he tried to pretend as if Mitch didn't exist.

Briefly, Nick wished his dad could have been there to see his moment of glory, but then again, maybe not. There was always an underlying sadness in his dad when it came to baseball. A wistfulness about what could have been, if things had turned out differently.

The batter tapped the plate with his bat, then held it at the ready, waiting for Nick's pitch.

Nick put all his concentration into the ball. He wound up and—

"Hey batter-batter-batter—swing!" yelled Mitch.

Nick's pitch went wild. It didn't even come near the strike zone.

The catcher grappled on the ground for the ball, and the coach said, "Don't worry about it. Try again."

Nick knew he was up to this. He had watched the team practice. He was a better pitcher than Theo, their goosenecked prima donna, and more agile around the bases than any of them. He knew he'd have to pay his dues, but when he finally shone, it would be all the more satisfying.

He wound up for the second pitch, and for an instant, only an instant, he wondered if anyone here had bought something from his attic. And that momentary mental hiccup flew off the tips of his fingers along with his pitch.

"Hey batter-batter-batter—swing!"

The second pitch wasn't quite as wild as the first, but was way too high for the catcher to reach. It hit the backstop and bounced off with a rattle.

This time the coach said nothing. He just motioned for the catcher to give Nick one more chance.

Nick tried to pull in all his concentration, winding it down into the perfect pitch he always delivered when it was most needed. His mother had been in the stands at his last game. He had pitched a no-hitter. When he threw that final strike, and the team raised him over their heads, he remembered the way she stood in the stands cheering for him.

Now, as he wound up to throw the third pitch, all he could think was that she would never see him play again . . . and even though Mitch said nothing this time, it didn't matter. With thoughts of his mother clouding his mind, his pitch hit the batter.

"Ow! What's wrong with you?" yelled the batter, rubbing his bruised arm.

"Sorry!" Nick shouted. "I didn't mean to, it just . . ."

The coach took a few seconds to inspect the damage to the batter, then reluctantly came out to the pitcher's mound.

"Son," he said, taking off his hat like he was about to tell him his dog had died, "I hate to say this, but maybe pitching isn't your forte."

"But it *is*," stammered Nick. "It's what I do best."

The coach glanced at the batter, who was still rubbing his arm, then back at Nick. "I'm sorry, son, but I think you need to work on your game some. Maybe next year." Then he walked away.

Nick wanted to hurl the glove at his retreating head. But he wouldn't give Theo and the rest of the team the satisfaction of seeing his anger. Instead, he took off his mitt and tossed it to the first baseman, who bobbled it and dropped it at his feet.

"Keep it," Nick said. "Maybe you'll actually catch a ball with it someday."

"Guess what happened today!" Danny was bouncing with excitement as Nick came in the door.

"You got bit by a radioactive spider, and now you can catch thieves just like flies."

"No," said Danny. "I made the nine-and-under baseball team!"

Nick just stared at him.

"The coach says I'm a natural outfielder!"

There were many foul balls flying through Nick's head at the moment, but instead of saying something he'd regret, he dug down and forced a smile. "That's great, Danny. Mom would have been proud of you."

Then Nick went to his room, pulled the ladder up behind him, and didn't come out for the rest of the night.

9 SIT DOWN AND EAT SOME SQUID

Archimedes, the great mathematician, once said, "Give me a lever long enough, and I shall move the world." Of course, another time he ran naked through the streets shouting "Eureka!"—which only goes to show that even history's greatest minds have issues.

Take Euclid, who, even after proving that the shortest distance between two points is a straight line, was habitually late to everything. And let's not even mention Pythagoras.

We rarely consider that the great minds that have changed the world at one time or another suffered heartbreak, loss, and exclusion from their chosen sport. We forget that they were human.

Nick Slate had no clue how important a part he was soon to play in the grand scheme of things. But one thing is certain: none of it would have been possible had he not suffered the course of his own human events.

Events like Petula Grabowski-Jones.

Eight o'clock sharp, Petula had said. Although Nick didn't want to appear eager to have anything to do with her, she did claim to have information he desperately needed. So he showed up five minutes early.

Petula, of course, had shown up ten minutes early.

Before he saw her, Nick thought he must have gotten the address wrong. The place was a restaurant. Not the sit-down-and-pig-out kind, but the kind where the food was ridiculously expensive, the portions were ridiculously small, the menu was in another language, and the waiters were dressed better than you.

Petula sat alone at a table with her hair up, wearing a stylish dress designed with curves in all the right places on a body that, unfortunately, had no discernible curves at all, so it hung like a red satin toga.

She looked up at Nick as he entered. "What do you think you're doing?" she asked sharply. "They don't allow jeans in here. Sit down before anyone sees you."

Nick looked around. No one was watching them but an elderly couple, who grinned at them with an "Ah, young love" look in their eyes.

"What's the deal?" Nick demanded.

Petula grinned. "You want information, you're going to have to romance it out of me. But I'll tell you right now, I don't kiss on the first date. Unless you actually want to."

A waiter arrived and smoothly placed before Nick a plate of some kind of food he had never seen before. They looked like miniature onion rings, but Nick doubted they were.

"Your date took the liberty of ordering the calamari appetizer," the waiter informed Nick.

"She's not my date," Nick said, then turned to Petula. "You're not my date."

"Let's not argue semantics," she said. "Now sit down and eat some squid."

Nick thought of a million reasons why not to sit, but they paled in comparison to the one reason he needed to, so he plopped himself down in the chair and, as he angrily gnawed on a calamari ring, said, "Whatever you've got to tell me had better be worth it. And by the way, I can't pay for this place."

"Calm down; I have a gift certificate." She waved it in his face. "Of course it's expired, but we can feign ignorance."

"Fine." Nick grabbed another few fried rings. "But your information had better be as good as this calamari."

Petula smiled victoriously. "Patience," she said. "It's only the first course."

And so Nick had to endure not just the calamari, but a salad and small talk that was almost as microscopic as the portions, before Petula would divulge anything.

Nick, on the other hand, was anxious to share what he had learned in his own research: that Tesla and Thomas Edison hated each other; that Tesla had accomplished things that to this day haven't been duplicated; and that he made his first million by the age of forty, but gave it all away.

To all of these things, Petula merely said, "Tell me something I don't know."

It was as they awaited their entrées that Petula served up the stuff that wasn't common knowledge. "Tesla was a very private man," she told him. "Rumor was he had a secret love shack, because he was carrying on with some Colorado Springs socialite, but no one in the old social columns I read knew who it was."

Nick considered this. It didn't take Euclid to connect the dots. "My great-aunt Greta?" he asked. The thought of his great-aunt having a romantic anything with anyone made him shudder.

"Apparently so," Petula said. "She was what you would call a floozy."

"So that explains why his stuff was in my attic."

"Yes and no," Petula said, enigmatically.

Their entrées arrived: Petula's blackened ahi with a lavender-infused beet rémoulade, and Nick's grilled cheese sandwich.

That's where the conversation ended, as Petula had a strict rule about not talking while chewing.

Between her seventh and eighth forkful, however, she said, "The question you need to ask yourself is . . . why did he put it in *her* attic, and not his own?"

As Petula had predicted, acting clueless about the expired gift certificate got them a free meal, and although Petula requested a walk home, Nick only went as far as the corner of her street, as any farther would definitely make this feel too datelike for comfort.

The information Petula gave him was worth enduring the meal, but there was still something she was holding back. "You still haven't told me what the old camera does," Nick pointed out, before they parted. "Besides taking pictures, I mean."

"I don't know what you're talking about," she told him. "It's a camera—it's not like it's going to grow legs and do the hokey-pokey."

And although Nick wasn't so sure about that, he didn't want to inflame Petula's curiosity any further. "Never mind. It's just that it belonged to Tesla, and like you said, he was a genius."

"Sometimes," said Petula, "a camera is just a camera."

She held out her arms, expecting a good-night hug, but Nick kept his hands in his pockets and said, "Well, see ya," then made a successful escape.

Although he knew there must be more to the camera than met the eye, if Petula hadn't discovered it yet, that could only be a good thing.

When he got home, Vince was lurking on the porch. The kid was very good at lurking, Nick decided.

"Here," he said as Nick approached, and held out an object that Nick recognized from the garage sale: an electric fan with odd hexagonal blades. "I was trolling the police net, and I heard about an apartment complex where the air-conditioning went haywire. Froze the place out. Snow in the hallways and stuff. This thing was running in apartment Four-G. People had no idea it was the cause of their freeze-out."

"Good going, Vince."

"Wanna see if we can cryonically freeze your neighbor's dog?"

"Tempting, but no."

"You're no fun." And with that, Vince slouched his merry way home.

Nick brought the fan up to his room, where he found that his dirty laundry had been collected in the center of the attic floor. Weird. He hadn't left it that way. When his mom was alive, she would occasionally gather his soiled clothes and shove them underneath his covers, as a not-so-subtle reminder to put them in the hamper. But now that she was gone, his dirty laundry carpeted much of the floor until he got so sick of it he finally washed it.

Was Danny playing some sort of game? Regardless, since the clothes were all in one convenient pile, he brought them down to the old washing machine that was certainly not designed by Tesla, because it did nothing abnormal—if you didn't count the way it jumped during spin cycles. Once out of sight, the laundry was out of mind—and when he returned to his room Nick didn't notice that his bed and desk had moved three inches from the wall, toward the center of the room.

10 A CASE OF MURLÓ

Mitch Murló, despite popular opinion, had a life.

It wasn't an enviable one, though. At least not for the past year. His mother, who had always been there for him, was rarely around now, because of the two jobs she had to hold down to keep food on the table for Mitch and his younger sister. His father, who had also always been there for him, was now elsewhere.

When Nick showed up in town, it was Mitch's chance to have a friend who knew nothing of his family's considerable baggage, so of course he tried a little too hard. Who could fault him? Mitch knew it wouldn't last forever—after all, people talked— but for now he and Nick had something in common: a sudden interest in the lost inventions of the original mad scientist.

And maybe, thought Mitch, it might even withstand a Murló "family day."

At eight o'clock on Saturday morning, Mitch sat at the kitchen table, staring at the Shut Up 'n Listen before him. He loosened his tie, as it was already beginning to choke.

The device waited with patient, intimidating silence for the opportunity to finish his thoughts. The little ivory ring on the end of the string was practically taunting him to pull it.

"Can I play with it?" asked Madison, his five-year-old sister.

"No," he told her. "It's not a toy."

"It looks like a toy."

"Well, it's not."

"Then you can't play with Mr. McGrizzly." She wiggled her stuffed bear tauntingly in his face, then strutted out of the room, leaving Mitch alone with the device that was anything but a toy.

He took a deep breath, pulled the string, and held it taut. "My father . . ." he said, then let the string go.

And the machine said, ". . . *can't wait to see you.*"

Mitch sighed. Not what he wanted to hear. Again his tie seemed to be turning into a noose, and he tugged it looser. He pulled the string and tried again. "My father only needs . . ."

". . . *to see you and your sister.*"

Mitch pounded his fist on the table in frustration. One more time he grabbed the ring and pulled.

"I can't visit my father today . . ."

". . . *without wearing a smile.*"

Mitch put his head in his hands. There was no getting out of this, and the damn machine only rubbed it in.

It wasn't that Mitch didn't love his father—he did—but the weekend visits had been getting progressively more difficult, more awkward. Mitch knew it was petty of him. But the things happening around him now were bigger than his personal problems. The connection between Mitch and this device was growing stronger. It was almost as if he had become a part of the mechanism. A crucial part of it.

He didn't understand it any more than he understood how the machine could do what it did. All he knew was that he, Nick, Caitlin, Vince, and everyone else who had been affected by the weird crap from Nick's attic were part of some invisible clockwork that was activated by the garage sale and was churning its gears toward some dark, mysterious end.

"Or maybe I'm just nuts," he said out loud. Hearing himself say it made him feel a whole lot better. *How weird*, he thought, *that I'd rather be nuts than right.*

Mitch's mother walked into the kitchen, her ear glued to her phone, as usual. "Honestly, Maria, the weather's been so unpredictable like the sudden downpour last week and my tires are bald and I don't have the money to replace them so one of these days we'll just fly off the road and land dead in a ditch and no one will find us for months and you know what else . . . ?"

Mitch found it amazing that she could talk without stopping for breath. The only way to get a word in edgewise was to talk on top of her at an increasingly louder volume. It was like merging onto a non-yielding freeway.

"Mom, I got too much homework and a major project due on Monday and I can't work in the car you know I get carsick so if I go today I'll fail and—"

"—the 'check engine' light keeps coming on what does that mean anyway 'check engine' why doesn't it just tell me what's wrong because if it did—"

"—and you and Dad will have no one to blame but yourselves for keeping me from doing my work which is due on Monday AND I'LL END UP GETTING SENT TO THE ALTERNATIVE SCHOOL ALL BECAUSE OF YOU!"

"Hold on, Maria." And finally she took the phone away from her face. "What are you going on about?"

"My homework, which is—"

"Very easy if you don't wait until the last minute," his mother said, subverting his thought. Then she returned to the phone, still without taking a breath.

The alternative school, thought Mitch, which was named after none other than Nikola Tesla, the man behind the machine that lately seemed to be controlling his life.

He picked up the Shut Up 'n Listen and headed for the door, pulling the string as he did.

"I'll be back," he called to his mom. "I'm going . . ."

". . . *to see Nick,*" finished the machine.

For once, the machine said exactly what he was going to say.

At that very moment, however, Nick was considering an unexpected proposition.

"So, you wanna come over?" Caitlin asked him over the phone, after about nine seconds of small talk. He didn't even know how she'd gotten his number.

"Huh?" he said like an imbecile. Then he fumbled the phone but caught it before it hit the floor.

"I need some help with my new art project," Caitlin said. "It involves blowing up paint cans with M-80s, and none of my other friends are willing to take any more shrapnel for the cause."

At that moment he would have dived on a paint grenade for Caitlin, but he wasn't about to admit it out loud. "Sure, I guess," he said.

"Do you have insurance?" Caitlin asked.

"Uh, yeah?" Nick said, which was better than saying, "Let me consult my portfolio of things I am clueless about."

"Good," Caitlin said brightly. "See you in half an hour?"

"Okay. And if you don't like my contribution to your project, you can always blow me up." But unfortunately the call dropped somewhere before he finished his sentence, leaving Nick to agonize for many years over exactly which words Caitlin had missed.

After dressing himself in clothes that were nice, but not too nice, and putting on cologne and then washing it off, Nick left the house for his explosionist-art encounter with Caitlin.

Nick was so caught up in his own thoughts that by the time he saw Mitch riding up on his bicycle, it was too late to hide.

"Hey," said Mitch, "goin' somewhere?"

"Yeah," said Nick, determined not to go into the details, because then he'd never be able to get rid of Mitch. "What's with the shirt and tie? Is it a religious thing? Are you going to knock on my door and leave a pamphlet?"

He'd meant it as a joke, but there was a certain sadness in Mitch when he answered, "Nah. Nothin' like that."

Mitch seemed awkward. It wasn't like him. Usually he would just barrel into conversation, oblivious to whether the other person wanted him to or not.

"Listen, Mitch, I'm kind of busy right now, so . . ."

"I'm gonna go see my dad today. I was hoping you might come with. I bet he'd really like to meet you."

Let's see, thought Nick. *Quality artistic time with Caitlin, or hanging out with Mitch and his father?* It was like comparing apples and no freaking way.

"Maybe some other time," he said.

"Yeah, yeah, I understand." Again that uncharacteristic look on Mitch's face. Something between nausea and puppy-dog eyes. "It's just that my dad thinks I have no friends. I want to show him he's wrong, y'know?"

Nick took a deep breath to steel himself against Mitch's desperation. *Let's see,* he thought. *Quality artistic time with Caitlin, or my conscience?* The decision was a little bit harder this time, but Nick's mental scale still tipped toward Caitlin. "Another time," he said again, and added, "I promise." And the fact that he really meant it was enough to satisfy his conscience.

To Nick's absolute surprise, Mitch didn't put up a fight. He just caved.

"Right," he said. "Okay, then, see ya."

He turned around and began to pedal away. It was as if knew he was defeated even before he began.

It was clear that Mitch needed this, and needed it now, not "some other time." So the question was, how on earth could Nick shift the balance to Mitch, when Caitlin sat so firmly on the other side?

To Nick's surprise, the answer came easily.

"Mitch, wait up!" He trotted out to Mitch in the middle of the street. "Tell you what. I'll go with you today on one condition."

"Yeah?"

"When we get home, you give me back the Shut Up 'n Listen."

For a moment Mitch looked like he had been stabbed through the heart. But then he looked Nick in the eye, held out his hand, and said, "Deal."

It is well known that the microwave oven was invented by accident, when a scientist walking near a huge microwave array discovered that a candy bar in his pocket had melted.

The first artificial sweetener was discovered when a researcher sat down for dinner and found his bread so unexpectedly sweet he was compelled to retrace his steps, touching every chemical his hands had come in contact with that day, until he found the ones that combined into something that tasted like sugar.

And the Slinky? It was invented when a naval engineer knocked a spring off a counter and watched it climb its way down to the floor.

Of course these all could just as easily have gone awry. The microwave guy could have fried his heart instead of the chocolate in his shirt pocket. The sweet genius could have had the good sense to wash his hands before eating, never discovering anything. And the Slinky sailor could have abandoned his wife and kids to join a Bolivian religious cult, never to be heard from again. (Well, actually, he did—but not until after inventing that which walks down stairs, alone or in pairs, thus changing childhood forever.)

Happy accidents and unexpected revelations are the rule rather than the exception in the world of science. For example, Petula Grabowski-Jones made a shocking discovery when she developed a photo she had snapped of her Chihuahua, Hemorrhoid, sitting on the corner table in the living room in broad daylight. Instead of getting an image of her dog, she got an image of her mother—taking money from her father's wallet in that very same location, in the middle of the night. This accidental find provided Petula with much-needed insight into her "malfunctioning" box camera—and a great income opportunity through blackmail.

The last thing Caitlin Westfield expected to discover was that blowing up paint cans was really no fun at all without Nick's help, which in turn gave her the unexpected revelation of her own secret motivation. She suddenly realized that she had concocted the whole art project as a means of spending the afternoon with Nick.

And as for Nick, the last thing that he expected to discover was that, much like the asteroid that had killed off the dinosaurs, thereby clearing the way for the evolution of mammals, there was more to Mitch than his overbearing, tactless surface might suggest.

"My dad lives in a gated community," Mitch told Nick as they made the long drive to wherever they were going.

They were in the backseat of Mitch's family car, his mom driving with her cell phone pressed quite illegally to her ear as she talked nonstop. Mitch's little sister was in the passenger seat next to her mom, kicking her feet against the plastic dash like she wanted to kill the glove compartment.

"What does your dad do?" Nick asked.

"Well, he was into computers," Mitch answered, "but now he works for the state."

Nick nodded, but that was already more information than he needed when he was still cursing himself for choosing the Murló family's Pontiac of Pain over a day with Caitlin.

Mitch fidgeted with the Shut Up 'n Listen but didn't pull the string. Nick wondered if his restraint was due to having sworn on Vince's Damnation Bible, or if there was a thought he didn't want finished.

"You know it's best if it goes back into my attic, right?" Nick said.

Mitch didn't look at him. "It doesn't matter what I think. I made a deal, didn't I?" Still, he ran his hand along its cold metallic shell. "Lately I've been feeling like it knows what I'm going to say before I even say it. That's crazy, right?"

"Yeah, crazy," Nick said. But he knew better.

Mitch's father's exclusive gated community had an extensive guard gate. In fact, it had two. It also had an electrified fence. And towers with armed guards. All things considered, few gated communities could be more exclusive than the Colorado State Penitentiary.

"Why didn't you tell me?" Nick asked Mitch as they waited in line to pass through the metal detector.

"I did," said Mitch. "You just failed to read between the lines."

Nick didn't want to ask the nature of the crime that had landed Mitch's father in a maximum security prison—although the term *serial killer* did cross his mind precisely twenty-three times between the gate and the metal detector.

"My father's a computer genius," Mitch finally said. "He designed electronic fund-transfer protocols for international banks. Somewhere along the line he discovered that the banking web was even more tightly connected than the Internet, so he created an untraceable program that could go into any random account and take a single penny. He tried it out, and it landed him here. Guess it wasn't quite as untraceable as he thought."

"He got thrown in prison for stealing a penny?"

"Sort of," said Mitch. "He stole one penny from every bank account in the world."

"No way," said Nick. "That's got to be—

Mitch pulled the string on the Shut Up 'n Listen. "—*$725,452,344,*" said the device. *"And thirty-nine cents."*

Nick was speechless.

"I never liked my dad's business partners," Mitch said, unloading junk from his pockets into a plastic bin on the security station's conveyer belt. "They were mega-creepy."

The Shut Up 'n Listen was not the usual sort of personal effect that prison security came across in their routine checks, and Mitch had the hardest time getting it through. Nick was troubled that Mitch had brought it in at all, but with the whole prison experience, he hadn't noticed until they were already inside under armed surveillance. The X-ray machine didn't reveal anything of obvious criminal intent inside the device, but it was too unusual for the officer on duty to let pass.

"It's my shop project," Mitch told him. "I promised my dad I'd show it to him."

"Mitch, why don't you just put it back in the car," his mom

said, collecting her cell phone and jewelry from the plastic bin. "And next time make something plastic."

Obviously, Nick's mother had no clue as to what the thing really was. But Mitch's sister had figured it out, even if Mitch hadn't told her—because she pulled the string just as the guard said, "I'm afraid I can't—"

"—*get a date without lying about myself.*"

The officer was flabbergasted, but Mitch's little sister laughed in delight.

"That's funny," she said.

The officer clearly did not know what to make of this. "Is that so?" he said as Madison pulled the string again. "Well, I don't think—"

"—*anyone needs to know that I still live with my mother.*"

Madison laughed again. "You want to hear what else it says?"

"No!" The guard, his face reddening, handed the thing back to Mitch. "Just move along."

Nick thought there'd be bulletproof glass between the prisoners and visitors, but there wasn't. It was just a room with tables and a whole lot of guards. The room smelled like old gym equipment—slightly metallic and slightly foul—and the only way you could tell the prisoners from the visitors was by who wore bright orange uniforms.

"We're hoping we don't have to come here much longer," Mitch said as he scanned the room for his father, who had not yet arrived. "My dad goes before the parole board next month. His lawyers are asking for time off for good behavior, and my dad is really well behaved."

Nick didn't know if he should sit or stand or run for his life. This was not the kind of white-collar Club Fed where one would expect to find a computer hacker. This place was the real deal. The men here were grizzled by hard time and harder crimes. Most of them had extreme tattoos that seemed to cover more space than they actually had flesh to put them on.

A guard finally escorted Mitch's father in, and Madison jumped up and down excitedly. Mr. Murló was slimmer than Mitch, but he had the same curly hair and gruff voice. He also had a deerish look of bewildered innocence, as if, after all this time, he still couldn't comprehend his circumstances. The man seemed overjoyed to see his family, but with every breath Nick sensed an abiding melancholy—perhaps the only thing he had in common with his fellow inmates.

They sat at one of the few vacant tables in the room, Nick pulling up a chair with the others, feeling more than awkward. Mitch introduced him as "my best friend, Nick," which seemed to please Mr. Murló a great deal. Madison spoke about her class play and her crucial role as a dental filling.

Mitch's father regarded the Shut Up 'n Listen curiously. "Whatcha got there?"

But since his mom was sitting right there, Mitch put it beneath the table and changed the subject, asking about the quality of food and his father's chances of parole. It was only when his mother left to take Madison to the bathroom that Mitch pulled out the Shut Up 'n Listen.

"Mitch," said Nick, "I don't think—"

"That I should use it," Mitch finished. "I know you don't, and I know I swore. But it's still mine as long as we're here, and I have to do this."

Nick looked to Mitch, then to Mr. Murló. Whatever Mitch was about to do, Nick couldn't stop him.

"I used to have one of these when I was a kid," Mr. Murló said nostalgically.

Mitch shook his head. "Not like this one."

"Your mom said you made it in shop class."

"Not exactly."

Mitch didn't try to explain. Instead, he looked around to make sure no one else was close enough to hear, then gave his father a crash course in unfinished thoughts. "The Colorado Rockies . . ." he began.

"*. . . will go 83 and 79 this year,*" the machine finished.

"The unemployment rate . . ."

"*. . . will drop by 3.2 percent.*"

"Your favorite restaurant . . ."

"*. . . is going out of business next month.*"

"Tomorrow's winning Lotto numbers . . ."

"*. . . will all be divisible by three.*"

Mitch looked away for a moment, trying to wipe his eyes without being obvious about it. Mitch's father gave him an awkward grin. "That's cute," he said. "You programmed the responses yourself?"

"You try it," Mitch told him.

Nick wanted to say something to stop this before it could go any further, but the scene unfolding before him had the momentum of a bullet train with Mitch at the controls. Mitch, who had always been two parts nuisance, one part screwup, was now pure steel intensity. He had full command of the moment. He knew exactly what he was doing.

When Mitch's father didn't reach for the string, Mitch pulled it again and again, a little more forcefully each time.

"Your business partners . . ."

"*. . . used you.*"

"You deserve . . ."

"*. . . better than this.*"

"You need this machine . . ."

"*. . . to give you a crucial answer.*"

And then Mitch pushed the machine closer to his father. "Ask it where they hid the money, Dad. Because once you can prove those creeps have it, and you don't, it will prove that you're innocent, and they were the thieves, not you. Ask it, Dad. Please."

Mr. Murló, skeptical and yet a little scared, touched the ring, toying with it, but still not ready to pull it.

"There are stranger things in heaven and earth . . ." he said.

"Let's just stick with earth," said Mitch.

Mitch's dad took a deep breath and looked around to make sure the other inmates weren't watching. Then, with electric anticipation, he pulled the string and let it go. "My parole . . ."

And the machine said, "*. . . will be denied for the rest of your life.*"

The last little bit of the string pulled in, and the machine whirred itself silent. Mitch looked down, unable to meet his father's eyes. "That wasn't what you were supposed to ask," he said very quietly.

His father said nothing. He just seemed to be lost in himself. Then Mitch's mother came back with Madison, in the middle of a one-sided conversation about the proper sanitary use of a public restroom.

Seeing the silence between Mitch and his father, his mother began a nonstop soliloquy that bounced in free association from personal hygiene to personal training to the training wheels on Madison's bike.

Mitch now clutched the Shut Up 'n Listen close to his chest, and Nick realized that, regardless of what it could do, there was one sentence the machine couldn't finish: Mitch's father's.

"You shouldn't have done that," Mitch said softly. Nick couldn't tell if he was talking to his father or the machine. All of Mitch's confidence had derailed at high speed, leaving behind this wreckage.

"Mitch, I'm sorry," Nick said.

"Don't!" Mitch snapped. Then, more calmly, "Just don't."

When they returned to the car, Mitch kept his promise. He handed the Shut Up 'n Listen to Nick. "It's all yours," he said.

And although Nick knew that it, like every other object, belonged back in his attic, there was something about the way Mitch commanded the thing that made him realize it wasn't so simple.

The security-check X-ray machine had revealed the mechanism inside. What it hadn't revealed was the mechanism on the *outside*. Somehow Mitch was a part of that now.

Nick knew what he had to do.

"No," he told Mitch, putting it back in his hands. "Keep it for now."

Mitch looked at Nick with the same expression his father had worn right before pulling the string that had decided his fate.

"Really? No kidding?"

Nick nodded. "No one can use that thing better than you," he told him. "And besides, I think he wanted you to keep it for a while."

"Who, my father?" Mitch asked.

"No," Nick said. "Tesla."

That night Mitch skipped dinner and went to his room without even the hint of an appetite. He had been so sure that the Shut Up 'n Listen would give him and his father enough direction to tweak everything just enough to reverse his father's sentence. It was all a matter of starting the proper thought. True, the

Shut Up 'n Listen didn't always take the thought in the same direction you were going, but even traveling at a tangent was better than being stuck at a brick wall.

But now it was more than a brick wall. It was a tomb. Fact: Mitch's father was never getting out of prison. The machine could not have been clearer.

Hope is a terrible thing to lose. Sometimes that wounded space gets filled with scar tissue, bitter, ugly, and angry. Yet other times, like the gash on Nick's forehead, it is washed clean, stitched with care, and becomes a decisive part of one's character.

And so, alone in his room, Mitch held the Shut Up 'n Listen in his arms, rocking back and forth, weeping silent tears, because he didn't want his mother to hear him. But even in his grief he was making a powerful pact with himself. He would know who his true friends were—and once he knew, he would make that friendship mean something. And he would never let himself be taken advantage of the way his father had been, by rich, shady business partners in pale pearlescent suits.

11 OUT OF LEFT FIELD

Danny's first baseball game was the following morning.

Nick's father was like a little kid with tickets to the World Series. He'd never been quite as excited for Nick's games. It wasn't that he loved Nick any less; he always took it for granted that Nick would play good ball. On the other hand, Danny playing any ball whatsoever was cause for celebration.

Nick truly wanted to support his brother, but after the troubling day with Mitch, he had tossed and turned in bed with all manner of nightmares. Billions of stolen pennies hailing from the sky, lightbulbs that attracted man-eating moths, and Petula's red satin dress—these were the dark specters of his dreams.

That being the case, he had no intention of going anywhere that morning—but at 7:54 a.m. Danny somehow managed to pull down the attic stairs. He climbed up and began bouncing on Nick's bed with his brand-new cleats, somehow forgetting that Nick's shins were directly under the covers. Nick knocked him off of the bed and onto a pile of dirty clothes that was gathered in the center of the room.

"Safe!" Danny said.

"Out!" Nick demanded, pointing to the ladder.

"Not until you come, too." Then he looked at Nick a little bit oddly. "Why's your bed here?"

"What do you mean?" But when Nick looked around, he saw what Danny meant. His bed was no longer against the wall—neither was his desk. Both had migrated about two feet away from their respective spots, toward the center of the attic. It was too early to think about such irritatingly unexpected things, so he just pushed the furniture back where it was supposed to be, shooed Danny out, and reluctantly got dressed for his brother's game.

Nick tried to make the best of it. Maybe, he thought, a Pee Wee baseball game would be just the thing to distract him from the weirdness that had surrounded him ever since arriving here.

Sadly, this was not to be the case.

The local community athletic park was one of those massive suburban sports McComplexes, boasting four baseball diamonds, six soccer fields, too many tennis and basketball courts to count, and even a hockey rink. Unfortunately, there were only about twelve parking spaces. So, after a half-mile trek from the parking lot of a Taco Bell, Nick and his overenthusiastic father took their seats in the stands.

All around them were strangers—but here and there a face seemed familiar. Nick wondered if maybe some of these people had been at the garage sale, and if there might be a sneaky way of finding out what they had bought, and what the object in question did.

They all rose for "The Star-Spangled Banner," and Nick was filled with the classically conditioned anticipation of the first pitch. True, he was feeling some sour grapes over the fact that he wasn't pitching for the team he had tried out for—which was now playing on the next diamond over—but he had to admit he felt excited and also a bit anxious for his brother's debut.

Especially when Danny, playing right field, ran out to left field by mistake.

"If the ball goes over my head, do I get a do-over?" Danny had asked that morning.

"Just catch it," Nick had told him, "and you'll never have to worry."

The first batter on the opposing team got on base with a line drive that the shortstop bobbled. The second batter was walked. The third batter, however, hit a pop-up into shallow right field.

Danny, with the steely concentration with which he might do a long-division problem, held up his mitt, and—wonder of wonders—the ball dropped straight into it, as if somehow that had been the batter's intent.

Nick's father leaped up so suddenly it sent a neighboring parent's popcorn flying. "Yay, Danny! Woo-hooo!"

Nick looked over at their stunned neighbor, who now had little butter stains dotting her blouse. "Uh . . . Dad?"

Seeing what he had done, Nick's father sat down, a little embarrassed. "Sorry," he said, grabbing the empty popcorn tub and handing it to his son. "Nick, do me a favor: go to the snack bar and get this nice woman a refill. My treat." As incentive, he gave Nick enough money to get something for himself.

But as he left, Nick heard the woman say, "Not to worry—my son got me this electric stain remover at a garage sale. Never saw anything like it!"

Nick was so busy pondering the possible misuses of an electric stain remover designed by a mad genius that he didn't even notice who was coming up beside him in the concession line, until he felt a hand tap his shoulder.

"Okay if I cut in line?" Caitlin asked. "After all, you owe me for standing me up yesterday."

Anyone else might have looked over the top in a shocking-pink T-shirt and matching sunglasses, but Caitlin made it work.

"I didn't stand you up," Nick reminded her. "I left you a message. Trust me, Mitch would have been a basket case if I didn't go with him to visit his father."

"In the pen? You're braver than I thought." She stepped forward to stand next to him. "So what brings you out here?"

"My little brother's game. How about you?"

Caitlin glanced quickly at the adjacent diamond, then back at Nick. "I'm a soft pretzel addict, what can I say?"

Nick knew better. "You're here to watch Theo, aren't you? Don't tell me you're still together with him?"

"No. Yes. I don't know." She folded her arms, frustrated by the question, or maybe a little frustrated with herself. "Honestly, it may be force of habit more than anything. I was taught to recycle instead of throw things away."

"So melt him into a lawn chair and donate it to Goodwill."

Then she gave Nick an accusing look. "Why do you care? I heard you went on a date with Petula the other night."

This was wrong on so many levels, Nick didn't know where to begin. "Who told you that?"

Caitlin shrugged. "Nobody. She posted the restaurant's surveillance video on her SpaceBook page."

"It wasn't a date! I was just getting information."

"If you say so." Then she ordered her soft pretzel and was triumphantly smug. Nick got the replacement popcorn and a soda for himself. He was ready to head back to the bleachers alone, when Caitlin rested her hand gently on his arm.

"Lead the way," she said.

"Huh?"

"I want to be part of your brother's cheering squad. It'll be much better than watching fans of the opposing team throw peanuts at Theo."

"What?"

"He's allergic to peanuts. Apparently there's no rule against anaphylactic heckling."

The fact that Caitlin chose to come back to the stands with him rather than go to watch Theo's game made Nick's day. He thought of offering her his hand to help her over the staggered bleacher rows, which are hard enough to navigate even without a hundred people in the way, but he decided that such a move would be a little too forward.

The second inning had started, and Danny's team was in the field again. Still no score—but there was a man on second and no outs. Nick hoped the double wasn't due to an error on Danny's part.

"Line drive right past the third baseman," his father told him, as if reading his mind. "It was a solid hit—lucky it was just a double."

"Dad, this is my friend Caitlin," Nick said.

"Hi," his father said absently, keeping his eyes on the game.

"I hear you played major league," Caitlin said.

That was enough to get him to turn toward her. "For a couple of years, once upon a time."

"That's more than most people can say."

He accepted the compliment graciously, then looked at Nick and, with an extremely embarrassing wink, said, "Glad to see you're making friends."

Before it could get any more awkward, they heard the crack of a bat. A ball soared deep between the center fielder and Danny. Both ran toward the fly ball. It was clearly the center fielder's catch to make—in fact, he even called it—but as the ball came down, Danny held up his glove, and it slammed into the sweet spot with a satisfying thud. It was as if the baseball had curved ever so slightly in midair. As a pitcher, Nick knew that spin could make a ball do mystical things, but that usually happened when it was flying *toward* a batter, not away. But why look a gift horse in the mouth? If today was Danny's day, then it was his day!

Nick's dad jumped up again, this time careful not to bump into the woman's popcorn, and he cheered louder than any parent. Nick joined in, although not quite as loudly.

"Your brother's pretty good," Caitlin said.

Nick swelled with pride. Warming to his brother's success was easing his own disappointment at not making a team.

The next ball that came toward Danny was in the following inning: a missile smacked by a kid who looked way too old to be in this age group. The ball was clearly going out of the park—and through one of the twelve windshields in the parking lot.

Danny backed up as far as he could until he hit the outfield fence. He held up his glove futilely—

—and then, in midflight, the arc of the ball suddenly changed. It plunged downward like a crashing plane, landing right in Danny's glove.

The crowd gasped.

"No way!" someone shouted. "Did you see that?"

"Did it hit a bird?" someone else asked.

"Maybe it was the wind."

Caitlin looked at Nick with a kind of fear in her eyes, and that's when he knew.

"Dad," he asked, "that's not your old glove, is it?"

And his father said, "Nope. It's from your garage sale." He grinned, all puffed with pride at his prodigy in the field. "I put five bucks in your box. Worth every penny."

Nick stood up.

"How many outs is that?" Nick asked.

"Two," his father said. "Try to pay attention."

Nick looked back at Caitlin. They weren't just on the same page; they might as well have been reading each other's mind.

"We can't take it from him in the middle of an inning. . . ." Caitlin said.

But it was more than that. "We can't take it from him at all. . . ." Because how could Nick tell his brother that his moment to shine wasn't really his moment? That he was nothing but an accessory to the glove?

There was a grounder to the shortstop, and the batter got on base. Then a short pop that the pitcher dropped. Man on first and second. A line drive past the third-base line and the bases were loaded—but Nick wasn't worried about the guys on base. He was worried about the next batter—a big kid who was clearly planning on a grand slam.

He swung at the first pitch, connected, and the ball sailed high into left field. The crowd was on their feet, screaming with anticipation. The left fielder positioned himself—but the ball began to curve like a boomerang away from left field, over the head of the center fielder, and straight toward Danny.

Danny's jaw dropped practically to his knees. He positioned his mitt as the ball sailed toward it. . . . But then something roared more loudly than the crowd, and from out of the sky came a ball of fire trailing a plume of black smoke. The plummeting fireball hit the baseball, instantly incinerating it, then slammed into the sweet spot of Danny's glove.

The force of the impact ripped Danny off his feet. He flew backward, dragged through the grass, and actually dug a trench before he finally came to a stop inches from the right-field fence.

For a moment no one moved. The crowd had fallen into

silent shock. Then, all at once, the kids in the field screamed and started running in different directions in a panic. Nick, his father, and Caitlin leaped over rows of people and out onto the field, where they sprinted toward Danny, who lay on his back, his mitt still smoking.

Their dad reached him first. "It's okay, it's okay, it's okay," he said, cradling his son.

Danny looked up at them with dazed eyes. "Did I catch it?"

"Yeah, Danny," Nick said. "You did."

He gingerly pulled the glove from Danny's hand. There, smoldering inside it, was a chunk of red-hot stone about the size of a grapefruit. Danny had caught a meteorite.

As there was nothing in the rule book about unexpected cosmic events, the game was called due to "severe weather conditions." Police were brought in to hold back gawking crowds, who had abandoned all the other sports being played that day. As for the field in question, it was cordoned off as a disaster area—and it looked like one, with abandoned gloves and hats lying on the field, forgotten by panicking players, as well as a single forlorn cleat that appeared to be trying to steal third base.

Paramedics arrived to evaluate Danny, who should have, at the very least, suffered a shoulder dislocated to the next county, but he didn't seem to be injured at all.

"Could you tell us exactly what happened?" the paramedics asked him while his father paced, still unable to wrap his mind around it.

"I held up my glove and caught a shooting star," Danny said brightly. "Do I get on the news?"

Nick and Caitlin watched all this unfold without any power to control or direct it . . . but it seemed that someone else was doing the controlling.

"There's something odd here," Caitlin pointed out to Nick.

"Understatement of the millennium," Nick replied.

"No—I'm talking about what your brother said. He's right—he *should* be on the news. But we've been here for nearly an hour, and have you seen a single reporter?"

She was right. No reporters, no news vans. A piece of sky just fell into some kid's hand—that's not just a local human-interest story, that's national news. World news! But no one was reporting it. Why?

What they got instead of news vans was a fleet of shimmering white SUVs bursting onto the field, all identical to the one that had showed up at Nick's garage sale.

Out of the SUVs stepped at least a dozen people, men and women, all well dressed. Their clothes, just as at the garage sale, were pearly pastel shades.

Nick grabbed Caitlin's wrist.

"I know these guys," he said. "Some of them, anyway."

"Who are they?"

Nick thought about the business card that kept reappearing no matter how many times he'd thrown it away. He couldn't remember the name on it, and suspected he had intentionally blocked it out.

"Creepy dudes with a lot of money," he told her.

Caitlin grimaced. "That's the worst kind."

On a crazy hunch Nick reached into his pocket, and he felt something in there that had the shape and texture of a business card. He refused to pull it out to see if it really was.

Sports-park security, the first line of defense, intercepted the approaching team of men and women. The tall man from the garage sale was in the lead. This time the way his suit caught the light, it appeared more pale peach than vanilla. He showed some kind of badge, and the security guard backed off, as if the guy were radioactive. Next, the police tried to stop them as they crossed the field. The man flashed his badge again. The cops seemed apologetic and waved them through.

The well-dressed team fanned out with equipment that looked like metal detectors and dowsing rods. While they examined the field, Mr. Peaches-and-Cream made a beeline for the Slates.

When Nick's father saw the man approaching, he left Danny sitting in the back of the ambulance.

"Can I help you?" Mr. Slate asked.

Nick and Caitlin watched, keeping a little distance.

The man flashed his badge, and his father looked at it.

"You're from the Department of Defense?"

"So it would seem," the man said, flipping the badge holder closed. "I understand there was an incident here today. I'd like to talk to you about it."

"It wasn't an *incident*," Nick's father said, already defensive. "It was a meteorite, not a missile attack. Not exactly a matter of national security. If you're from the DOD, then you're wasting your time."

The man gave Nick's father a patronizing grin. "Just doing our jobs, sir. Is it true that your son caught this meteorite?"

Nick's father looked away. "So? Stranger things have happened." Which wasn't exactly true, and they both knew it.

Right about then the paramedics pulled Nick's father away to fill out some paperwork. As he went, Mr. Slate gave Mr. Peaches-and-Cream a suspicious look.

Then the man turned his head smoothly, like an owl, zeroing in on Nick, and Nick felt his blood temperature drop a few degrees.

"Hello, Nick," he said. "Good to see you again."

Nick turned to Caitlin for support, but she was gone. The man put his hand out to shake, but Nick didn't take it.

"You don't trust me. I don't blame you. Trust must be earned."

"If you're from the Defense Department, why didn't you say so at the garage sale?" Nick asked.

"Defense?" said a passing policeman. "These guys are with the FBI."

Nick put his hands on his hips. "So which is it?"

The man whipped out his badge, flipping the cover open. "You tell me."

Nick looked at the official ID and read it out loud: "Dr. Alan Jorgenson, Dark Lord of the Sith?"

Jorgenson sighed and rolled his eyes. "So it would seem."

"What is this, some kind of joke?"

A little embarrassed, Jorgenson put the badge away. "It's not an ID badge. It's a neuro-antagonistic mirror. When you look at it, it reflects back the most intimidating thing you expect to see."

"Sorry," said Nick. "I don't believe in magic."

"Good for you," said Jorgenson. "Neither do we. It's science. It may appear as magic to the less enlightened, but people like you and me can see through it to the truth. Scientific smoke and mirrors, practically applied." He smiled. "It's like that quantum business card I gave you. I'm sure it's turned up in unlikely places, has it not?"

He waited for an answer, but Nick refused to give him one.

"Well," Jorgenson continued, "quantum physics dictates that it will remain a part of your life until you physically hand it to someone else. Then it becomes their problem."

"How about the funky suits?" Nick had to ask. "More smoke and mirrors?"

"Yes," said Jorgenson, without hesitating. "They're made of the fabric of time and space." He paused for a beat, then said, "That's a joke." And when Nick still didn't laugh, he smoothed out his suit jacket. "It's Madagascan spider silk. Very rare. Very comfortable. I could get you an outfit if you like."

That succeeded in making Nick laugh. Mainly because Jorgenson was serious. Nick looked around at the man's colleagues and the odd devices they were using on the baseball field.

"So who are you really?" he asked.

"We're scientists from the University of Colorado, nothing more or less sinister than that." And then he cut to the chase. "Now, maybe your father and everyone else here thinks this was some random event, but you and I both know it wasn't. So please, Nick, in the name of science, why don't you tell me exactly how that meteorite was pulled out of the sky."

Suddenly, from behind them, Danny said, "It was me. I caught it all by myself." He climbed out of the ambulance.

"Danny, be quiet," Nick said.

"I've been catching stuff all day. I'm really good at it. I never thought I'd catch a falling star, though. Hey, don't I get a wish or something?"

Jorgenson knelt down to Danny's level. Nick watched as the man's eyes, smooth as spider silk, slid to the glove sitting on the bumper of the ambulance behind them. Then his gaze turned back to Danny and he smiled broadly.

"And what might that wish be, young man?"

"Excuse me," said their father angrily, stomping away from the paramedics. "Who gave you permission to talk to my sons?"

Jorgenson stood, a bit flustered. "I apologize if I was a little forward."

"Since when does the DOD interrogate children?"

Jorgenson put up his hands. "Let's not get carried away."

A woman from Jorgenson's team, as sharply groomed as he, brought him the charred chunk of space rock. Jorgenson held it up, turning it in his hand, regarding it like it was a crystal ball.

"Is this it? Remarkable."

"And," said Danny, reaching up and grabbing it from him, "it's mine."

"That's right," said Mr. Slate. "First rule of baseball—you catch it, you keep it."

"Besides," Nick said, "a meteorite is like a piece of land, right? It belongs to the first person who claims it, fair and square."

"Can't argue with that," said their father with a smug grin. "Now, if the United States government wants to seize my son's property, I'm sure there's some slow, painful, legal process that can get you what you want."

Jorgenson gave an exasperated sigh. "No one said anything about seizing your property. We're willing to pay for the meteorite." Then he nodded toward the bumper of the ambulance. "And the glove that caught it, of course."

"Dad, no!" said Danny.

Jorgenson pulled out a pad and wrote down a number.

"Will this amount be sufficient?"

He showed the paper to Nick's father. His eyes widened, but only slightly.

"Well . . ."

"No way," said Danny.

So Nick's father stood firm. "Sorry. It's not for sale."

"How about now?" Jorgenson showed him another, higher number.

Nick's father was like a house of cards ready to fold, until he saw Danny's eyes filling with tears.

That's when Nick jumped in.

"Which is more important, Dad? Money or your son?"

Their father took a deep breath and turned his house of cards into a stone fortress. "I'm sorry. My decision is final."

And Nick thought it was over . . . until Jorgenson produced a checkbook.

"I'll tell you what, Mr. Slate. I understand you've been out of work. As it so happens, I know of an opening at NORAD for a man just like you. With your qualities."

"A job?" their father said.

"The benefits are excellent. This check represents your first month's salary."

He filled out the check and handed it to his father.

Nick didn't see the amount of the paycheck, but whatever it was, it made his father turn to Danny and say, "Give the man his rock."

Jorgenson wrenched the meteorite out of Danny's hands against the boy's protests.

"And the glove," reminded Jorgenson.

"Forget you!" Danny cried, although *forget* was not precisely the word he used.

"Let it go, Danny," said Nick. "It's probably better with them anyway." He went to retrieve the mitt, then held it out to Jorgenson. "If this gets Dad a job, then it's worth it."

Jorgenson took the mitt, but he seemed a little suspicious as he looked it over. "Rather unremarkable, isn't it? It's clearly old, but it shows very little sign of wear . . . and the pocket—it's perfectly clean."

Nick took a deep breath. He knew that the mitt showed absolutely no sign of having caught a red-hot hunk of iron. This fact wasn't lost on Jorgenson, an observant man. Very observant.

"What is that you have there, Nick?" Jorgenson asked.

"I don't know what you're talking about."

"Come now—what are you hiding behind your back?"

Jorgenson reached behind Nick and found the other mitt

that he was hiding. This one was also old, and it showed heavy wear, as though it had been through a war.

Jorgenson smiled. "I believe that is the glove I just purchased," he said.

Nick looked down, his face going red.

"Well played, Nick," Jorgenson said, taking the glove and dropping the first one on the ground. He studied the stretch marks in the glove's pocket. "You almost had me." He handed it to one of his associates, who slipped the mitt in a plastic bag and quickly trotted back to where the SUVs waited.

Back in control and infinitely pleased with himself, Jorgenson turned to Nick's father. "The job is real, the salary is real. You and your boys will come to see that we are very much your friends."

Then he turned and left, while Danny looked at the ground, kicking up sod with his cleats. Nick still looked away, red in the face.

Caitlin came running back from wherever she had disappeared to. "Nick, I saw what happened—I'm so sorry."

Nick glanced at the scientists getting back into their vehicles and driving off the field.

"Don't worry about it," he said.

"Well, maybe this will make you feel better," she said. "I was going around doing my best to be a general nuisance and find out from the other scientists what they were up to. They gave me the garbage you might expect: 'We're taking readings,' 'We're looking for anomalies,' blah blah blah—basically trying to sound scientific without saying much of anything. And then the guy who was measuring the trench Danny created tripped over a clump of sod, and this fell off his lapel."

She held out to Nick a gold pin, smaller than a thumbnail.

It looked like the letter *A*, but the crossbar, instead of being a straight line, was a figure eight—the symbol of infinity.

"Wait a second," Nick said. "Jorgenson had a pin, too."

"They all do," whispered Caitlin. Then, with a smile, she said, "So, they have something of yours, and now you have something of theirs."

Nick looked up and watched the last of the SUVs pull off the field.

"Who says they have something of mine?" Then he reached down to the grass and picked up the baseball glove that Jorgenson had dismissively discarded. This was the glove that Nick had so freely offered Jorgenson. The one that showed no signs of ever having caught anything, much less a meteorite.

The corners of Caitlin's mouth curled into a smile. "You didn't!"

"Hey," said Nick, shrugging, "he's the one who specifically requested the one I was holding behind my back . . . which was, I believe, dropped by the second baseman when he ran screaming off the field."

Caitlin looked at him admiringly. "That," she said, "was masterful."

"No," Nick said, "just smoke and mirrors, practically applied."

12 FOOD FOR THOUGHT

While Nick and Caitlin were experiencing baseball on a cosmic level that Sunday, Petula was experiencing her own personal world of wonder. Although she tried to keep a low profile as she took a number of photographs downtown that morning, the box camera was cumbersome—and an oddball object held by an oddball girl had an exponential quality about it that was bound to square, or possibly cube, any amount of public attention.

Well, let them gawk. I don't care. She wished she could aim the camera at the people who looked at her strangely and snap away their souls, as some cultures believed cameras had the capacity to do—but alas, that was not one of the box camera's qualities.

Acacia Park, located in a part of Colorado Springs that brochures called "quaint," offered many opportunities for experimental photography. Uncle Wilber Fountain, for instance, the source of joy for small children who desired to catch their death of cold, was a fine photo op. Even this early in April it was surrounded by . . ., perhaps reliving past summers when the many spouts and blowholes of the irritatingly whimsical fountain had drenched them and allowed them to claim they didn't need to take a shower when they returned home.

Petula was curious to see if, at night, the fountain was frequented by drunks, derelicts, druggies, and dealers—the four

D's of every downtown American park. Would the pictures she took in the child-infested light of day, when developed, show Uncle Wilber's nighttime seedier side?

To her delight, Petula discovered that the camera's "focus ring" was marked from one to twenty-four, giving new meaning to the word *focus*. All the pictures she had taken thus far were set at twelve, which clearly meant they snapped pictures twelve hours in the future. But to see tomorrow instead of just tonight would be a fine thing indeed!

Near the corner stood a newspaper kiosk, clinging to a dwindling hope for a nondigital future. The attendant of the little wooden booth was a man so old he could probably already smell the embalming fluid. Petula observed that he already spent so much of his time in a small wooden space, the transition to a coffin would be none too difficult. She laughed out loud. These were the kinds of lighthearted observations that made her so enjoy being out in public.

"A candy for you this fine day, young lady?" the old man said, seeing her jovial demeanor.

"No," Petula told him, "just a picture."

"Well, I guess it'll be CHEESE, then!" He chuckled at his own joke and gave her a smile. She snapped a picture that only caught half of his face, because he wasn't the actual subject of the photo—the newspaper next to him was. She had already set the focus ring to twenty-four. It would be most interesting to read tomorrow morning's headline this afternoon when she developed the negative, and to think of a way to exploit her foreknowledge.

Then from behind her she heard, "Is that an old-fashioned box camera? My grandfather had one of those!"

She turned to see someone who looked familiar, and yet not.

"Petula Grabowski-Jones! I should have known you'd be the one holding such a blatantly anachronistic object."

Only now did Petula realize this was Ms. Planck, the lunch lady. It was the first time Petula had seen her out of her natural habitat. And without a hairnet, even. It was disturbing. The fact that she was carrying several bags from a gourmet food emporium further messed with Petula's grasp of reality.

Ms. Planck caught Petula's astonished gaze and, guessing the reason, laughed. "Honey, I may serve slop for a living, but that doesn't mean I take my work home with me."

"Sorry," said Petula, looking away in uncharacteristic embarrassment.

Ms. Planck put down her bags. "So let me see this camera of yours."

Petula hesitated, then realized that refusing might mean inferior lunches for the remainder of the year. If there was one thing she had learned in her years at school, it was that there were two people you needed to befriend: the Lunch Lady and the District Superintendent. Currently Petula had the latter in her pocket should she need to influence a districtwide vote. But Ms. Planck had always put up a food-service wall when it came to Petula. Here was an opportunity to tear it down.

"Of course," Petula said, handing her the camera. "Careful, it's old."

Ms. Planck turned it in her hands like it was a puzzle box. "My grandfather's was a Seneca Scout—but this one has no company name."

"I think it was a beta model. You know, a prototype." She was glad Ms. Planck didn't notice the initials scratched on the bottom.

"Exquisite!" Ms. Planck handed the camera back to Petula.

"Take good care of it, honey—a prototype in such good condition could finance your college education."

Which, to Petula, was an insult. "I'll be getting a scholarship," she announced. "Academic or badminton."

"Is that so? I didn't know anyone played badminton anymore."

"They don't," Petula responded. "Hence the ease in getting a scholarship."

Ms. Planck nodded in seeming approval, then bent down to pick up her bags. Apparently her fennel-infused truffle oil had sprung a leak, and when she lifted her bag, it split open, dumping everything from foie gras to porcini mushrooms all over the pavement.

Ms. Planck shouted a word she often heard in reference to the lunches she served, then knelt down to pick it up. Petula, not wanting to appear unhelpful, joined in the recovery effort, using her foot to stop a bottle of kalamata olives from rolling into the street.

The old man in the news booth handed them several small plastic bags, but without the gourmet shop's oversize shopping bag, it was clearly too much for Ms. Planck to handle herself.

"Are you going to help me home with all this?" Ms. Planck asked Petula. "Or are you going to make me struggle on my lonesome? I just live across the park."

"Hmm . . ." Petula said with a grin she hoped was disarming. "Larger lunch portions, and I get to choose my own pizza slice?"

Ms. Planck returned the smile. "I think that goes without saying."

"And my choice of dessert?"

"Now you're pushing it."

Petula accepted the terms, they shook hands, and the deal was struck. With the box camera in one hand and a few bags in the other, Petula crossed through Acacia Park, making a point, as she always did, to sneer at Uncle Wilbur ensconced in his fountain.

"So how long have you been interested in photography?" Ms. Planck asked.

"As long as I can remember," Petula said. "Slices of life are easier to digest than the unedited version."

Ms. Planck laughed. "I couldn't have said it better myself."

She lived in a trendy town house that was far from what Petula expected a woman of her nature to inhabit—but as Petula set the groceries down on the kitchen counter, she was coming to realize that the nature of a lunch lady is a very unpredictable thing. A point brought home even more when Ms. Planck said, "Come downstairs, I'll show you my darkroom."

When a semi-stranger invites you inside to see her darkroom, any sensible human being would break the land speed record running in the other direction. However, with her perpetually present pocket pepper spray and a brown belt in theoretical jujitsu, Petula felt well able to protect herself should Ms. Planck turn out to be serving up local children in the beef ragout, like that lunch lady down in Phoenix.

As they descended the stairs, Petula noted numerous framed black-and-white photos of an artistic nature.

"So you're a photographer, too?"

"I dabbled," said Ms. Planck. "But in the end it didn't pay the bills." Then she swung open the door of a basement to reveal that it had been converted into the darkroom of Petula's dreams. All nature of high-end equipment, from an Omega diffusion enlarger to an Arkay print washer, filled the room. But it was all covered in dusty plastic.

Ms. Planck sighed. "I always said I'd get back to it, but when Charlie died, I just didn't have the heart for it anymore."

"Was he your husband?"

"My Chihuahua."

Petula gasped. "I have a Chihuahua!"

Ms. Planck folded her arms and leaned against the door frame. "Interesting. Do you believe that things happen for a reason, Petula?"

"No."

"Well, let's consider it happy coincidence, then," said Ms. Planck, "that I have a darkroom that longs to be used, and you have a camera that has never even heard of digital photography."

13 MARK OF THE ACCELERATI

Nick leaned back from his computer and held the gold pin up to the light streaming through the attic skylight. The tiny *A* sparkled.

He had spent half the afternoon searching online for anything resembling it, and he had come up blank. He even scanned the face of the pin and tried a Google match. Nada.

The *A* had to stand for something, and the infinity symbol was probably significant, too, but without any clues it was all just guesswork.

"I'm not surprised you didn't find anything," Caitlin said when he called her, which may or may not have implied that she thought he was inept. Nick couldn't say for sure, but he wasn't about to use the reel-to-reel to find out. That would be far too sneaky. "All right," said Caitlin. "Then we'll go with plan B."

"I didn't know there was a plan B."

"There's *always* a plan B."

She explained there was a jeweler in town who was *the* expert in personal adornment.

"I really don't feel comfortable showing the pin to anyone else," Nick told her.

"Don't worry," Caitlin assured him. "He's a family friend; we've been going to him for years. He's the model of discretion."

"Whatever that means," said Nick.

"It means we can trust him. Anyway, I already set up an appointment. He doesn't usually work late on Sundays, but I think he has a crush on my mother, and he keeps hoping she'll come in one day to have her wedding ring appraised. So he made a special exception. We have a meeting with him at seven thirty tonight."

Caitlin liked to believe she lived for adventure, but any adventure in her life had been limited to drama she created herself. Here, however, was something real. Or surreal, as it were. Here was an event that was larger than life, and relatively speaking, in her own backyard. Now she had a real mystery that involved shady, well-dressed people, a secret symbol, and a boy who was both smart and cute. Caitlin suspected he might even evolve from cute into seriously good-looking when the rest of his face caught up with his ears and he did something about his per-petual hat-hair.

She was resigned to the fact that there would be no such evo-lution for Theo. Yes, he had the good-looks part down, if you didn't mind the extra vertebrae in his neck, but as for smarts, well, he was eternally mired smack in the middle of the bell curve. He wasn't stupid, just woefully average—which might have been fine if he wasn't always so pleased with himself.

Perhaps the between-the-lines conversation played over the school loudspeakers was a blessing in disguise.

Nick showed up on foot at seven.

"Don't you have a bike?"

"Lost it in the fire."

"Right. Sorry. You can borrow my dad's." And although it was a bit big for him, he handled it well.

They rode side by side, hogging the bike lane as they made their way to Svedberg & Sons, Fine Jewelers.

"So how are Danny and your father dealing with what happened?"

"They're not," Nick told her. "Danny's the kind of kid who takes things as they come, and my dad—well, whenever there's something that he can't understand, he gets weirdly busy with stuff he does understand. When I left he was weed-whacking."

"At night?"

"Exactly."

They made their way into the business district, where elegant, newly restored shops nestled beside original businesses that hadn't changed a window display in recorded history. There was a fabric store that sold hideous remnants from the seventies, and a shoe store that had a sun-faded poster for Hush Puppies, whatever those were. Even in daylight those older stores could feel creepy, or at the very least depressing—but on a Sunday night, void of any foot traffic, those dark plate-glass windows were bleakly foreboding.

Caitlin coasted to a stop in front of Svedberg's jewelry store, with Nick right behind her. The shop was as dark as all the others.

"Are you sure he's here?" Nick asked. "Maybe he forgot."

Caitlin got off of her bike and tried the door, fully expecting it to be locked—but it opened when she pulled on it. A warm breath of air pulsed out from inside. A bell above the door jingled, uproariously loud in the silence, and Caitlin flinched. Nick snickered at that, and she gave him a dirty look. No doubt if he had been the one opening the door, he would have flinched, too.

She should have remembered the bell from her childhood—although it had been many, many years since she'd been here. Her father, always in a panic, used to take her to pick out a last-minute Valentine's Day gift for her mother. Then Caitlin would go again, when her mother returned the gift and picked out something she actually liked. It was a secret known only to Caitlin, her mother, and Mr. Svedberg, so she felt an odd sort of camaraderie with the man. Co-conspirators in a secret intrigue of jewels.

"Come, come," said a voice from the back. "Is that you, Miss Westfield? Come, come!"

There was a faint light from the rear of the shop, creating long, tiny shadows of rings, necklaces, and bracelets in the jewelry cases. There was not enough light to make them sparkle, though. There, in the very back, as always, sat a tired fiftyish man in his little workspace. He looked exactly the same as he always had to Caitlin—maybe only a little dustier. His eyes were a bit too small for his face, which he tried to compensate for by opening them wide whenever he spoke. It gave the impression that he was always astonished to find himself in a conversation.

"Hello, Mr. Svedberg. I can't thank you enough for taking the time to meet us like this."

He looked up and smiled with more warmth, it seemed, than the place allowed.

"This can't be right," he said. "Last I recall, young Miss Westfield was just so high, clinging to her mommy's pant leg with ice-cream-sticky fingers." And he winked. He always winked at her. Further proof of their jewelry conspiracy. The wink made her look away awkwardly, as it had all those years ago. "How is your mother?"

"She's good," Caitlin said, making a mental note that he didn't ask about her father.

Then Svedberg turned to Nick. "And this must be the young man you told me about."

"Nick Slate. A friend." Nick offered his hand to shake.

"Well, Nick Slate, a friend, it's very chivalrous of you to escort a young lady on a dark night."

"It's not so dark," said Caitlin, already tired of the small talk. She and Nick sat down on stools beside the workstation. With Nick sitting beside her, she imagined they looked like a nervous young couple about to choose an engagement ring, which made her irritated at Nick even though it wasn't his fault.

The old jeweler looked silently back and forth between them. Caitlin began to worry that there was some protocol to such private transactions, and she was blowing it.

"So . . ." she said.

"So," Svedberg answered, "you mentioned some jewelry you wanted appraised, yes?"

Nick reached into his pocket. "It's a pin. I have it right here." He had wrapped it in a tissue, and Caitlin rolled her eyes. You don't bring a jeweler something precious wrapped in a tissue. He should have at least located a velvet pouch somewhere. Surely his mother's jewelry collection would have one. . . . Then, all at once, she remembered Nick had lost his mother. She wanted to apologize, even though she hadn't actually said anything.

Nick held the pin but didn't extend it toward Svedberg yet. He looked to Caitlin. "You sure about this?"

Caitlin turned to Svedberg. "My friend needs reassurance that this consultation will remain strictly confidential," she said.

"Of course," said the jeweler. Now he seemed almost greedy to see what Nick held.

Nick unwrapped the pin and placed it on the felt workstation, where it glistened under Svedberg's lamp.

If Caitlin had expected any kind of reaction from Mr. Svedberg, she was disappointed. He simply picked up the pin and looked at it through an enormous magnifying lens.

"Hmm . . ." the jeweler said thoughtfully, touching the pin lightly with his fingertip. "Most likely gold, very fine quality; I'd guess twenty-four karat. The workmanship on the pin, too, is very fine, the insignia molded, not stamped." He sighed, and felt the pin in his palm. "But it's very light, I'm afraid. So even if the gold is pure, it would not be worth very much."

"Do you recognize the symbol on it?" Caitlin asked. "Maybe it has more value as an objet d'art than its weight would suggest."

As the jeweler studied the front of the pin, Nick mouthed the words *Objet d'art?* at her. Caitlin studiously ignored him.

"It's a *V* letterform with traditional stems," the jeweler murmured, "bisected by a figure eight. There's something familiar about it. . . ."

"Turn it over," Nick prompted. "It's an *A*, not a *V*. And isn't a sideways figure eight the infinity symbol?"

Svedberg turned the pin right side up, and the moment he did, his eyes—already wide—peeled a bit farther, and he suddenly stopped talking. Caitlin imagined that all the watches in the glass cases stopped as well.

"What is it?" Nick asked.

A brief hesitation, then Svedberg shifted uncomfortably in his chair. "Indigestion. My doctor says I should stay away from spicy foods, but I do love the occasional jalapeño."

Then he stood and handed Nick back the pin. "I wish I could be of more help. Best of luck to you, though."

"But wait," Nick said, and he looked to Caitlin as if the jeweler's sudden shift in demeanor was her fault, then back to Svedberg. "You said it seemed familiar. . . ."

"I was mistaken," Svedberg said quickly. "One sees so many designs in this business, one symbol is bound to be confused with another."

But Caitlin could sense unspoken volumes. The question was, how to extract whatever information Svedberg was hiding. When the answer came, it was far easier than she imagined and far too devious for comfort—but this was one case where Caitlin concluded that the end justified the means.

"My mother will be so disappointed," she said.

At that, Svedberg perked up. "Don't tell me this is your mother's!"

"Well, it was a gift."

"From whom?"

"That's the thing, she's not entirely sure. It arrived anonymously."

Then Svedberg looked suspiciously at Nick. "So if it's your mother's, why did *he* have it?"

"Are you kidding me?" said Nick, not even missing a beat. "Look at how tight her jeans are. You can't get anything in those pockets."

"That's right," said Caitlin, smiling through the sting. "So I asked Nick to hold it, considering his clothes are so ill-fitting." She smiled sweetly at Mr. Svedberg. "It would mean a lot to my mother if she knew just what it was—then maybe we could figure out who sent it."

Svedberg looked at the two of them, and Caitlin could sense his resolve to stay silent had begun to crumble. Just one more nudge . . .

"She always speaks of you so fondly—that's why I came to you . . . because I thought you'd be kind enough to help her."

That did it. Svedberg put his hand on a glass jewelry case as if to keep himself steady. "I don't suppose you've heard of"—his voice dropped to a whisper—"the Accelerati?"

Caitlin looked at Nick, who only shrugged.

"Suffice it to say that whoever sent this to your mother is not to be trifled with. Bring her here tomorrow night, and I'll tell her what I know."

"Bring her here?"

"Yes."

"Tomorrow?"

"Am I being unclear?"

Caitlin's head was already reeling at the thought of having to involve her mother in this, but Nick rose to fill the void.

"Thank you, Mr. Svedberg," he said, shaking the man's hand. "I'm sure Mrs. Westfield will be grateful for your help."

And they left, the jingling bells announcing their exit to anyone who might be nearby.

History is filled with a sordid assortment of secret societies, each dedicated to either the betterment or the destruction of humanity. Regardless of their aim, however, all secret societies have one thing in common. They all have a stupid pin. Or a stupid hat. Or a ridiculously stupid handshake.

When it came to secret societies, the Accelerati were at the pinnacle of the pyramid. Their interest in Nick Slate was no small thing, and if Nick knew what grand events now revolved around him, he might have run to the farthest side of the globe. But in this instance, ignorance was his greatest asset.

Nick hurried up to his room the second he got home, and he tried to do a Web search of *Accelerati*—but the moment he hit enter, his computer crashed. He rebooted, tried again on a different search engine, and his computer crashed again. And again. He wondered if Caitlin had a similar problem, but he didn't want to call her, because she was miffed by his comment about her jeans.

"I had to come up with something!" Nick had told her. "And it worked, didn't it?"

Nevertheless, any affront to Caitlin's fashion sense, no matter the motivation, destined him for the doghouse. At least until morning.

It was maddening, because Nick had no one else he could discuss this with. He couldn't talk to Mitch about it—Mitch already had enough on his mind after the fateful visit to his father. And although Vince was aware that something was up, he didn't exactly engender a warm feeling of trust.

There was always Petula. But hadn't Nick suffered enough already?

On Monday morning, as Nick was leaving for school, Vince showed up at his door with a baseball bat.

"For you," he said.

"Very funny." Nick figured he had heard from Caitlin, or maybe Mitch, about Danny's involvement in the falling-star incident.

"I don't do funny," Vince said. "This came from your garage sale."

Nick hadn't even remembered it. "How did you find it?"

"There is a dark underworld of mailbox smashers," Vince told him, "and baseball bats suffer high casualties in the enterprise. The smashers are always looking for cheap ones. Once I remembered that there was a bat in your garage sale, I knew exactly where to look for it."

Nick took it from Vince gingerly, as if it were made of glass. "It doesn't look damaged."

"Smashing only happens on alternate Tuesdays, so we were lucky," Vince said. "You owe me fifteen bucks."

Nick was more than happy to pay up. He returned the object to a corner of his attic, satisfied that, for once, all was well.

At school, however, all was not well with Mitch. Nick noticed that he was uncharacteristically silent in class, and during lunch, he didn't finish anyone's sentences. Nor did he have loud conversations, or inject himself into anyone else's business. He just sat, ate, cleaned up after himself, and quietly observed the world around him. When Nick had finished his own lunch, he went over to Mitch.

"Hey," he offered tentatively.

"Hey."

"So you left it at home?"

They both knew what Nick was referring to.

"It's not like I need the thing to survive." Then Mitch added, "I don't even miss it."

Although Nick could tell that he did. "It's good you don't have it," he told him. "It proves you control it, and not the other way around."

That actually made Mitch smile. "Yeah, that's true, isn't it? I mean . . . the thing is what it is . . . but I am what I am, with or without it." Then he got a little somber again. "So . . . who am I again?"

Nick shrugged. "A half-Hispanic, half-Irish kid with a French-sounding last name."

"Right," said Mitch ruefully. "Even my name doesn't know who I am."

Nick hadn't intended to make Mitch feel worse. "I'll tell you what. When we find Tesla's identity-crisis can opener, you can be the first to use it."

"Nah," said Mitch with a reluctant grin. "It'll probably open up a can of worms."

But Nick knew the can of worms was already open. And those worms were rapidly evolving into cobras.

After school, Nick invited Mitch to join the second excursion to Svedberg's. It thrilled Nick that Caitlin balked slightly at the idea of Mitch coming along—it meant that she preferred quality time with Nick alone, but he felt that Mitch deserved and needed to be included.

"So let me get this straight," Mitch said as they sat on a bus heading downtown. "You found a pin that belongs to a secret society, and some jeweler who's in love with Caitlin's mom is gonna tell you all about it?"

"Well," said Caitlin, "he agreed to tell my mother."

"And your father feels about this how?" Mitch asked.

Caitlin hesitated. "Well, he doesn't know. . . ."

"So you set your mom up on a date with some dude behind your dad's back?"

"You're missing the point, Mitch," Nick told him. "Her mom's not going to be there."

Mitch was quiet for a moment, then asked, "Does she know that?"

Nick gave up. Mitch was grinding more gears than their bus as he tried to get up to speed. However, he had actually brought up a good point, whether he realized it or not. Svedberg *did* think this was a date, of sorts. Nick turned to Caitlin. "What if he refuses to tell us anything when your mom doesn't show?"

"You worry too much," Caitlin replied curtly. "I'll sweet-talk him. Watch and learn."

When they got off the bus, one corner from the shop, Nick's anticipation began to spike. Was it too much to hope that Svedberg's explanation would encompass not only the Accelerati, but the items in his attic as well?

"Here we are," Caitlin said as they approached the shop.

It was Nick who first realized that something was very wrong, when he saw a disturbingly familiar green-and-black sign above the entrance. He touched Caitlin's arm to get her attention. She looked at him, noted the sheer disbelief in his eyes, and then she looked at the shop.

What had been Svedberg & Sons, Fine Jewelers yesterday was now a Starbucks.

"So," said Mitch, "are we getting Frappuccinos first?"

"This can't be right," said Caitlin, the pitch of her voice rising slightly. "It was right here between the bank and the barber-shop, remember?"

"Yeah, I do." If Nick hadn't seen it for himself, he would have thought she'd lost her mind.

"You guys must be wrong," said Mitch. "I mean, Starbucks don't just pop up overnight out of nowhere, do they?"

Nick pushed his way into the store, followed by Caitlin, then Mitch, who was already getting his wallet out for a purchase.

The smell of freshly brewed coffee hit Nick instead of the musty odor of the old jewelry store. The display cases on the right had been replaced by people with drinks and laptops, and the counter to the left was now the barista station.

Nick went straight to the cashier, not caring that he had cut in front of half a dozen people in line.

"Who are you, and what's going on here?" Nick demanded of the teenage clerk, a girl just a few years older than him. "And don't you dare tell me you have no idea what I'm talking about."

To which the clerk replied, "I have no idea what you're talk-ing about."

"Svedberg's jewelry store. It was here exactly . . ." He looked at his watch. "Twenty hours ago."

"Don't know anything about it." The clerk shrugged. "I work at the Fourth Street store, but they told me to come here today."

Caitlin, who had been quizzing the barista at the other end of the counter, shook her head toward Nick as if to say, *These clowns know nothing.*

"Who's in charge here?" Nick asked the cashier.

"That would be me. Now, if you'll excuse me, there are people waiting to order." Then she turned to the woman standing behind Nick.

Nick took a step back and let the clueless cashier wait on the equally clueless customers.

When Caitlin came to him, she was trembling at this new caffeinated reality.

"So, can I buy you a drink?" Nick asked.

"Cappuccino," she said. "Make it a double."

"Guys?"

They both turned to see Mitch, looking about as troubled as they were. "I thought you both were yanking my crank, until I found this in the corner."

And he held up a diamond ring.

In the end they chose to forget the drinks in favor of getting out of there.

They spent the rest of the afternoon at Beef-O-Rama, and although they ordered, their basket of fries was ignored.

Caitlin was still visibly shaken, avoiding eye contact.

"Listen, there's a . . ." Nick began.

Caitlin pounded her fist on the table, dislodging a flurry of fries. "If you say 'logical explanation,' I'll slap you so hard they'll find your eyes in Denver."

Nick shifted his baseball cap, a little nervous and a little impressed.

"Guys," said Mitch, still holding the ring, "I think this diamond is real. Check it out." He reached over and used the diamond to make a scratch on the window, large enough to be cause for a lawsuit if the owner had seen. "How much do you think it's worth?"

Caitlin snatched it from him. "It doesn't belong to you. It belongs to Svedberg. And when we find him, we give it back. Got it?"

Nick took a deep breath, feeling it was his duty to state the obvious. "He's been disappeared. We have to accept it."

Caitlin folded her arms and looked out the window rather than at Nick. "I accept nothing!"

"Disappeared by who?" asked Mitch.

But Nick knew it was best not to involve Mitch any deeper than he already was. "You don't want to know."

Maybe it was Nick's tone of voice or the look on his face, but Mitch's curiosity was shut down as effectively as Svedberg's jewelry shop. He cast his eyes to the cold, limp, and lonely fries. "What a waste." But still he didn't eat.

Caitlin stood up abruptly. "I'm done. I'm going back to my art projects, and my school projects, and my cheerleading projects."

"And your Theo projects?" Nick asked, regretting it immediately.

Caitlin pursed her lips. "At least I know *he* won't be a coffee-house tomorrow."

"No," said Mitch, "but he might be a perko-later."

Caitlin gave him a flesh-incinerating glare. "That's not even funny." Then she turned and stormed toward the restroom.

Nick went after her, and he paced the restroom hallway, not sure what to say to her when she came out. How could he talk her down when he was on the same ledge beside her?

Caitlin came out a moment later, but she wasn't angry anymore. She was in tears. She looked up to see him there. He thought she might try to hide her face, but she didn't.

"Abnormal things don't happen to me," she told Nick through her tears. "I happen to them."

And although Nick had no idea what that meant, he knew

exactly how she felt, and he found himself putting his arms around her.

"It's not the end of the world," he told her.

"I know," she said, "it's just . . ." But she never finished her thought because Mitch had arrived, and he was putting his arms around both of them.

"Good idea," said Mitch. "Group hug."

And they stood there like that until somebody needed to get past them to use the restroom.

Nick went straight up to his room when he arrived home. He pulled the attic trapdoor closed behind him and slipped beneath his covers, determined to escape into unconsciousness. For ten minutes he tossed and turned, unable to get warm, and too wired on his own adrenaline to find relief. He couldn't tell how much of his exhaustion was physical and how much was emotional. He wished there was a device from his attic that could make him forget any of this had happened. But if a blissful ignorance machine had ever been in his attic, it had been sold for a bargain at his garage sale.

He sat up, thinking he might try getting on his computer to über-Google Tesla again, and find out things even Petula didn't know. It was then that he noticed his dirty clothes were gathered in the center of the attic once more, and his bed and desk had moved away from the walls again. Not only that, but the original attic items that he had retrieved seemed to be frozen in mid-migration toward the center of the room.

He reached beneath his mattress and pulled out the baseball mitt, just to make sure it was where he had left it. Then he stood up and approached the center of the room. He could no longer deny that there was some sort of gravity pulling things to the center of his attic.

He could feel heat emanating from the spot. It was directly beneath the skylight, so perhaps it had been warmed by the sun. But it shouldn't still be warm now that it was twilight. . . .

Nick lay down on his back amid the laundry, using the baseball glove as a pillow, and soaked in the warmth. It was more than just warmth, however. As he lay there he had an undeniable sense of . . . connection. That was the only way he could describe it. He thought about all the items that had been in his attic. He had no idea where they were or how they were being used, yet somehow he *felt* them out there, just as clearly as he could feel his fingers and toes. They were a part of him—or more accurately, he was a part of them. It was a deeply satisfying sensation. So satisfying that his whole body relaxed, and he drifted off into a contented sleep.

Danny shook him awake.

"You were hiding up here all along! I knew it!"

Nick took a moment to gather his wits. He was still beneath the skylight, only now the twilight sky had given way to night.

"I wasn't hiding," Nick told his brother. "I just took a nap."

"Dad thinks you didn't come home, that you stayed away on purpose." There was a sadness to Danny's voice that didn't seem right. "What are you doing with my glove? I thought they took it."

"Yeah," said Nick, "*they* thought they took it, too." He was worried that Danny might make a big deal out of it, but he didn't. Again, that seemed odd.

"You missed dinner," Danny told him. "Dad cooked a roast, but it burned, so he called it Cajun Blackened Beef."

Nick could not recall a single instance when his father had used a kitchen appliance. "Why? What's the occasion?"

Danny just stared at him, then started to get red in the face. "Nothing," he said. "I guess it doesn't matter." Then he left. A few moments later Nick heard him slam his bedroom door one floor below.

When it hit Nick, it hit him with such a wave of misery and regret, he almost doubled over in pain—but the pain wasn't just in his gut, it was everywhere.

Today was his mother's birthday.

It wasn't like they spoke of it. Nick's father certainly hadn't mentioned it—and the weight of her absence was such a constant, their day-to-day lives gave no hint that a dark milestone was looming on the calendar.

How could he have forgotten his mother's birthday? What kind of person was he? He could almost see her shaking her head at him. "Nicky, Nicky, Nicky, where is your head?" She was the only one he had allowed to call him Nicky. Now no one was allowed to call him that, and no one ever would be.

He left his room, practically falling down the attic ladder, which retreated back into the ceiling, its springs activated by his final bound.

Down in the living room, his father had hooked up a video recorder to the TV. He was watching an old baseball game. Although the figures on the field were too far away for Nick to be able to see their faces, he could tell by the number on the pitcher's jersey, and the way he moved, that it was a younger version of his father.

Mr. Slate took a quick look at him, and then his eyes went back to the TV. "This was one game before I blew out my elbow. Almost a no-hitter."

Nick watched his father throw a perfect pitch. It was ten years ago, but it felt like it could have been a hundred.

"Dad, I'm sorry—"

"Shhhh," his father said. Then he added, "Nothing to be sorry about."

Nick sat beside him on the sofa. It was only a few minutes in when Nick realized why his Dad was watching the video. His father had always been the one to man the camera—but this time he was on the field. Which meant someone else was holding it.

"Nicky, stop squirming!" he heard his mother say. The image jostled and went momentarily skyward before refocusing. He heard his younger self complaining about being thirsty and cold, and wanting a hot dog. He must have been what, four? Danny hadn't even been born yet.

"Nicky, watch Daddy."

"I'm watching, but he's not watching me."

"That's because he's watching the batter."

"But he just looked away."

"Because he's checking the runner."

"So he doesn't steal?"

"That's right!"

Then his father struck out the batter, and the fielders came running in to thunderous applause.

Nick knew there were plenty of videos of his mother, but he also knew why his father had chosen this one. If he saw her—if he watched her smile at the camera, and do the casual, everyday things a person does, it would be too much to bear. But hearing her, that was something he could handle.

"She would be happy you were out with your friends today," Nick's father told him. "She'd be glad to know you're getting along so well in a new—" He choked up before he could finish.

Nick could feel his own tears threatening to become volcanic, but he couldn't let it happen. When one of them cried, the other two remained strong. That's the way they kept one another afloat. So Nick leaned into his father as he had when he was little. "Can you start it over, Dad?" he asked. "I want to see the whole game."

"Sure thing, Nick."

His father rewound the tape to the beginning, and together they listened to Nick's mother try to keep little Nicky content for the better part of two hours.

It wasn't until after the video had ended that they realized Danny had vanished from the house.

14 MAKES NO DIFFERENCE WHO YOU ARE

Nick's first thought was that Jorgenson had taken Danny. That he had figured out the glove was a fake and he'd come back for vengeance. But if that were the case, Nick would have heard something. Plus, Danny's jacket was gone, which meant he had left the house on his own. Where he had gone, and why, was anyone's guess.

"Your brother barely knows this town!" his father raved. The man was already an emotional wreck tonight; he didn't need this. "Where could he possibly go?"

"It's good that he doesn't know the area—that means there aren't many places he knows to go," Nick told his father.

They drove to his school and walked the perimeter, looking for signs of Danny. They went to the ice cream shop they had already been to twice since moving in. It was just as Mr. Slate was getting ready to dial 911 that a bright flash in the sky caught their attention.

"Was that—" But before Nick could finish the thought, something else streaked brightly down from the heavens, landing somewhere nearby. By the time the third one came, they were back in the car, speeding toward the sports complex.

They arrived in time to see yet another shooting star rocket down and smack into Danny's glove, giving off a sound like a tiny sonic boom. He was thrown back and dragged through the dirt, leaving a trench, just as he had the first time. Only this time there were multiple trenches around him.

"Danny!" called their father, sprinting across the field toward him. Danny was already up again, raising his mitt, assuming a ready position.

"Go away!" he yelled, keeping his eyes fixed on the sky. "I gotta do this! I gotta do this."

Before their father could get to him, another meteorite came plunging out of nowhere, drawn toward Danny's glove.

"Dad!" yelled Nick.

His father turned just in time to see it and dive out of the way. A flaming meteorite dragged Danny even farther than before. And yet, in an instant, Danny dropped the smoking wad of iron to the ground and got up again.

"For the love of God, what's going on?" their dad yelled.

Nick reached Danny before he could put the mitt up once more, but Danny struggled against him as if his life depended on catching just one more flaming fly ball.

"There's got to be something to it, Nick," Danny said desperately. "There's got to be."

"What are you talking about?"

Danny's eyes, wide and pleading, glistened with tears. "Wishing on falling stars. They're falling for a reason, and I know why." Fighting Nick, he thrust his gloved hand into the air again. "To make the wish come true. To bring Mom back."

Suddenly the night sky looked brighter than daytime. When Nick turned, he saw a huge fireball roughly the size of a washing machine hurtling toward them. Nick ripped the glove from his brother's hand, hurled it into the air, and threw himself and his brother into one of the ditches to get out of the way.

With the roar of a bullet train bearing down on them, the huge meteor hit the glove and just kept on going, shaking the earth around them.

When the thunder subsided and Nick looked up, he saw a trench at least ten feet deep. It had torn a huge hole in the right-field fence and taken down several trees. He could see the angry piece of sky lying at the end of the ditch, white-hot, slowly smoldering to red as it cooled. The glove had somehow protected his brother from the other meteorites, but he doubted it would have saved him from this one.

And there, lying in the ditch with him, his eyes closed tightly, Danny muttered, "I wish she was back. I wish she was back," pleading with a field full of shooting stars to grant him his heart's desire.

Then his words faded into gentle sobs.

"It's all right, Danny. It's all going to be all right."

Nick turned to see their father coming up to them, his eyes filled with a kind of numb disbelief, but it didn't stop him from reaching down, grabbing Danny in his strong arms, and carrying him off the field with Nick close behind.

Danny fell asleep even before they reached the car, going limp in his father's arms, and Nick and his father were silent on the way home, for what was there to be said? His father knew that the questions he would ask Nick couldn't be answered.

It was only after Danny was tucked in that Nick's father, leaning against the door frame of Danny's room as if he needed it to hold him up, looked at Nick and said, "I think your brother's through with baseball."

Nick thought he might say more, but instead he just gave Nick a hug, told him he had school tomorrow, and went off to bed himself, apparently preferring the madness of dreams to the current madness of reality.

Nick couldn't blame him, because he felt exactly the same way. Up in the attic, he pushed his bed back against the wall and lay down on it, choosing to avoid the center of the room. He twisted the Accelerati pin in his fingers, knowing he was in over his head, but also knowing that there was nothing he could do about it. His one consolation was that the rain of meteorites had stopped before it could do any real damage.

Of course, he didn't know that forty-three million miles away, an asteroid roughly the size of Rhode Island had changed its trajectory by a single degree while Danny's glove was still held high in the air. A single degree—tiny in the grand scheme of things—but large enough to put it on a collision course with planet Earth.

15 THE BURDEN OF BEYOND WEIRD

The meteor shower that hit the sports McComplex was all the talk at school the next day. Even though there was absolutely no news coverage, word of mouth had spread, quickly devolving into misinformation, until a few simple chunks of rock had become Aliens in the Outfield. Ralphy Sherman claimed to have actually seen one.

"All three of its heads looked me in the eye, then it ripped off my wallet and escaped on a public bus."

But no one believed him, because everyone knew the buses didn't run past nine.

For Nick, the mundane workings of middle school were a pleasant, if somewhat numbing escape from issues of cosmic intrigue. Then Vince arrived with a set of croquet mallets.

"Here," he said, handing the whole set over to Nick. "I picked these up on the way to school. You owe me forty-three bucks."

They looked like ordinary croquet mallets. There was a reason for that. "These weren't from my attic," said Nick.

"What? But I heard the guy telling people he got them at a garage sale."

Nick shrugged. "Not mine."

"So what am I gonna do with croquet mallets?"

"Stop right there!" They turned to see Petula glowering at them with steely intensity. "Are those croquet mallets?"

"Indeed they are," said Vince.

"No one plays croquet anymore," Petula said. "Which means more scholarship money for me. How much do you want for them?"

Ultimately Vince cut his losses by selling the mallets to Petula for twenty bucks.

It was during the last period of the day that Nick was called in once more to Principal Watt's office. He offered Nick his deepest condolences.

"What do you mean?" asked Nick, gripping the arms of his chair. "What happened?"

"It's your mighty morphin' permanent record," the principal said. "I have good news and bad news. The good news is you are no longer from Denmark. You did, in fact, attend Tampa Heights Middle School."

"Okay, and . . ."

"The bad news is you were labeled 'deceased' as of February twelfth."

The significance of that date was instantly clear to Nick. It was the date of the fire. The air-conditioning in the room suddenly felt very cold.

"My brother, too?"

"You'll have to take that up with the elementary school." Then, from a manila folder, he withdrew a sheet of paper and handed it to Nick. It was a death certificate. "I must say it disturbs me that you're officially dead, Mr. Slate. This is not that kind of school."

Nick looked it over. Whoever created it had taken great pains to make it look real. But why? He found the answer at the bottom of the page, where there was a small, hand-printed *A* crossed by the symbol for infinity.

It was a warning. A threat. The Accelerati, whatever they were, now knew that Nick knew. And if they had the power to mess with his school records, there was no telling what else they could mess with.

"It's someone's idea of an April Fools' joke," Nick told Principal Watt. "That's all."

"It's a few weeks late for April Fools'."

"Not Chinese April Fools'. Keep watching my file," he told the principal as he got up to leave. "I'm sure next week I'll be alive, but from Mars."

The sound of clattering pots and pans when Nick arrived home meant that his dad was cooking again. Nick realized that the end of the world must be upon them, because his father preparing a home-cooked meal two nights in a row was surely a sign of the apocalypse.

On his way toward the kitchen, Nick caught sight of Danny in the living room, sitting on the floor and wrestling with a video-game controller—which Danny often did these days, because of their lamentable lack of cable. On the screen, heads were exploding; the result of some supercharged weapon that might or might not have a real-life cousin from Nick's attic.

It was the first time Nick had seen his brother since last night's flaming parade of heavenly bodies. He hesitated at the arched threshold of the living room, knowing that any move toward Danny would feel like walking on eggshells.

"Hey," he said softly.

"I don't want to talk about it!" snapped Danny.

"That's okay," said Nick. "I wasn't going to ask."

Danny paused the game and looked at Nick. His eyes were searching for something in his brother, but whatever Danny was searching for, Nick knew it wasn't there.

"I want to pretend it never happened, but I can't," Danny said. Then he gazed down at the faded carpet for a few moments before saying, "There's something wrong with this place, isn't there?"

"Not wrong," Nick answered. "Just weird."

"No," Danny said, a little irritated. "My principal's comb-over is weird. Our neighbor and her dog in matching sweaters are weird. But this?"

"Good point," said Nick, thinking back to Mitch's appraisal. "Let's just say, 'It is what it is.'"

Danny returned to his game, but his heart wasn't in it, and his avatar accidentally blew up his own head.

"So, was it just the baseball glove? Or all the stuff in the attic?" Danny asked.

Nick thought about lying in order to shield his brother, but Danny had probably figured out the answer already.

"I know this is scary, Danny," he said, "but you know what? Everything in the world is scary until you understand it."

"Do you understand it?"

"No," Nick said. "So I'm scared, too."

"Really?"

"Yeah . . . but I think it would be easier if you let me be scared for both of us."

Danny considered the wisdom of that, and he nodded. "I can do that." Then he restarted his game, content to let Nick bear the burden of all things beyond weird.

Nick stepped into the kitchen, where his father was now singing. It sounded almost Italian, but it fell short with a lot of dum-de-dums where the Italian words were supposed to be. Pasta was obviously on the menu.

"I found a meat-sauce recipe online. It got five out of five stars from four hundred and twelve people globally."

"Right . . ." said Nick. "You okay, Dad?"

"More than okay." Mr. Slate stirred the sauce so hard it splattered the wall behind the range. "The job that Jorgenson guy was talking about? Turns out it's the real deal. Somehow they'd heard I'd been a technician in Tampa. Now I'm repairing copy machines at triple the salary for NORAD!"

"NORAD?"

Nick had heard of the North American Aerospace Defense Command, and he knew it was somewhere near Colorado Springs, but he couldn't wrap his mind around the idea of his father working there. It was as unlikely as . . . well, as Svedberg & Sons, Fine Jewelers, disappearing into thin air.

"I started today. I actually get to go into the mountain!" Nick's dad grinned like a kid. "I have security clearance and everything. At least to the places that have copy machines."

He drained the pasta while Nick tried to sift through his father's big news. Jorgenson must have connections nosebleed high if he could put Nick's father into a NORAD job.

"Oh, the folks at NORAD explained to me what's going on," his father said. "The baseball mitt is part of some old experimental weapons system. The mitt has a homing chip in it. And the meteorites were actually test missiles in disguise. I guess the idea was to attack an enemy but make it look like a random cosmic event! Very controversial. I guess that's why it was scrapped."

Nick said nothing. *They're lying to you, Dad,* he wanted to say. *They're lying to you to keep you from asking questions.* But when the alternative was believing that your eight-year-old son was pulling real meteorites out of the sky, a lie—any lie—becomes a welcome relief. If his father hadn't been so desperate for a simple explanation, he might have realized that if it *were* true, they never would have told him. Who gives classified military information to the copy-machine technician?

"Don't know how the thing ended up in our attic," his father continued as he poured the meat sauce on the spaghetti. "Maybe your great-aunt Greta won it in a poker game from some general. I hear she was a wild one back in the day."

Nick sat with his father and brother, eating his five-star spaghetti in silence. Yes, his father now had a job, but slipping him into this job was not an act of generosity on the part of Jorgenson. It was a way of keeping an eye on the whole family. A way of telling Nick that if he didn't get with the program, his father might pay the price.

Nick had to face the fact that this was all too big for him. It would be wise for him to simply bow out now, before someone got hurt. Just give Jorgenson whatever he wanted, and never speak of the Accelerati again.

Things might have gone that way, too, if Nick hadn't picked up the sports pages after dinner. When he flipped over the section to check the baseball scores, he found himself looking at the obituary page instead.

Nick never read obituaries. He had a funny superstition about it, fearing he might see his name, have a coronary, and fulfill the prophecy of his own death. He knew it was ridiculous, but still the thought of it was enough to keep him from looking. Except this time. And out of the various local dead folk staring back at him from the newspaper, one looked familiar.

Nick excused himself and went upstairs to call Caitlin.

"Uh . . . I found Svedberg," he told her when she answered, the obituary page still in his hand.

"That's great! Where is he? Will he talk to us?"

"That might be a problem," Nick said. Then a thought occurred to him. "Then again, maybe not . . ."

■ ■ ■

Vince's house and his mother were just as cheerfully bright as ever. "Vincent!" she called down to the basement after greeting Nick and Caitlin at the door. "I'm sending your friends down. Please make sure you're decent."

"Friends?" Nick heard Vince say, as if this were a foreign, and perhaps unwanted, concept. "Sure, send 'em down."

Vince was, in fact, not decent. He was wearing briefs in police-line colors, and the slogan read: CAUTION! THIS PACKAGE IS EXPLOSIVE!

Caitlin immediately shielded her eyes. "Vince!"

"Sorry!" He quickly stepped into a pair of torn jeans. "Better?"

"Only partially," Caitlin said. "Until you have some pectoral muscles, I insist you wear a shirt. Are we clear?"

Vince sighed, and he slipped on a shirt. "Nobody appreciates malnutrition chic anymore." The shirt slogan read: EAT YOUR HEART OUT . . . BEFORE I DO IT FOR YOU. Which was only slightly better than his underwear.

Through all of this, Nick chuckled nervously, traumatized by the thought of Caitlin seeing Vince in his Skivvies, while simultaneously jealous of Vince for having such a level of optical intimacy with her—even though it was unwanted.

"Where's the wet cell?" Nick asked.

"I knew you had an agenda," Vince said. "I knew you wouldn't visit unless you wanted something."

"We respect your privacy," said Caitlin. "Don't we, Nick?"

"Yeah—I mean, we wouldn't bother you unless we really had to."

Vince looked back and forth between them a few times and then said, "I haven't used it for anything stupid. If you must know, I've been conducting experiments with it so I can understand exactly how it works." He sat down on his bed and pulled out a notebook, which he began to flip through. "It can animate roadkill, but only the parts that haven't been crushed."

Caitlin began to look mildly green. "Oh, yuck."

"That goes for possums, raccoons, squirrels . . ."

"We get the idea," said Nick. "What else did you find out?"

Vince flipped the page. "I tried it on a steak. Cooked, no— but raw, yes. My specimen, a raw New York steak, twelve ounces, began to squirm when the electrodes were applied."

"Squirm?" said Caitlin.

"Yeah, it started to crawl off the plate and . . ." Caitlin gave him another look, and he quickly turned the page. "I took it to the museum the other day, and when no one was looking, I attached it to a dinosaur skeleton."

"You what?!" Nick exclaimed.

"Don't worry, it had no effect on the bones." He shook his head wistfully. "Yeah, that would've been sweet. So my theory is the battery can reanimate something when the tissue is in decent shape and still has some sort of muscular integrity."

"Like the freshly dead," suggested Nick. Both he and Caitlin leaned in closer for the answer.

Vince smiled broadly. "Where are we going with this, guys?"

16 MAN IN A DRAWER

The fact that Vince knew the location and religious affiliation of every mortuary in town was one of those things he never thought would come in handy—unless, of course, he was ever lucky enough to witness a multicar pileup or a high-casualty natural disaster. Still, he couldn't help but know. His mind was a spring-loaded, bloodstained steel trap when it came to tidbits of morbidity.

Being that Svedberg was a Scandinavian name, and that all the Scandinavians he knew were Lutheran, Vince reasoned that Svedberg would be chilling at the Clausing & Corkery Mortuary, in preparation for a funeral later in the week.

"Hey, Nick," said Vince as they approached the quaint Victorian mortuary. "Looks kind of like your house, doesn't it?" And noticing Nick's discomfort at the suggestion, he said, "Don't worry, I'm sure any bodies at your house are unintentional."

"Let's just get in and get out," Nick said.

"So," asked Caitlin, "how are we going to get in?"

Vince handed the heavy wet cell to Nick. "The side door has a sticky lock when the weather's been wet," Vince said. "Sometimes it doesn't fully engage and can be jimmied open with a credit card."

"How do you know this?" Caitlin asked, a slight tremor in her voice.

"Well, sometimes when I can't sleep—"

"Stop right there." Caitlin put up her hand. "My disturbing-image meter is already in the red with the first half of that sentence."

Vince shrugged, and he reminded himself that personal information should really only be shared on a need-to-know basis.

The side door, not used by the general public, was neglected and weather worn. Vince put his hand on the doorknob to steady it, and just as he said, the door opened with a little credit-card tinkering.

"Voilà," Vince said, holding the door wide. The others hesitated, not yet ready to step into the dark space beyond the open door. "Don't be such lightweights," he said. "There's nothing in there but death." And he strode into the void, knowing they would follow if he led the way.

Vince felt his way down the hall until he reached the alarm panel. From experience he knew he had thirty seconds to disarm the security system. He had once tripped it accidentally, and then he hid and watched the security guard enter the code.

Vince heard the others enter the hallway behind him and the steel door creak closed as he punched in the numbers by the light of his iPhone.

"They've got a rent-a-cop who comes by once an hour or so," he explained.

"There's no security here now?" whispered Nick, looking around.

"Nah," Vince said. "It's not like the guests here need hand-holding. We should be okay, but keep your ears peeled in case anyone comes in."

"*Eyes* peeled; *ears* to the ground," Caitlin corrected him, unnerved. "Keep your expressions straight."

"Just be listening," Vince told them.

He led them down a stairway and into the prep room. Various tools of the trade hung on the walls, and a sink table was set smack in the middle of a green tiled floor.

Vince held out his hands. "This is where it happens, people. The Egyptians did it with sea salt and linen. But now it's formaldehyde and stainless steel."

"Dude," said Nick. "Enough."

"Right." Vince noted that not everyone had as healthy a perspective on life and death as he did. "Let's take a look in the chill drawers, shall we?"

He led them across the room to a series of square refrigerator doors set into the wall. Nick and Caitlin kept a nervous distance.

"Just tell us when you find him," Nick said. Caitlin's eyes were closed, and Nick was looking down at the oversize battery in his hands, clearly to avoid having to look anywhere else.

Vince sighed. "I guess I'll do this part." Without hesitation, he opened the first of many doors holding the mortuary's current clientele.

The first two drawers held women. Vince could tell without even having to look at the toe tags.

The third and fourth drawers were empty. And the fifth held the prize.

Vince pulled the steel tray out all the way. "Ladies and gentlemen," he said, "I give you the late Mr. Svedberg." And he pulled off the sheet with the flourish of a magician.

Nick and Caitlin cautiously approached as Vince inspected him. He had the standard look of death. Nothing remarkable about him or the disposition of his remains.

"Sometimes," Vince said, pointing to Svedberg's face, "they've got one eye open and it's like they're winking at you."

Caitlin let out an audible shudder at the thought.

"Just do it," said Nick, holding out the battery.

Vince fished in his pockets for the insulated wires, attached one end of each to the wet cell, and held the other ends over Svedberg's chest. He took a deep breath, realizing this was nothing like a fish, or a frog, or a possum. Vince knew this would truly be a life-defining moment for him. Life-defining and death-defying, he thought, in a very literal way.

Then he touched the electrodes to Svedberg's chest.

The most annoying thing about being reanimated, Alfred Svedberg was quick to discover, was not the foul mood one finds oneself in; nor was it the acrid smell of embalming fluid. Instead it was a sudden and overpowering craving for corned beef and cabbage, both of which are good sources of iron. Since the dead are anemic, what with their blood being drained and all, the oft-referred-to zombie penchant for human brains is nothing more than a legitimate craving that could easily be satisfied with spinach.

"What the hell is wrong with you?" Svedberg asked. "Can't you see I'm busy?"

Svedberg spontaneously knew that he was dead. Realization of one's own death must be a universal component of reanimation, although further research would be required to prove it.

"Mr. Svedberg," said a girl. He didn't recognize her at first, because of the angle of his view: somewhat upside down. "We're sorry to bother you. But you were going to give us some important information before you . . . that is to say, before you . . ."

"Before I was murdered? Is that what you're trying to say?"

"So it *was* murder," said a boy standing next to her, holding some square apparatus that Svedberg immediately knew was the source of his unexpected life energy.

Now he identified two of the kids. They had come to see

him shortly before his death. Young Caitlin Westfield and Nick something. And it made him furious.

"Why should I talk to you? It's because of you that I was killed! I had so many plans, so many years ahead of me—"

"Not anymore," said the boy holding the electrodes to his chest. "The best you can do now is make a difference. Maybe even point the finger at the people who did this to you."

Svedberg had less interest in vengeance than in getting back to being deceased, from which he had been so rudely interrupted. But it was obvious this trio was not going anywhere until he gave them something.

"Fine," he said. He tried to cross his arms, but he found them both very stiff, as if he had double tennis elbow that no amount of physical therapy could cure. And though his jaw felt a little bit looser, this conversation was a struggle no postmortem personage should be subjected to.

"Please, Mr. Svedberg," said Nick. "We need to know about the Accelerati."

"Do you have any idea what they'll do to me?" Svedberg asked.

"Uh, what more could they do to you?" asked Caitlin.

Svedberg had to admit she had a point. "If I tell you, will you let me rest in peace already?"

They nodded, and so he began.

And whoever said, "Dead men tell no tales," had never met Alfred Svedberg.

"My grandfather wasn't just a jeweler. He was a gemologist. He studied precious gems. He actually synthesized the first artificial diamond, which you call cubic zirconia. Of course, he never got credit. As a member of the Accelerati, he was bound to a code of anonymity. Although he was never supposed to speak of it, not even to his family, he confided in me just a few days before he died.

"The Accelerati began more than a hundred years ago, according to my grandfather. It was an honor society, created by the man history claims to be the greatest inventor of all time: Thomas Alva Edison.

"As the story goes, Edison grew tired of the pompous posturing and mundane concerns of other wealthy businessmen. He wanted a society of intellectuals, scientists, inventors, and great thinkers who could and would change the world. But from the very beginning, Edison had an agenda. The Accelerati were never about enlightenment. They were the dark side of genius, the secret shadow of invention. For the Accelerati it always was, and always will be, about power. Not some vague, idealistic grasp at control, no—but power in the literal sense. Electricity, fuel, the very energy that drives our world. Edison's goal was to control everything from production, to delivery, to consumption—and he almost succeeded. There is a reason why nearly every American power company has Edison as part of its name.

"Oh, there was no question that he was brilliant, both as an inventor and a businessman, but he fell one level short of the genius it would take to truly master the world's energy supply. That's why he created the Accelerati, co-opting the brainpower of some of the world's greatest minds. Minds who were the equals of Einstein, Fermi, or Bohr, but names you'll never hear because of the Acceleratis' vow of anonymity.

"It was they who detonated the first atomic bomb, a mile beneath Harvard, years before Oppenheimer began his experiments. It was they who broadcast the first television signal, when the public was just beginning to accept radio. And when a member went astray, it was they who, like the hand of God, would wipe that person out, and sometimes their entire neighborhood, in a freak 'accident' or natural disaster that had nothing natural about it at all. It was a warning to its members that crossing the Accelerati was met with the severest of consequences.

"Even after Edison was gone, the Accelerati continued their quest for energy—with results as glorious as microwave transmission, and disasters like Chernobyl. My grandfather played the loyal member to protect his family, long after he realized what they were. Once they had the secret patent on the artificial diamond—one of many ways to finance their cause—the Accelerati had little use for him, so they let him be.

"It was an attempt to harness geothermal energy that did them in. In their arrogance, they had gathered in 1980 to witness the dawn of a new era, toasting their own brilliance as their geothermal engine tapped the core of a dormant volcano. It malfunctioned, and the Accelerati were killed in the resulting explosion—an event known to the world as the 'eruption' of Mount St. Helens.

"Some years later my grandfather died thinking the Accelerati were gone, disappearing into their own most-deserved anonymity. I thought so, too, until you brought me that pin. I should have picked up and left that very moment. I was foolish enough to think they might not be watching. But they're always watching. I saw him through the glass door of my shop, shortly after you left. A tall man in a white suit, with a remote control in his hand. Did you know that a universal remote control could be recalibrated to the electrical signature of a human heart? No? Neither did I."

The dead man was silent after that, looking rather sour about the whole thing. Nick was both relieved by the light he had cast and terrified of its scope.

"Tesla and Edison hated each other," Nick pointed out.

"Envy," Svedberg said, "is a powerful motivator. Tesla had what Edison lacked: that highest level of transcendental genius. He was the one scientist who could have made all of Edison's dreams come true. The Accelerati were always trying to get their hands on his secret inventions, but they never could."

Nick looked at the others, but they kept their eyes fixed on Svedberg, who laughed as something seemed to occur to him.

"My grandfather told me a legend that the greatest of Tesla's inventions are hidden right here in Colorado Springs, disguised as ordinary household items." He shook his head. "People will believe anything."

Then he paused for a moment, his smile fading as he turned his eyes to the wet cell that was, for the moment, keeping him alive.

"Oh," was all he said.

Caitlin then pulled the diamond ring out of her pocket—the last remnant of the man's shop—and she placed it in his hand, forcing his stiff fingers to close around it. Nick could see her eyes were filled with tears.

"I'm so sorry, Mr. Svedberg," she said. "You're here because of me. I did this to you, and I'll never forgive myself."

"Well, young Miss Westfield, because you and your mother have always been so kind to me, I'll give you something few people, if any, ever receive. Absolute forgiveness from beyond the grave."

"Technically," offered Vince, "you're not in the grave yet."

"You shouldn't be so rude to a man in my condition," said Svedberg. "Now, if you'll excuse me . . ." Then he reached out, pulled away both of the electrodes touching his chest, and got back to the business of being permanently out of business.

17 WHAT HAS THE HUBBLE DONE FOR US LATELY?

Regardless of its other properties, Petula's box camera had a simple one-to-one magnification ratio. With its temporal focus ring set to zero, a picture of the sky would yield nothing but the moon, some birds, and the occasional passing aircraft. To see what was in store for the planet Earth, she would need to spin the focus ring a week forward, and it might give her a completely different story. Unfortunately, the focus ring had a maximum zoom of twenty-four hours into the future.

Thus, only a telescope of extreme proportions could detect the sly approach of what was known as Celestial Object Felicity Bonk. It bore that name for the simple reason that it was sold to a fifteen-year-old girl on a field trip to New Mexico's National Radio Astronomy Observatory, home of the very large array of radio telescopes known, quite uncreatively, as the Very Large Array.

Felicity had purchased the asteroid one year earlier, because naming an asteroid only cost ten bucks, whereas a star was a whopping seventy-five.

As any Realtor can tell you, when purchasing real estate, there are only three things that matter: location, location, and location. Celestial Object Felicity Bonk could be found in the low-rent district of the solar system. That is, until just a few days ago, when it began a dramatic relocation.

As most of the world's telescopes were trying to catch such cosmic celebrities as glitzy Magellanic Clouds, camera-shy black holes, and the haunting habits of cannibalistic galaxies, it was a while before the astronomical paparazzi turned its lenses toward quiet, unassuming Celestial Object Felicity Bonk.

It was the Hubble Telescope, free from the nuisance of atmosphere, that first caught the asteroid's movement in its peripheral vision. And a quick calculation by NASA, twice corrected because of metric conversion errors, confirmed its collision course with the Boardwalk of solar real estate, namely planet Earth.

At a speed of sixty-eight thousand miles per hour, its impact in seven days' time, while thankfully putting an end to reality TV forever, would also put an end to reality.

Taking into account its speed and the earth's rotation, the impact point was projected to be a neighborhood sports complex in Colorado Springs. The astonished astronomer who made the discovery was left with one all-important question: is it more appropriate to e-mail, call, or text your boss that the world is about to end?

18 NO ROOM FOR MAYBE

The mathematician Gödel said no equation is complete, because a perfectly complete equation must contain the seeds of its own destruction. In other words, every equation must have its own troublesome variable. Every ointment must have its fly.

Petula Grabowski-Jones was that fly. Although she was more like a mosquito hawk, due to her ability to suck the blood of lesser flies. She had spent most of her free time on Monday and Tuesday taking pictures that were far less pointless than they appeared. Petula found that the most annoying thing about knowing the future between one and twenty-four hours in advance was that the future was mostly uninteresting.

She could take a picture of the school cafeteria, and after developing it, she could tell you what any given kid would be eating for lunch and who they might be sitting next to tomorrow. But who really cared? Everyone knew what was for lunch tomorrow, and everyone knew who they would be sitting next to anyway.

Taking interesting pictures of the future meant trying to guess not only *when* something would happen, but *where* it would happen, too. In addition, as Petula developed her many photos in Ms. Planck's darkroom, she discovered that it wasn't the grand vision of the future she should be focusing on, but the unobserved minutiae. The little details are what make all the difference between *now* and *then*.

Before school started on Wednesday, Petula pulled aside Heather North, who was substantially more popular than she was.

"Don't ask me how I know," she whispered, "but Tommy Woodruff is going to ask you out today. In fact, by the end of the day, I wouldn't be surprised if you're wearing his jersey. If it's true, you owe me one."

Between second and third period, Petula cornered Principal Watt. "I know you've been trying to find a way to fire Mr. Brown. Don't try to deny it. Some things are public knowledge."

The principal said nothing, just stared at her with a slightly bemused and slightly terrified expression.

"Well," Petula whispered, "during his prep period, if you happen to find him alone in his room, he'll be guzzling a bottle of Jack Daniel's. I hope you'll remember who gave you the info."

Then she winked at him and went on her merry way.

And when woefully thin-skinned Cindy Hawthorne came down with one of her epic nosebleeds during lunch, who was there to perform triage with a huge stack of napkins that she just "coincidentally" happened to be holding?

"Thank you, Petula," said Cindy. "I really owe you."

Petula found that she enjoyed doing good deeds when she knew there would be a return on her investment.

It wasn't until the end of the day that she began to worry about the fabric of the universe, because Heather North was not wearing Tommy Woodruff's jersey seven minutes before the time her picture showed she would be. In fact, Tommy Woodruff was already in the boys' locker room, getting ready for football practice. If it didn't happen, it meant the camera didn't really take pictures of the actual future, just a possible future. And if there was any concept Petula could not stand, it was the great "maybe."

"Maybe there'll be something worth watching on TV." "Maybe people will actually come to your equinox party." "Maybe your parents will remember your birthday this year."

No, the hard cubic reality of her box camera had no room for uncertainty.

So she stormed into the boys' locker room, selectively ignoring things she did not wish to see, ferreted out Tommy Woodruff, and told him point-blank, "I hope you know that Heather is waiting for you to ask her out. Now get out there, give her your jersey, and seal the deal."

Somewhat bewildered by the news, Tommy Woodruff put on his pants, left the locker room, and with far more charm than Petula expected, told Heather North he liked her "a real, real lot" and handed her his jersey as a token of his sincere affection. Heather put on the jersey and a moment later was strolling down the hall, looking lighter than air, as she passed the exact spot where Petula had snapped the picture precisely twenty-four hours earlier.

It was at that moment that Petula realized the *true* power of the camera, and this grand revelation could, and eventually would, change everything. Because although it was clear she had no power to *change* the future, if she knew what that future was, she had every power in the world to *create* it.

Her first premeditated attempt to exploit this knowledge involved her current object of obsession: Nick Slate. Her plan was simple: find a way to lure Nick into her living room while her parents were still at work, and call forth his raging hormones through provocative conversation and her feminine ways. One thing would lead to another, and the afternoon would result in a make-out session worthy of the record books—or at least YouTube.

All that remained was to take a photo of the sofa precisely twenty-four hours before so she would know whether or not her plan had succeeded.

If Nick wasn't with her on the couch, it would save Petula the trouble of having to set the whole thing up. In this way, she could save valuable time by only going through with schemes that she knew in advance would succeed. For what greater power is there than being able to abandon your failures before you even attempt them?

And so, with the camera's time ring set precisely to twenty-four hours, she snapped the picture of her sofa, then hurried over to Ms. Planck's, whose darkroom she had become pleasantly addicted to.

"My parents are awful snoops," she told Ms. Planck. "And my photography is my business."

"As well it should be," Ms. Planck said, and she proceeded to do her own snooping, looking at the various prints that hung from strings around the darkroom, like laundry in neighborhoods of old. Somehow it didn't bother Petula the way it did when her parents stuck their noses into her darkroom back home.

"Slices of life," Ms. Planck said. "You certainly have an eye for catching people candidly. And I even like the still lifes," she said, pointing to photos of empty hallways and vacant tables, where Petula failed to capture anybody doing anything. "You have a curious sensibility."

Then Ms. Planck left her alone to get to the business of developing her future.

Processing the negative took the longest. Spooling the film into a little drum, filling it with chemicals, and shaking it like one of her father's cocktails. Developing solution first, then the stop bath and fixer. She was supposed to let the negative dry, but Petula didn't have the patience—not this time.

Instead, she put it right into the enlarger. And, to her joy, the negative image did show two people on the sofa, one leaning toward the other. With her heart racing, she brought the image into focus. The redness of the safelight only added to the intensity of her emotions, which bloomed from joyful anticipation into something very different. . . . Then she let out a scream when she saw exactly who was on the sofa with her.

It wasn't Nick sitting beside her—it was Mitch. And they were, indeed, making out.

Caitlin's experience that afternoon, while not quite as horrifying as Petula's, was nonetheless profoundly abnormal. It seemed odd to her that, after having spent her evening talking to the dead, she should have to go about the busywork of school, but the simple fact of knowing about the Accelerati didn't give her a way to do anything about it. In fact, if anything, it made things worse. Now she knew that the Accelerati were many generations old, and like a tree whose roots had wormed their way into the sewer system, they had grown strong by unpleasant means. She knew they could not be battled by normal methods.

At lunchtime, Caitlin sat with Theo rather than with Nick, trying to lose herself in simpler times, and all times with Theo were simple. He was the white bread to her PB&J, and the fact that he would still sit with her in spite of having suffered public humiliation was somehow admirable. Either he was sure enough about himself not to care, or he simply didn't know what else to do.

Or maybe he sat with her because he knew that as long as she was with him, she wasn't with Nick. Although today, Nick was the last person she wanted to sit with, because rehashing the night before would not exactly be conducive to digestion.

So Ms. Planck served up her usual slop, and then Theo served up his usual fluff. And for a while Caitlin could pretend that the extent of her problems lived and died within the hallowed halls of Rocky Point Middle School.

"Meteor showers suck," Theo proclaimed.

"Not all of them," Caitlin pointed out.

"Well, the ones that shut down the baseball fields do. All our home games are canceled until further notice, and all because of a bunch of rocks." Theo carved a river of gravy through his mashed potatoes and directed it into a series of rapids using chunks of beef stew. Theo, Caitlin had learned, was the absolute master of playing with his food.

"So are we still, like, going out?" he asked.

"Ask me again next week," Caitlin told him.

"Fine," said Theo, "enjoy your lunch."

And he up and left, taking his gravy river with him. If nothing else, this had made it clear to Caitlin that there was no going back. Whatever trajectory her life was on, she knew her white-bread days were over.

When she got home, Caitlin found none other than Mr. Accelerati himself—Jorgenson—sitting in her kitchen as if he belonged there, sipping a cup of tea.

This was odd enough, but what made it even more disturbing was that her mother, in one of her food-show frenzies, had decided to attempt a fancy meal. Moving at the pace of a contestant in a culinary competition, she was opening and closing drawers, setting pots and bowls everywhere, and leaving ingredients precariously balanced on counter ledges.

All of this was going on around Jorgenson as if he weren't even there.

"Mom, what are you doing?" Caitlin asked.

"It's called Brandy Peppercorn Duck, or at least it will be when it's finished," her mom said, plopping a silver bowl down right in front of Mr. Jorgenson, who only looked at Caitlin and smiled.

"What's he doing here, Mom?"

"He who?"

"Don't you see there's a man sitting in the middle of our kitchen?"

"Well, yes, obviously there is," her mother said, focusing her eyes on Jorgenson for a moment before returning to the multitasks at hand and opening the refrigerator. "Now, let's see, do we have enough butter?"

Jorgenson simply grinned at Caitlin.

"Mom, did you invite him into the house?"

"No, he was here when I got home," her mother answered absently. "Now, Caitlin, you're either going to help me with this dinner, or go do your homework. But please don't distract me, it's a complicated recipe."

"But, Mom—"

"I wouldn't bother," said Jorgensen softly. "Anything you say will just confuse her and complicate the matter."

He held up a small fob on the end of his key chain.

"It's quite simple, really," Jorgenson said jovially. "The chip inside this device projects a signal that affects the logic center of the brain of the person it's been keyed to, telling her there's absolutely nothing unusual about her current circumstance. Observe."

Jorgenson turned to Caitlin's mother. "Mrs. Westfield, I'm going to place your cat in the microwave."

"Be my guest. Make sure you turn him halfway through."

Jorgenson turned to Caitlin with a pleasant smile. "You see?"

Caitlin found herself fuming. "If you so much as *touch* Caliban . . ."

Jorgenson put up his hands. "Banish the thought. I merely proposed it as an example."

"Why are you here?"

"I want to save your friend Nick a world of pain, and I was hoping you might help me." He glanced at her mom, then back at Caitlin. "It's a lovely day. Shall we sit out on your patio?"

And although it was the last thing Caitlin wanted to do, she agreed.

As Jorgenson stood up, he picked up the small teapot in front of him and poured a cup of tea for her. Caitlin looked at the brew warily.

"How do I know you're not poisoning me?"

"Actually, Miss Westfield, it's quite the opposite. The leaves of this coenzyme 'Oolongevity tea' are from select plants, genetically engineered for the highest medicinal value. An instant herbal cure for whatever ails you, from the common cold to various and sundry malignancies."

"What if *you're* what ails me?" Caitlin asked.

"Well, we're here to discuss the cure for that, aren't we?"

He handed her the cup, and they headed outside to the patio.

She was admittedly curious, so she tasted the tea. It was sweet and flavorful, and she instantly felt more relaxed. Healthier, even. Caitlin suspected it was the first of many bribes Jorgenson would offer. She put the cup down and crossed her arms.

"Oh, one more thing," said Jorgenson. "You will find that this tea has a profound effect on memory—and it will make you feel inclined to tell the truth about the things you suddenly remember."

"Truth serum?"

"Please, it's herbal. At most, it's truth chai."

On an empty stomach, it was hitting her system quickly. She suddenly remembered where she had left her lunch box. In the third grade.

"So, how is this going to work?" she asked.

"Very simple," Jorgenson said. "I ask you a number of simple questions, and you tell me what I need to know. If you cooperate, I can assure the safety of Nick, his family, and all of your friends."

"And if I don't answer at all?"

"Then no amount of Oolongevity tea can assure anyone's health."

It was a thinly veiled threat. Considering what the Accelerati had done to Svedberg, she knew Jorgenson wasn't bluffing. In fact, she had begun to wonder if she would get out of this encounter alive.

On the other hand, Jorgenson didn't know how much dead Svedberg had told her and Nick about the Accelerati. She realized the only way she stood a chance was to play this like a game, and so she said, "If I answer your questions, it's only fair that you answer mine. And since you had the same tea that I did, I know you'll be truthful."

Jorgenson bristled, but only slightly. "Fair enough." And he leaned forward. "Where is the Ballistic-Gravitational Glove?"

Caitlin considered how she might somehow sidestep the truth, in spite of the sudden urge to tell it. Then it occurred to her that the answer was obvious and would only give Jorgenson information he already knew. He was testing her.

"Probably still beneath that two-ton meteorite, if it didn't get incinerated."

Jorgenson nodded. "We will know once we're done excavating it."

"My turn," Caitlin said. "How did you turn Svedberg's shop into a coffeehouse so quickly?"

"Selective time dilation," Jorgenson responded without hesitation. "We can travel between the seconds, doing in five hours what would normally take five days. We actually have a very lucrative contract with Starbucks to put in shops overnight." Through all of this, he held eye contact with her. "Now," he said, "tell me the location of the Far Range Energy Emitter."

Caitlin was about to say she had no idea what he was talking about, but then realized that his question had just revealed something important. She briefly considered how to respond honestly and said, "If I had the answer to that, this would be a very different conversation, wouldn't it?"

Jorgenson clearly wasn't pleased with the answer, but before he could say anything, Caitlin asked, "What will you do with it when you find it?"

"We'll do what Tesla was never able to do. Make it work." And then he added quickly, "For the betterment of mankind, of course."

"Of course," Caitlin responded. "As *you* define it."

Jorgenson brought his hand down on the small table with enough force to make her teacup jump. "Now tell me about each of the items you already have, and what each of them actually does."

If this were a game, Jorgenson had just flipped the board.

"Thank you for the tea," said Caitlin, sounding far calmer than she actually felt. "But there is nothing more I wish to say to you. And that's the truth."

"How . . . *very* . . . unfortunate," Jorgenson said, drawing out each word to make clear how unfortunate it really was. And then he said calmly, "I could reach out and slit your throat right now, you know, and your mother would happily give me a hand towel to clean up the mess. You realize that, don't you?"

Caitlin took a deep slow breath and then said, quite evenly, "Killing me won't help you any more than killing Svedberg did."

Jorgenson's eyes glinted, but the truth in her voice stopped him. He stood and straightened his pearlescent coat. "When one stands in the way of the greater good, Miss Westfield, one is often ground up by the wheels of progress. Don't say you haven't been warned."

After he left, Caitlin returned to the kitchen, where her mother was head-and-shoulders deep into the cupboard.

"What are you looking for?" Caitlin asked.

"Garlic press," her mom replied.

Caitlin followed a string of muffled meows to the microwave oven. Quickly throwing open the door, she found her cat, Caliban, sitting inside, safe and sound, placed there no doubt by Jorgenson, traveling in between the seconds.

19 A TRUNK OF LOST MEMORIES

Nick had been terrified of the Accelerati before he heard
Svedberg's tale. And yet, finding out that the Accelerati were
even more powerful and dangerous than he had imagined—
rather than increase Nick's terror, it gave him an uncanny sense
of relief.

Knowing they could easily crush him like an insect posed
the all-important question: why hadn't they? After all, if you see
a spider in your room, you squash it, plain and simple—unless
you have a reason to let that spider live. So it can catch flies,
perhaps, or maybe, as in the case of the Madagascan silk spider,
so it can weave valuable webs.

For whatever reason, the Accelerati needed Nick—which put
him at a distinct advantage, because he definitely did *not* need
them.

"They're looking for something called a Far Range Energy
Emitter," Caitlin said.

She had come over unexpectedly late that afternoon, racing
upstairs and into the attic. It was the first time in the universe's
thirteen-billion-year history that a girl had been in Nick's
bedroom.

Luckily Caitlin was doing all the talking, or she might have
noticed how, for at least the first couple of minutes, Nick found
himself incapable of speech. She first told him of her chilling

encounter with the Grand Acceleratus himself—or whatever you call the leader of a lethal secret society. Then they began to discuss the mystery of the Far Range Energy Emitter.

"You think it was something I sold at the garage sale?" Nick asked.

Caitlin shook her head. "It sounded like something bigger. Not a thing, but a place."

"Some place Tesla built, maybe?" Nick suggested. "Like Wardenclyffe Tower?"

In crunching facts about the mad scientist who now ruled his life, Nick had learned that Tesla began building a tower in New York, nearly two hundred feet tall, with a giant copper sphere at the top. He quickly relayed the facts to Caitlin: how it was supposed to transmit electricity from the United States to Europe through the air, how it would have been the world's first "wireless" network, and even though he designed it nearly a hundred years ago, it would have blown today's technology out of the water . . . if it had worked. Unfortunately, Tesla ran out of money before it was finished.

"Well, whatever this thing is," Caitlin said, "they're desperate to find it."

"Which means we need to find it first."

"There are a lot of things we need to find first," Caitlin reminded him.

"Right. So what else did Jorgenson do?"

"Well, he gave me some sort of crazy mind-warp tea that made me remember all the places I hid my pacifier when I was, like, two. It also made me tell the truth, but only about the things I felt like talking about, so he didn't get much out of me. I suppose if he had used a second tea bag, I might have remembered previous lives."

Nick heard the sound of a car in the driveway—Nick's

father returning home after his second triumphant day as the copy-machine repair king of NORAD. He looked over at Caitlin sitting right there on the edge of his bed, thought of his father coming into the house, and he felt that knee-jerk reaction of being caught doing something he shouldn't. Which annoyed him, because he wasn't doing anything. And it annoyed him further that he wasn't.

"Whatever Jorgenson wants from me," Nick told Caitlin, "I can't give him—even accidentally. Because once I do, I'm in the drawer next to Svedberg."

And then he heard Danny shout from the bottom of the attic ladder.

"Hey, Dad—Nick's got a girl up in his room, and they're whispering secret stuff."

To which he heard his father respond, "About time!"

Nick would have turned beet red, but somewhere deep down, his subconscious mind decided it wasn't worth the effort.

Caitlin stood up. "I'd better go before any of my pets end up nuked."

"Huh?"

"Long story."

He would have seen her out, but his phone rang. Although caller ID claimed that Eleanor Roosevelt was on the line, it turned out to be Petula.

"I just want you to know," she growled at him, "that I'm holding you personally responsible for what is going to happen tomorrow afternoon."

Then she hung up loudly in his ear.

Nick woke at dawn with an idea. It sent such an adrenaline rush through him that he didn't have his usual morning sluggishness. He was dressed and racing down the stairs in five minutes—only to be stopped by his father, who, thanks to actually having a job, was also up at the crack of dawn.

"Where are you headed off to?" his father asked, looking far more professional than usual in a coat and tie.

Outside, Nick heard the rumble of trash trucks, and the loud complaint of garbage cans being raised and unloaded into the hopper. With a sickening groan, he realized that this was trash day, which meant he didn't have much time to implement his plan.

"Morning run," he blurted.

"Really? Since when?"

"Since now," Nick said, and he burst out the door before his father could ask any more questions.

Trash trucks swarmed everywhere, like some sort of metallic-green invasion. Some of the streets Nick passed had already had their big plastic trash bins emptied, while some still awaited the inevitable.

A truck was already on Caitlin's street when he arrived. Without a moment to lose, Nick flipped open the lid of Caitlin's trash bin and thrust his hands into the unpleasant-ness. Chopped onion and potato peels, duck skin in a dark red sauce. The mess clung to his arms and squished between his fingers.

What were the chances he could find it? What were the chances it was even here? Nick dug through another layer of trash. The garbage truck was now at the next house, and the driver was eyeing him with malice, as if he might use his big hydraulic claw to pick up Nick along with the trash and deposit him in the hopper.

When Nick looked up, Caitlin was standing there in *Starry Night* pajamas, looking at him like he had lost what little sanity he had left.

"Mind telling me what you're doing Dumpster-diving on my doorstep?"

"It's not your doorstep, it's your curb."

Finally his fingertips touched a fine mesh with a familiar consistency attached to a tiny string, and he extricated it from the trash. A tea bag dangled from his fingers, and the little tab had the tiny *A* symbol of the Accelerati.

"Teatime!" he said cheerily.

A minute later, Nick was washing his hands in the kitchen sink, and Caitlin was setting the teakettle to boil. They had quickly concocted a semi-plausible story for her parents as to why Nick was at her house so early. Something about having to document the calls of birds at dawn for science class.

"Would you like something to eat, Nick?" Caitlin's mother asked. "I can't imagine you had breakfast before coming here at this ungodly hour."

"No thanks," Nick told her brightly. "Just some tea would be fine."

The brew that Caitlin poured for Nick, however, barely resembled tea. It was pale and weak.

"I'm not feeling anything," he whispered to her after the first cup.

"Well," she pointed out, "the bag's already been used."

"What am I supposed to feel?"

"First you'll feel . . . healthy. Then you start remembering weird stuff and have an urge to tell the truth about it."

After the fourth cup, with the weak tea sloshing around in his stomach, Nick finally began to feel a mild but undeniable sense of well-being. And then, a minute later—

"I was eating chocolate the first time I actually tied my own shoelaces! My favorite kind of baby food was string beans! I used to pick my nose and hide it under the kitchen table when I was five!"

"Ew!"

Nick really didn't want to be telling Caitlin these things, but once he started, he found it hard to stop. And then something that was both joyful and sorrowful came to mind. "My mom smelled like magnolia blossoms at my sixth birthday party."

Caitlin looked excited. Nick just felt weird. Like he had opened a trunk of things he never realized he had lost. He closed his eyes and got to the task at hand—the reason he had come over before the trash was collected. He thought back to the day of the garage sale.

"We sold thirty-two items from the attic. . . ." And then he started to remember to whom they had gone.

"There was a woman with red hair and a flowered dress who bought an old-fashioned dome hair dryer."

He pointed at the notepad on the table, reminding Caitlin to write down everything he said.

"There was a brown Cadillac. Dented fender. License plate FGT385."

"Is that the car that almost hit us?" Caitlin asked.

"No, that was a gold Buick." He hesitated as the scene came back to him, the closeness of Caitlin, the warmth of her cheek against his as he saved her life.

"Got it," said Caitlin. "Keep going."

Nick reluctantly let the moment go and got back to remembering. "The old washboard went to a bearded man in a Hawaiian shirt. He wore tortoiseshell glasses and drove a green Saturn that made a funny noise when it dropped into reverse."

The effects of the tea lasted for about fifteen minutes before Nick's memory began to slip. Soon he was back to normal, although normal felt pretty dense after a bout of total recall.

"You feel stupid now, right?"

"Yeah," he confessed. "Even more than usual."

She laughed at that.

Together they looked at the information he had spouted forth. Descriptions of people, vehicles, license-plate numbers, and a whole list of objects that he hadn't even remembered selling. He didn't have addresses, he didn't have locations, but at least now he had dozens of clues.

"If you saw those people again, do you think you would recognize them?"

Nick closed his eyes and tried to imagine the people he had dredged forth from his memory. Now that they had been brought to the surface, he felt confident he could pull them out of a crowd.

He nodded, and Caitlin smiled.

"That's quite a list of birdcalls you got there," her father said as he passed through the kitchen, casually glancing at the notepad.

"Yeah," said Caitlin, smirking at Nick. "You won't believe the things I've heard in this kitchen."

As a rule, Nick was not the type to skip school, unless you count the pretending-your-runny-nose-is-the-plague-because-you-didn't-study-for-your-science-exam ploy.

However, on this day, he was a blatant scofflaw, an unrepentant truant, spending his day on a reconnaissance mission around his neighborhood. He searched for the makes, models, and license plates of cars parked on streets and in driveways, and for faces in the markets and strip malls, refusing to despair when he couldn't find anything or anybody all morning.

Finally, around noon, his efforts began to pay off. After recognizing a license plate in a driveway, he rang the doorbell. He was greeted by a woman he remembered from the garage sale. According to the cheat sheet Caitlin had written up, she had purchased a set of old-fashioned hair rollers.

Nick explained that he had accidentally sold some items that were of sentimental value, and he would be happy to buy them back at one and a half times the original price. The woman was more than happy to hand him back the set of hair rollers.

"Never had the chance to use them anyway," she told him. "I don't know what possessed me to buy them." Then she casually told Nick that one of her neighbors had purchased the dome-style salon hair dryer and was "having problems" with it.

Nick discovered that the woman who had purchased it appeared to have a head slightly larger than standard human proportions. He had no idea if this predated her use of the hair dryer or not. Buying it back was costly, because, although the woman claimed it gave her migraines, she sensed Nick's desperation and insisted on being paid three times what she originally paid for it. In the end, he made the deal and struggled home with the bulky, egg-shaped device.

As the day wore on, he managed to find the flat-paddled electric mixer. It was being sold at a substantial markup in a thrift shop. But after that it all started to go downhill.

He recognized an old man coming out of the grocery store and followed him home. "Excuse me," Nick said, as politely as he could, just before the man went into his house. "I think you might have been at my garage sale."

The old man suddenly became jittery. "You'll have to speak to my son," he said. And when he opened the door, standing there was a man in his forties, clearly from the same gene pool.

"It's him," said the old man.

"I can see that," said the younger one.

In the shadows behind them, Nick could see a boy about his age, watching him suspiciously.

Nick tried his tall tale about sentimental value of the glass vacuum tube the old man had purchased, but they weren't buying it.

"If my father did buy something at your garage sale," said the middle-aged man, "and I'm not saying that he did—it's our property now."

"Yeah," said the kid behind them. "So get lost."

Nick heard a baby crying somewhere deep in the house.

"Now, if you'll excuse us, we have family matters to attend to." And he slammed the door in Nick's face.

Nick made a note of the address. The man who bought the tube clearly knew what it did, and he had shared that knowledge with his family. It might take some work getting it back, but at least now he knew its location.

His final encounter that day was the strangest.

He found the brown Cadillac with the dented fender sitting in front of an ordinary suburban tract home. A woman answered when he knocked at the door.

Before he could say anything, the woman gasped.

"No!" she shouted. "It's mine!"

"If you'll just let me explain—" said Nick.

"Go away or I'll call the police!" And yet another door was slammed in his face.

This time Nick was not going to be brushed off so easily. He pounded on the door. "I just want to talk!" he shouted. No response. He pounded again, a little louder this time.

Then he heard a strange high-pitched warbling noise from inside. He reached to pound on the door a third time, but his hand fell upon empty air. The door was gone. The woman was gone. In fact, the entire house was gone.

All that remained was the cement stoop he stood on, a hole where the basement used to be, and pipes gushing water into the air like a fountain, still believing there was a sensible place to pump it.

"You there!" said a voice from behind him. Nick turned to see a pudgy man walking a pudgier dog. "What the hell did you do to that house?"

Nick ran and didn't stop until he got home. It wasn't until he was up in his attic room that he began to calm down. He had secured his bed and desk to the wall, but that didn't stop the "sweet spot" in the center of the attic from drawing him to it.

More and more lately he'd taken to lying on the floor in that curious spot directly beneath the skylight whenever he felt uneasy. The warmth and uncanny sense of connection soothed him. They put his concerns in perspective.

He knew this must have been by design as well. He could imagine Tesla sitting in the middle of the room, using this nexus like a relaxing bath for his hyperpowered brain. If it could somehow pull furniture from the wall, surely it could gather the disorganized thoughts of a genius.

But not even the calming nature of the attic could give Nick perspective when an entire house did a quantum leap out of his neighborhood.

"Breathe in, breathe out," he told himself. "Don't overthink it." And soon he had his racing thoughts under control. It was amazing how many unthinkable things he could store in his mind when he had no other choice.

Petula, on the other hand, was deeply embittered by the things she had to store in her mind. All day she had wandered through school like a sulking zombie, partially because she had gotten no sleep, and partially because she now knew the future, and it was not pretty.

To add insult to misery, halfway through the day she had lost her purse. This meant she'd had to walk home, because the bus driver refused to let anyone on without a pass, even if he knew the passenger.

She arrived home at T minus 15 and counting, and with a mounting sense of inevitability and dread, she fluffed the pillows on the couch and waited. At T minus 5 the doorbell rang. She answered it to find Mitch at the door.

"Gee," she said flatly, "what a surprise."

"I found this at school," said Mitch, holding out her purse to her. "I think it's yours."

"Wonderful. A member of a crime family attempting to be honest."

"We're not a crime family. My dad was set up."

"Whatever," said Petula. "I suppose you want a reward?"

"Well, I wasn't expecting one, but hey, if you're offering."

"Just get in here and let's get this over with."

She led Mitch to the couch, and when he didn't sit, she pushed him down on it. Mitch seemed a bit startled and perplexed, which just annoyed Petula further.

"So," said Mitch, "nice house you got here."

"Really?" said Petula. "Is that the best line you have?"

"It's not a line. I really think it's nice."

"I know what you're here for, don't try to deny it. But you'll have to wait precisely one and a half minutes."

"Oh," said Mitch, "really?" And then he added, "What am I waiting for?"

"As if you didn't know."

She reached over and grabbed a crystal bowl of peppermint candies she had prepared in advance.

"Have a mint," she said.

"No thanks," Mitch told her.

"I SAID, HAVE A MINT."

And Mitch, like a weak mind manipulated by the Force, obeyed.

"I prefer wintergreen," he said, chewing the mint to oblivion.

"Deal with it," Petula told him. Then she tossed her hair in that come-hither way that models do on TV, and her left pigtail smacked Mitch in the face.

"Hey, watch it with that thing," said Mitch.

She grabbed him by the shirt. "I want to be clear about this," she told him. "No matter what ideas you get in that pea brain of yours, this means absolutely nothing."

Then she checked her watch, pulled him closer, and got down to the business of kissing.

At first Mitch resisted, perhaps overwhelmed by the sheer intensity and skill that Petula had cultivated, having practiced kissing her Chihuahua on numerous occasions in preparation for the real thing. Everything being relative, Petula found Mitch's kiss to be far more appealing than her dog's—and she found it went on much longer than she had planned. Indeed, much longer than was necessary to prove the validity of the camera.

Mitch had long since gone limp, perhaps having fallen unconscious from lack of oxygen.

Finally Petula pushed him away, handed him another mint, and herded him toward the door.

"So," Mitch said, "want to go to the movies or something?"

And although she found the thought disturbingly appealing, she told him, "This didn't happen. You will speak of it to no one."

Then she kissed him again and pushed him out the door.

■ ■ ■

The imaginary number, *i*, is defined as the square root of negative 1. It's a quantity that mathematically cannot exist, because no number times itself is a negative number . . . unless that number happens to be Petula Grabowski-Jones. After her encounter with Mitch, Petula found herself so completely confused and illogical, she was the very embodiment of *i*.

This sudden and unexpected attraction to Mitch Murló flew in the face of all her plans. Her true goal was Nick. Furious at the treachery of her own emotions, she stormed out of her house with her camera, desperate to take pictures of a tomorrow with Nick she knew she could create.

She resolved that at precisely four thirty tomorrow she would walk up to Nick's front door. He would answer it. Then she would crush his resistance with the same practiced power-smooch that had rendered Mitch into mint jelly. She would steal his heart away from that flighty, artsy-fartsy Caitlin. Petula had no doubt in her mind she could make this happen.

Now all she needed were the pictures to prove her success.

And so, standing in front of Nick's house, she snapped a series of shots of his front door. Then she ran off to Ms. Planck's darkroom to develop them, convinced that there was nothing imaginary about her fantasy.

But, oh, what a difference a day makes. Because the pictures, when developed, did not reveal a scene of romance triumphant at Nick's threshold. Instead, they revealed policemen. And an ambulance. And someone covered by a sheet being wheeled out of Nick's front door on a stretcher. Someone who, both in and out of focus, was very much dead.

20 BONFIRE OF THE PROFANITIES

Theo had no illusions that his relationship with Caitlin was going anywhere. They were from two different worlds, after all. She lived in a world of creative expression. He lived on earth. She spent her time dreaming of how things might be. He spent his time on earth. And although she kept making lukewarm overtures of wanting to keep it going, he had already checked out, using the express lane. Because when it came to the list of reasons for being together, it was certainly twelve items or less.

Getting over Caitlin wasn't the issue, but he couldn't ignore the fact that she was giving her time to that new kid from Florida who couldn't pitch to save his life. Plus, Theo had to be reminded of him every day in science, because the goofus sat right across from him. It made the class unbearable. To Theo, Nick was like a peanut lurking in the trail mix. Not that Nick was deadly enough to send Theo to the emergency room the way a peanut would, but he was, in his own way, a threat to life as Theo knew it. There was some high-octane weirdness surrounding that kid—things that Theo couldn't figure out—like maybe he was in the witness protection program. Or an alien. Or an alien in the witness protection program. And the fact that Caitlin would abandon Theo for such a weirdo was a foul ball he simply could not field.

It was on the day of the science-lab earthquake that Theo decided to do something about it.

Mr. Hoffman, the science teacher, had determined that everyone would present their lab projects throughout the year, in alphabetical order, to the despair of Adam Aaronson and Heather Aardmore.

Theo, safely nestled among the L-M-N-O-P bloc, knew he could look forward to weeks of blissful procrastination before slapping together a half-assed "household magic" demo.

Today's science lab was being presented by Jason Boring, as Theo liked to call him, although he knew his name was really Berring.

"My project," announced Boring from the front of the room, "is a homemade, localized earthquake machine that I myself designed myself from spare parts I found at home, myself."

Boring put what looked like an old-fashioned radio on the table in front of him.

Across the aisle from Theo, Nick jumped up. "I object!" he said.

"This isn't a courtroom, Mr. Slate," said the teacher with a chuckle.

"Just sit down and let Boring get it over with," Theo said, pleased to see Nick back off and sit.

"Moving on," Boring said, twisting one of the device's two dials. "I just have to find the room's resident frequency."

"Don't you mean *resonant* frequency, Jason?" suggested Mr. Hoffman.

"Yeah, that too," said Boring.

As he kept twisting the dial, tuning in greater or lesser levels of static, Theo shouted, "If you could just rattle off Miss Flannigan's bra, I'll give you an A-plus!"

Laughter came from all around, even from the girls.

"Got it!" Boring said proudly, and he moved his hand to the volume dial.

Theo felt it, first as a low-level rumbling in his gut. He could tell from the expression on Nick's face that he felt it, too. Although Nick seemed far more panicked about it. Then Theo's desk began to tremble, and it skittered a few inches away.

"Now watch this," Boring said as he turned the dial up a few more notches.

The whole room started shaking, the light fixtures rocking back and forth as acoustic ceiling tiles dropped like giant snowflakes.

As the earth beneath the classroom floor rose up and then dropped, like the Kamikaze roller coaster at Six Flags, someone started screeching like a maniac. The Kamikaze was not Theo's favorite ride, and he wasn't one hundred percent sure that he wasn't the one screeching.

He was too terrified to do much of anything and could only watch as Nick leaped for the device. With all the shaking, Theo doubted Nick would even reach it, but he did, and he turned it off.

The tremors stopped, and the room returned to more or less normal. Before he could even catch his breath, Theo watched Nick grab the earthquake machine, throw a dirty look at Jason not-so-Boring-anymore, and run out the door with it.

Principal Watt, unsure how to deal with this incident, closed the science lab for the rest of the day and gave Jason detention, claiming "disruptive behavior." As a precaution, he also put Mr. Hoffman on probationary leave.

In the meantime, Nick had managed to save the day. As far as Theo was concerned, that was like pouring salt in an open grave. Both Nick and Caitlin disappeared from school. Rumor was that they had ditched together.

Now there was no question in Theo's mind that this was war—and it wasn't a matter of who ended up the object of Caitlin's affection. All that mattered to Theo was who didn't. As far as he was concerned, Caitlin could devote her time and attention to anyone she pleased—except Nick Slate.

Theo had already heard through the grapevine that Nick's dad had once been a professional baseball player. Such a thing, under different circumstances, could have brought him and Nick together as friends. And then Theo realized that indeed it still could, because it's like they say, "Keep your friend's clothes . . . in your enemy's closet."

Nick had no doubt that if he hadn't shut down Tesla's earthquake machine at that instant, the entire school, maybe even the entire neighborhood, would have come crashing down around them.

Tesla was clearly a genius. And he was also clearly out of his freaking mind.

"I can't believe you didn't feel it," he said to Caitlin as they hurried away from the school.

"Well, I was at the opposite end of the building."

"If it had gone on for another thirty seconds, there wouldn't be any building."

"Don't you think you're overreacting the teensiest bit?"

Nick stopped walking and looked at her. "I'm holding an earthquake machine in my hands."

Caitlin looked at him, looked at the radio-like device, and said, "Point taken."

They started walking again. "Can you imagine what the Accelerati would do if they got hold of this thing?" Nick asked.

"I don't suppose they need it to get an A in the Accelerati Science Fair."

Nick took a deep breath, his resolve setting in. "We have to destroy it," he said. "We have to destroy them all."

The scorched-earth policy is a time-honored tradition of war. Villagers about to be overrun by the enemy would burn their own homes and crops to deny the enemy shelter and food. Armies would destroy their own munitions to prevent their attackers from using their own weapons against them.

The Russians used this strategy very successfully against a very irritated Napoleon, burning everything they had and retreating into Russia. And since there was no end of Russia to retreat into, Napoleon was pretty much screwed.

Nick realized that he was now at war with the Accelerati. A very different kind of war, perhaps, but the principle was the same. They wanted to get their hands on this stuff, and like Napoleon's army, they were a force to be reckoned with. But, like Napoleon's army, they could be defeated.

The only way to beat the Accelerati was to get rid of the things they desired, fully and completely.

Two months ago, Nick had suffered through a fire that had taken the life of his mother. But today he was going to start one.

Nick still didn't have all the accursed items from the garage sale. Far from it. But at least he could create a bonfire out of the ones that he had.

He texted Mitch and Vince to come to his house with their respective items, saying that he'd explain when they got there—knowing that if they had any inkling about his plan to burn them, they'd never show.

He and Caitlin went out to his backyard with all of Tesla's inventions, plus an ugly end table left by Great-aunt Greta, because Caitlin insisted it was too hideous *not* to burn.

"Now," said Caitlin after they had piled the items up, "we need an accelerant."

"A what?"

"You know, gasoline or alcohol. Something that'll make it all catch fire."

"Oh, right."

Nick went into the house, but all he could come up with was a big jug of cooking oil. He came back out and showed it to Caitlin. "Will this do?"

"Any porch in a storm," Caitlin answered, "as Theo would say."

Nick untwisted the cap and prepared to pour the oil, but Caitlin reached out to stop him.

"You know," she said, "for a long time I've wanted to do a photo collage of random objects burning."

"Caitlin, this isn't one of your garbart projects. This is serious business."

She looked at him, insulted. "Art *is* serious business. At least it is to me. I thought you appreciated that."

"I do, but—"

"If we're gonna burn it anyway," Caitlin interrupted, "can we at least make it aesthetically pleasing? I'll take pictures, I'll do my collage, and not only will it be a work of art, it'll be a spite bomb for the Accelerati."

"Will this take long?" he asked, not bothering to hide his impatience.

Caitlin didn't answer. She just went over to the pile of stuff and began rearranging it.

"If we tilt the reel-to-reel like so, and hook the fan around the neck of the lamp, then we can perch the radio on top, its Gothic point recalling a church steeple."

Nick held the jug of oil by his side and watched Caitlin creatively rearrange the objects.

"They actually have grooves that help them balance on each other really well," Caitlin noted.

That's when something began to dawn on Nick. At first he couldn't be sure what it was—perhaps an inkling of intuition, perhaps a pattern that his unconscious mind had already begun to put together—but as he looked at the objects and the way that Caitlin was stacking them, it seemed he could tell where she was going to put the next object before she placed it. The notched base of the hair-curler caddy fit perfectly into the top of the reel-to-reel player. The two odd flat paddles of the electric mixer were perfectly spaced to fit in the toaster. This was not coincidence!

"I'm almost done," Caitlin told him. "I just can't find a place for the bat, or this big ugly hair dryer."

"Caitlin, what was that thing the Accelerati were looking for?"

"They called it the Far Range Energy Emitter. Why?"

"I think we may be looking at it."

Now as they stared at the collection of objects before them, there was a sense of things almost snapping into place. Sure, some placements were wrong, and there were tons of parts missing, but each of these items from the attic, Nick realized, in addition to what it did on its own, was somehow part of a larger whole.

Caitlin visibly shivered. "All the more reason to get rid of it!" She tossed the remaining objects onto the pile, no longer caring about aesthetic placement, then picked up the oil jug. She moved forward, ready to pour it, but Nick stopped her.

"Caitlin—this was his life's work. His greatest accomplishment. Right here under our noses."

Caitlin sighed. "We're not setting it on fire, are we?"

Nick shook his head. He realized they had the upper hand. They knew something the Accelerati didn't.

"Let's take it apart," he told her. "Let's take it apart before anyone can see."

21 CLOUDY WITH A TEN PERCENT CHANCE OF DEATH

At any given time, there are believed to be ten rogue waves somewhere in the world: massive mountains of water that exist for no particular reason other than the random compounding of small, chaotic forces—from gravity to tides to wind to the movements of fish.

When all this randomness converges, nothing in its path can withstand the surge, but since the oceans are so immense, the vast majority of rogue waves go unnoticed. Unless, of course, you happen to be in the path of one.

That afternoon the convergence of random forces upon Nick's house was going to leave one of those forces dead in the water. The only question was, who would it be?

Random Force number one: Danny.

Danny could not have been happier with the week's turn of events. People were already calling him Danny the Star Catcher, which could have been a bad thing, if people weren't really impressed by it.

Rumors were already circulating that he was part of a government project, and the fact that his father had a secret job "repairing copy machines" for NORAD gave the rumors some weight.

Whenever he was asked about it, Danny quoted a line from one of his favorite movies, *Ninja Nanny 3*, and told them, "I'm sworn to secrecy about it. All I can tell you is that I'm a registered weapon." It made the bullies too scared to do anything but sneer and most everyone else vie for his attention. In fact, several kids at school had their cell phones confiscated when they tried to take pictures of him to post online.

And just when he thought things couldn't get any better, today he'd gotten an A for his presentation on the Transcontinental Railroad, which included an authentic iron railroad spike that he had painted gold and secured to a wooden base, point up.

It was a pain in the neck to carry it home on the bus, but he wasn't going to part with something he had worked so hard on, no matter how dangerous the bus driver thought it was.

"You'll put somebody's spleen out," the driver had said, but Danny wasn't worried. It was destined for a shelf in his room at a safe distance from any random spleen. Of course, for now, he was satisfied to leave it in the front hallway along with his backpack, completely forgotten as he went to turn on the TV.

To his frustration, the TV screen still showed nothing but static.

"What?" He knew the cable guy was supposed to come that day, sometime between eight a.m. and the end of time, but with no one to let him in, who knew if they'd ever have cable?

As Danny pondered the hellish idea of a television-free existence, the doorbell rang, and he hopped up, almost tripping over the golden spike as he answered the door.

It was not the cable guy, however, but that creepy dude Vince, carrying something that looked like a car battery.

"Oh, it's just you."

"Where's your brother?" Vince asked.

"How should I know?"

Then Nick barged into the house from the backyard, with an armful of junk, allowing Danny to get back to the business at hand. Bemoaning his media blackout, he hurled himself onto the old sofa to wait for the cable guy.

He landed with such force that it summoned up a cloud of dust and shook the heavy portrait of Great-aunt Greta on the wall above him, loosening the framing hook.

Random Force number two: Vince.

Vince suspected that Nick was going to try to convince him to give up the wet cell. He almost didn't bring it, but there was the small chance that Nick was calling with a new and previously unconsidered way to use it.

Vince, of course, had his own thoughts about that. For instance, he could set up his own private detective agency. Solve crimes by secretly talking to the deceased, like a show he saw on TV once. There was definitely money to be made. Unfortunately, there weren't enough murders in Colorado Springs to really make a business of it. He'd have to go to a larger criminal capital, like Bogotá or Denver.

"Good, you're here," Nick said when he saw Vince. "You got it?"

Vince held the wet cell a little higher so Nick could see it over the stack of stuff he was carrying. All items from the attic, no doubt.

"Good. Bring it upstairs."

"Why, so it can go back into that attic and rot for another seventy-five years? I don't think so."

"Do it, Vince!" Caitlin said, on her way in with a few antiques as well. "I think he's onto something."

"*On* something, you mean. You can't have it back. Period."

"What do you think I'm gonna do? Burn it?" Nick said, and

Caitlin unaccountably laughed. "Just let me borrow it, okay? I promise you won't be disappointed."

"And if I am?"

"Uh . . . correct me if I'm wrong," said Caitlin, "but isn't disappointment where you live?"

Vince had to admit she had a point, and he followed them up to the attic.

Random Force number three: Theo.

Theo was not stupid. It took a huge amount of intelligence to calculate exactly how little schoolwork he could get away with doing and still pass all of his classes. In fact, he prided himself on manipulating his GPA to being exactly where he wanted it to be: C-minus. Because when it came to college acceptance, grades wouldn't mean a thing until high school, at which time he would start miraculously getting A's, which his overjoyed parents would reward by buying him a car. He would manage his GPA the way his father managed stock portfolios, and that would get him into at least half the universities he was interested in, with or without a baseball scholarship. Then once he was in college, he could go back to getting C-minuses again. He had this thing wired.

So skilled was Theo at being mediocre that he deeply identified with Nick's dad, who, according to Theo's research, was a pretty mediocre baseball player. "Whiffin' Wayne," as he was known during his two short years with the Tampa Bay Rays, was a pretty good pitcher, but his pitching wasn't stellar enough to shut down the nickname. Poor guy. What he needed was a fan. And what Theo needed was a way to wedge himself between Nick and Caitlin. As they say, "this could be the big inning of a wonderful friendship."

Theo lurked behind a hedge, out of view of Nick's home, until he saw Nick's father drive up and park. The man grabbed two take-out bags from the car, and Theo intercepted him before he got to the front door.

"Mr. Slate, could I talk to you for a second?" He put on his best "aw, shucks" expression, which worked well on girls, adults, and certain breeds of dog.

"Yes?" the man said, a little apprehensively.

"I know you're Nick's father . . . but I was just wondering . . . are you also *the* Wayne Slate, of the Tampa Bay Rays?"

Nick's dad stood just a little bit straighter. "You've heard of me?"

Theo took precisely three steps closer. "Heard of you? Are you kidding me? You're the only pitcher who ever struck out Tyler Spornak twice in the same inning."

Slate chuckled. "Nothing to be proud of, getting all the way through the batting order in a single inning."

"Naah—if you don't mind me saying so, you're seeing the grass half empty. You were the best thing the Rays had going for them back then. I bet you'd have taken them all the way to the World Series if you didn't blow out your pitching arm."

Mr. Slate looked at Theo in disbelief. "How do you know all this? You were a little kid when I played."

"I'm a pitcher, too. Historical perspective is an important part of the game." Then Theo took one more step forward and delivered the winning fastball.

"I would be honored if you'd sign this for me, sir." And he presented an official Topps baseball card featuring Wayne Slate looking a little bit leaner and a little bit younger than he did today. It had cost Theo a buck-fifty on eBay and twenty-five for overnight delivery. If all else failed, the signed card might earn him back his investment.

"Whaddaya know," the man said, shaking his head. "I used to have a bunch of these, but we lost them in the fire. You got a pen?"

Theo checked his pockets, which he already knew to be empty. "Darn, I forgot one. Duh."

"Why don't you come inside," said Slate. "I didn't get your name."

"Theodore," he said with a winning smile. "I'm a friend of Nick's."

"In that case, why don't you join us for dinner?" He held up the large take-out bags he carried in his card-free hand.

"Smells good—what is it?"

"Thai."

"Cool. Never had Thai before."

Which wasn't surprising, considering the fact that Thai cuisine relies heavily on peanuts.

Random Force number four: Caitlin.

At first Caitlin was sure Nick was out of his mind when it came to his new theory that all the objects fit together somehow. However, as they positioned and repositioned them in the center of the attic, Caitlin could see that the odd shapes and unnecessary grooves and divots in the framework of each device were not mere decoration.

Yes, they were individual inventions with remarkable properties, but they were also puzzle pieces, and Caitlin had to accept that the real reason for her denial was that she hadn't thought of it first. After all, she was the visual artist with a keen dimensional sense.

She had to admit, though, that since she had known him, Nick had had several moments of genius-like inspiration, grasping the big picture in a way no one else had. It made her like him all the more.

Nick and Vince figured out the placement of the wet cell, and not to be outdone, Caitlin finally made the missing visual connection. She lowered the clear egg-shaped salon-style hair dryer over the bulb of the stage light.

As soon as it was in place, it clamped on and stayed there, with the bulb in its center.

"Excellent," said Nick. The light was the only object that had a power cord, but he didn't plug it in. At the garage sale, it had attracted buyers by the dozens. Caitlin wondered exactly what it might attract now if he turned it on, and then she decided she'd rather not know.

"We're still missing too many pieces," Nick said.

"Are you sure you want to put the entire thing together?" Caitlin asked. "I mean, Tesla was a genius, but he was also a lunatic. Right? Who knows what this thing will do."

Nick didn't offer an answer. Maybe he was as uncertain as she was. Even incomplete, the strange device was taking shape, like the intricate gearwork of a clock. Caitlin could already imagine it humming and sparking with lightning, doing whatever it was that it did.

Nick, Caitlin, and Vince considered the objects for a moment more, and then Nick said, "Hey, what about the hair curlers?"

"They're still out back," said Caitlin. "I'll go get them." She went down the attic ladder and then the main staircase to the first floor. Then, as she hurried through the kitchen toward the back door, her brain did a serious double take.

Why was Theo sitting at the kitchen table with takeout in front of him?

She turned slowly, fully convinced it must be someone else, that her mind was playing tricks on her. But Theo was still right there, leaning back with a smug look on his face, just waiting to be noticed by her.

"What are you doing here?" she heard herself ask.

Theo shrugged, like it was nothing. "Can't I hang out with my friend Nick Slate and his famous father?"

Caitlin was rarely speechless. Her mouth opened and closed a few times like a fish gasping for air. Finally she wrangled her brain enough to say, "Huh?"

"Yeah," said Theo, crossing his arms. "I'm a regular friend of the family now. Mr. Slate's down in the basement at this very moment, digging up some sports paraphernalia as we speak."

"You can't be serious."

"Oh, I'm very serious," Theo told her. "And from now on, Nick and I are gonna be stuck together like toupees in a pod."

Caitlin gaped at him.

"In fact," Theo continued, "I plan to be here every time you are. Who said three's a crowd?"

The idea of Theo poisoning the air between Caitlin and Nick by his presence was unthinkable. Awkward didn't even begin to describe it: her sort-of-ex-boyfriend hanging out with her kind-of-prospective boyfriend was almost enough to make her head explode.

But of course it wouldn't. Making her head explode was the job of the miniature Tesla coils she was about to innocently retrieve from the backyard.

Random Force number five: Petula.

Petula had always admired Almira Gulch's perfect posture as she rode her bicycle up to Dorothy's house. With modern bicycles, however, such posture was impossible, unless one didn't hold the handlebars. Thus, Petula had become a master of what she called "Venus de Milo cycling." In other words, riding without arms. Of course, this left her with no brakes, but then Petula was not one to stop for anything—which is why she was nearly turned into roadkill by the LifeLine Cable truck that careened into Nick's driveway and screeched to a halt mere inches from her.

"What's *wrong* with you?" Petula screamed at Random Force number six: the cable guy, but she didn't wait for a response. He was the cable guy; it was a sufficient answer to her question. She jumped off her moving bike with practiced skill and let it roll onto Nick's lawn, where it lost momentum and fell over.

Here's what Petula knew: at precisely four thirty, a dead body would be carried on a stretcher out of Nick's house to an ambulance waiting in the driveway—but exactly when the death itself was to occur, she had no idea. Nor did she know who the victim would be. There was no way to tell from the image whether the lump beneath the sheet was male or female.

Frankly, she didn't care who it was, as long as it wasn't Nick.

She entered the house without knocking or ringing the doorbell, and she practically tripped over a mounted gold spike that was in the doorway for no reason she could figure.

Nick's annoying little brother brushed past her, shouting, "The cable guy's here! The cable guy's here!" like Paul Revere might have said had he been more interested in watching the British arrive on CNN.

There seemed to be quite a lot of activity in the house. She rushed through the rooms, taking quick stock of the situation. There were more people present than she expected. Vince was coming down the stairs from the second floor with Nick. Then there was a man, presumably Nick's father, shouting from the basement, "I'm still looking! I know it's down here somewhere." Caitlin was in the kitchen staring at Theo, and what Theo was doing there was anybody's guess.

This was actually good news. As the cable guy entered the mix, Petula quickly calculated the odds. There was only a one-in-seven chance that Nick would "buy the farm"—her father's favorite euphemism for "kicking the bucket." Of course, those were the odds if she didn't include herself.

And then it dawned on her that there was no reason to exclude herself. Now that she was there, she was equally at risk for a farm purchase.

She ran up the stairs toward Nick, shoving Vince aside. Vince fell the rest of the way, almost, but not quite, breaking his neck. Close, but no cigar.

"What's *wrong* with you?" cried Vince.

"Popular question today," said the cable guy as he walked toward the living room, giving Petula a wink that was just on the cusp of being creepy.

Petula ignored it and turned to Nick. "Come with me," she said. "You're in danger."

"What are you talking about?"

She grabbed him by the shirt and started shaking him. "Don't you understand, you idiot? I'm trying to save your life."

"From what?"

She slapped him, the way they do in movies, to knock some sense into him, but he just proceeded to slap her back, which made her so furious she slapped him again.

Caitlin, who was standing at the bottom of the stairs, apparently saw enough of the exchange to say, "Can I slap Petula, too?"

"Be my guest," said Nick, pushing past Petula so he could take the object Caitlin was holding out to him. Something resembling a set of old-fashioned hair curlers.

"What is she even doing here?" Caitlin asked Nick.

For Petula, it was one of her personal pet peeves to be spoken of in the third person—but before she could level a complaint against either of them, the two were hurrying back up the stairs. In an instant they had disappeared into the attic.

The idea of Caitlin and Nick being alone in an attic did not sit well with Petula, although it did make her feel better to know that Caitlin had a one-in-eight chance of dying today. Perhaps, she thought, Nick was a serial killer, and he was at this very moment strangling her in the attic. If so, Petula would keep his dark secret, and it would bond them together for eternity.

But Petula knew she couldn't count on that. What she needed was to improve the odds for Nick and herself by adding someone else to the equation. Someone who stood a much larger chance of spontaneously dropping dead.

And wasn't there a frail old woman who lived next door?

Random Force number seven: Mitch.

Mitch knew that Nick was going to ask him for the Shut Up 'n Listen, because the machine had told him so. But the machine also told him it was best to do what Nick asked, regardless of how Mitch phrased the first half of the sentence. So, with the device in hand, he went to Nick's house.

The last thing he expected to see as he approached the house was Petula practically dragging Random Force number eight, an old woman, across the lawn toward Nick's front door. A small dog in a knit sweater that embarrassed both the dog and the sheep that it came from angrily nipped at Petula's heels.

"We need your help! Hurry!" Petula screamed in the old woman's ear. "Someone's dying! Someone's dying!"

"Dying?" asked Mitch. "Who's dying?"

Petula looked at him, seemingly put off by the question. "I don't know yet," she snapped at him, and then she continued to the house with the old woman, pushing her through the front door.

Petula had so many endearing quirks that, prior to yesterday's kiss, Mitch might have misinterpreted as irritants. He smiled at the thought.

Popping a jawbreaker into his mouth that was curiously the exact same diameter as his windpipe, Mitch stepped into the house behind them.

Random Force number nine: Mr. Slate.

Mr. Slate rummaged around the cobweb-covered basement, filled with the bittersweet nostalgia that can come only from someone acknowledging who they used to be.

Among the few things that had survived the fire, there was a baseball signed by the entire Tampa Bay team. He had thrown it into a box, along with a few other singed knickknacks. But since everything in the box still smelled like smoke, he had stored it in the basement, because the memory of the fire over-whelmed any positive memories associated with the items.

Only now that he had his own personal fan did he even remember the baseball. Since Nick and Danny had grown up with it as just a decoration on a shelf, it didn't mean much to them—but he knew it might impress Theodore. If only he could remember which box it was in.

"I'll be back in a second!" he shouted up the stairs. "I've almost got it."

Then he reached for the farthest box, never knowing his hand was passing through a series of spiderwebs and disrupting the peace of several highly affronted black widows.

And Random Force number ten: Nick.

While Caitlin tried to figure out where the set of rollers fit in the device they were constructing, Nick went downstairs to see what all the commotion was about.

He found Petula running up and down the stairs with the neighbor woman. "Up this way," Petula told her. The old woman huffed and puffed as she hurried up the stairs, only to be told at the top that she had to race down instead. Although Petula was Colorado Springs's ambassador of the abnormal, this was bizarre even for her.

"What are you trying to do?" Nick said. "Give the poor woman a heart attack?"

"Shush," said Petula. "It's our little secret."

Nick grabbed Petula and pulled her down the stairs and out the front door, bumping into the cable guy, who was also leaving.

"Nick!" shouted Danny, bursting with joy. "We have six hundred and ninety-two channels! You wanna watch 'em?"

"Kind of busy right now," Nick responded. "You start and I'll catch up."

"I'll watch with him," said Vince. "Channel surfing is the only sport I excel in. In fact, someday I hope to go pro."

Once out on the lawn, Nick didn't give Petula a chance to launch into anything but the truth. "Tell me what's up with you!" he demanded. "In simple English, with no Petulisms."

Petula took a deep breath before she leveled this tasty little tidbit at him: "Someone in your house is going to die today. Never mind how I know, I just do. I came to save your life, so the least you could do is be grateful!"

"Die? What do you mean, 'die'?"

"Well, off the top of my head, there are three definitions I can think of, but none of the others are verbs. Get it?"

Nick put two and two together. "The camera you got at the garage sale!"

"Never mind that."

"It tells you the future?"

"Never mind that!"

Then she froze, and Nick followed her gaze to the driveway, where the cable guy was backing out way too quickly, never seeing the old woman and her dog behind him.

"Hey! Watch out!" Nick shouted. The old woman looked up, saw the truck, and jumped out of the way just in time. The truck rolled over the dog, but as it was such a small animal, the truck's belly passed over it, leaving the sweatered pug unharmed but even more annoyed than usual.

"WHY did you DO that!" Petula yelled at Nick. "This whole thing could have been over, but, no, you had to save the old lady!"

"So I was supposed to just let her get flattened?"

"Yes!" Petula told him. "Better her than me or you, or anyone else in your house!"

Nick didn't have time to argue the logic of death prophecies. He turned and ran back inside with Petula close behind, clicking the odds back to one in eight.

Mitch had never been accused of clairvoyance, or of being in any way in touch with the ripplings of supernatural frequencies. Indeed, he had trouble with the radio tuner in his mother's car.

But perhaps his symbiotic relationship with the Shut Up 'n Listen had fine-tuned his metaphysical awareness, so that now he felt a palpable sense of foreboding. Or perhaps it was just Petula announcing that someone was going to die. While everything around him was hectic, nothing looked particularly deadly. Except perhaps the deadly volume of the TV, which Nick's little brother didn't seem to be able to control.

"I can't change the channels, either," Danny said to Vince, sitting next to him on the sofa. "This thing is broken already." Then he banged the remote on the coffee table.

Vince practically had to scream over the TV. "It probably just needs batteries. Give it to me."

The TV and the conversation were so loud, Mitch felt his heart begin to race. He sucked harder on the jawbreaker, and almost reflexively pulled the string on the Shut Up 'n Listen.

"What I should do is—" Mitch began, and released the string. But the TV was so loud he couldn't hear the answer. So, putting the device right up to his ear, he pulled the string again. "What I should do—"

And the machine said, "—*is get out. Now.*"

Mitch was so shocked that he gasped, causing the jawbreaker in his mouth to roll back down his tongue toward his uvula, which stood like a single upside-down pin in a bowling alley.

And Mitch was about to score a spare.

For Petula there was no feeling worse than helplessness—to know something beyond a shadow of a doubt, and also know she couldn't stop it or control it. She had tried, but that blasted old woman simply wouldn't die.

"Nick! No!" She ran after him as he reached the front door, hoping that an adrenaline rush might give her the strength to grab him and hurl him across the lawn to safety. Instead, as she followed him inside the house, she had just enough adrenaline to make her walk a little bit too quickly, catch her foot on the threshold of the front door, and fall headlong toward a golden spike that seemed specifically placed there to impale her.

Down in the basement, Mr. Slate finally wrapped his hand around something cool and round. The familiar feel of a baseball in his hand was a sense memory that always brought a flood of good feelings. Theodore would most certainly be impressed by it. Perhaps, thought Mr. Slate, he could tell him about the time he almost pitched a no-hitter against the Cubs. There'd be no mention of "Whiffin' Wayne" today!

Wayne Slate was blessed, or cursed, as it were, with a sizable coat of arm hair, a nuisance when reaching through spaces crisscrossed with sticky webs, and right now his arm was practically cocooned in the stuff. But that was only the half of it.

There comes a time in every man's life when he must face the spider of his nightmares. But in Wayne Slate's case, bad luck came in threes.

Theo had no particular interest in a baseball signed by the Rays—except, perhaps, for the cash he could get for it on eBay should the opportunity arise. Nevertheless, ogling it in Mr. Slate's presence would endear him to the man and solidify his presence as a friend of the family. Caitlin's reaction was already priceless, and the dividends of this venture could only grow, proof of the old adage "Success is the pest's revenge."

He had nothing but high hopes as he dipped a skewer of chicken satay into a curious beige sauce that smelled nothing like peanuts, and he lifted it toward his mouth.

Caitlin was aware of none of this, as she was alone upstairs in the attic—and was only now beginning to wonder what was keeping Nick. By the looks of the half-built device before her, there were at least a dozen pieces still missing, but perhaps it didn't need every piece to work—or, at least, to partially work. For the life of her, however, she couldn't figure out where the hair curlers fit. She opened the case and pondered them. Six bluish-gray cylinders made of tightly coiled wire. Perhaps, she thought, the case was just a holder, and the coils fit on the device individually. If that were so, all she had to do was remove them from the case and find where to insert them.

As she reached for one of the coils, it didn't occur to her that electrical transformers were made of coiled wire—and that those made of tempered tantalum and designed by Nikola Tesla might be several degrees beyond deadly. In fact, touching them with bare hands would be far worse than being struck by lightning again.

The fact that the cable guy had left the TV in less-than-perfect working condition infuriated Danny. He continued banging the remote on the table, venting his frustrations at the stupid thing.

"Dad!" he shouted. "Do we have batteries?" He tried to pry open the battery compartment, but it wouldn't budge. He didn't even know whether it took AA or AAA, or one of those stupid little square ones that are supposed to make smoke detectors work but obviously didn't work well enough to keep their mom alive. For this reason, Danny hated batteries with a passion, so he kept banging the remote on the table while Vince went to the TV to lower the volume the old-fashioned way.

Nick came in, all upset about something, and looked at Danny like the blaring volume was his fault.

"Turn that thing down!" he yelled, as if Danny hadn't already tried. But before Danny could say anything, Nick grabbed the remote from him to try it himself.

Fine, thought Danny. *Let him get the batteries.* Exasperated, he hurled himself backward onto the old sofa, once more giving rise to a cloud of ancient dust, and once more shaking the portrait of Great-aunt Greta—this time hard enough to knock it off the wall.

Although Nick had no way of knowing this—the moment he grabbed the remote from Danny was the moment of convergence of multiple cosmic strings of human fate. Mitch had felt it coming, but now he was much more preoccupied trying to give himself the Heimlich maneuver. Petula caught a glimpse of it in that telltale print from her camera—but right now she was much more interested in a certain metallic object toward which her body was falling, which might or might not pierce her heart.

All Nick knew as he aimed the remote at the TV and hit the power button was that all hell broke loose. A picture came crashing down from the wall behind him; Mitch hurled himself at the corner of an end table; and Nick's father burst up from the basement, screaming like a little girl.

Many lives were saved that day because of Mr. Slate's high-octave scream, which was substantially louder than the blasting TV. The scream made Caitlin drop the curler container in the attic, and the curlers rolled on the floor, sparking and sizzling a warning not to be touched.

The scream made Theo freeze an instant before he put the lethal peanut sauce in his mouth.

And the scream made Danny jump up from the sofa just as the huge oak picture frame crashed down on the spot where he had been sitting.

As for Mitch, the corner of the end table did the trick. It sent the jawbreaker flying toward the front door, where it ricocheted off the golden spike—not powerfully enough to knock it over, but enough to move it slightly off center—so that as Petula came down on it, it didn't pierce her heart but instead tore her blouse and gave her a nasty scrape on her side.

In the kitchen, Theo, thinking quickly, used his uneaten chicken satay skewer to scrape the surly black widows from Mr. Slate's arm before they bit him, and they were quickly crunched underfoot.

And in the living room the TV blared, as Nick's attempt to turn it off had absolutely no effect.

At least not on the TV.

. . .

Vince had never liked the childhood games they had made him play in kindergarten. Even then he'd had enough objectivity to notice how almost all of them were designed to isolate and/or humiliate a single child. Namely him. Someone is always left holding the hot potato. There are lots of ducks, but only one goose. Some poor slob has to be "it." And, as everybody knows, the cheese stands alone. Somewhere along the way, Vince decided to embrace it, and he made dark isolation a badge of honor.

As far as he was concerned, today's unpleasant turn of events was just an extension of a running theme. The universe was singling him out as "it" once again.

Vince had no way of knowing that the remote would not work for Danny because it was coded to Nick's bioelectrical fingerprint, so it would only work for him. Vince also had no way of knowing that it was not programmed for LifeLine Cable's 692 channels, because it didn't come from LifeLine Cable.

It was a gift of the Accelerati.

When Nick hit the power button, it shut down Vince's heart, just as it had done to poor Mr. Svedberg. There was never any hope.

Vince was dead before he hit the ground.

22 AS SEEN ON TV

"**N**oooo!"

Nick realized a moment too late what had happened. He felt the strange invisible pulse leave the "remote" when he pressed the OFF button, and he instinctively knew this was no ordinary device.

Vince had been at the TV, trying to lower the volume manually. He was directly in the line of the bioelectric pulse. Nick dropped the device and ran to him. He did not know CPR, he had only seen it on TV. Still, he desperately tried chest compressions until his father arrived. Mr. Slate didn't know CPR either, but had the benefit of seeing it on TV for many more years. He tried while Caitlin, who watched in horror from the stairs, pulled out her phone to dial 911.

When it was clear there was nothing they could do for Vince, Nick felt his rage turn from the device to the one person who had known that death was coming to Nick's door.

Petula was still nursing her own wound when Nick stormed toward her. It had only just registered with her that Vince was the one who died, not her—but she found her relief to be short lived.

"You knew!" Nick yelled at her. "You knew, and you did nothing to stop it!"

"I didn't know *what* would happen," she tried to explain. "I just knew *something* would. And I couldn't have stopped it even if I tried!"

"That doesn't matter!" he screamed. "Even if there's nothing you can do! Even if it's hopeless, you try! You try, and you don't stop trying! YOU'RE the one responsible for his death!"

She attempted to reason with him—to explain to him that you can't change a picture of the future. The best you can hope to do is frame it. But no matter what she said, Nick blamed her.

This was not the turn of events Petula was expecting. When death's scythe came swinging down, she thought Nick would finally understand and be grateful. That he would see how deeply she cared—for she risked her own life to come here and save him. But instead—

"Get out of here!" Nick growled. "Get out, or I swear to you, there'll be *two* bodies to be hauled away!"

And although Petula knew from her photograph that such an outcome was impossible, she said, "Well, all right, then. I guess I'll be going."

Then she turned and left quickly before anyone could see her tears.

After Petula left, Nick turned back to the terrible scene. Only once before had he experienced the all-consuming revelation that something unthinkable and irreversible had happened. Something that would change him and his life forever.

Immediately he was brought back to the aftermath of the fire—standing there helplessly on the lawn as his father raced toward the porch after his mother, the porch exploding before he could get there, the flames like the gates of hell themselves had opened up to consume everything Nick knew. And here again was a shell shock that didn't numb him but made him hyperaware of everything going on around him.

The sound of his father's grunts as he tried hopeless chest compressions on Vince's limp form . . . the sound of Caitlin's sobs as she spoke to the 911 dispatcher . . . Mitch standing just a few feet away, having pulled the string on his stupid machine but too afraid to let go or even to start a sentence . . . and the back door slamming as Theo slipped out to avoid any blame that might be cast.

Danny picked up the remote and looked to Nick for an explanation. Nick just slapped it out of his hand. The remote hadn't worked for Danny, and Nick instinctively knew that it was designed for Nick's use and Nick's use alone. No, the Accelerati wouldn't kill him, but their warning was to kill someone close to him—*anyone* close to him—by his own hand.

Something told Nick, just as it had when his mother had died, that this was the end of the world. But this time it was more than just a voice inside him.

Raging above this living room tragedy was a television that could not be silenced. And the newscaster, looking far more serious than newscasters usually do, spoke of something that made the death of Nick's friend seem insignificant when compared to the big picture.

The world was, indeed, about to end—at the cold, stony hands of Felicity Bonk.

23 BONK

One might expect that the announcement of the end of the world would bring about widespread panic and the looting of electronics stores—but such wholesale chaos takes time to come to a boil. Celestial Object Felicity Bonk was like that unexpected relative who calls to announce she's coming for a visit just as her car pulls into the driveway, leaving you no time to so much as clean house.

The world was ending on Monday. Period. The end.

As soon as the announcement went public, places of worship were packed with souls seeking salvation, but movie theaters were also packed by people who wanted one last escape into someone else's reality. When it comes to facing the end of the world, there is no wrong way to do it. Except, perhaps, for the guy who, in fine Archimedes fashion, ran naked through the Colorado Springs Museum's cactus garden. It wasn't "Eureka!" he was shouting, however.

The weekend airwaves were full of blameful pundits accusing world governments of either (a) hiding the truth, or (b) being too inept to know the truth before it was too late. But in the end, blame didn't matter. This was going down. No amount of warning could have stopped it or changed the outcome. Felicity Bonk was huge and fast and, regardless of where on the globe you stood, would be putting your lights out at 5:19 p.m. Mountain time, give or take a minute.

Monday morning found Colorado Springs in an odd state of heightened normality.

School buses ran, paperboys biked their routes, patrons of the new Starbucks downtown lamented all the TV shows that they would never see the conclusions of. When faced with the end of all things, it was much easier to nibble at it than take it in large, indigestible bites.

By and large, people went about their Monday-morning business as usual, because what else could they do? Surprisingly, about half of the students showed up at Nick's school, because their parents claimed they needed time to prepare—as if the end of the world required careful planning and well-packed luggage.

"Under the circumstances," Nick's math teacher announced first period, "Friday's test has been canceled." Several kids reflexively cheered, not quite getting that the test wasn't canceled, Friday was. To his credit, the math teacher was devoted to his subject, and they spent the hour calculating the speed and trajectory of the asteroid while the more advanced students tried to project how many pieces the earth would split into. The general consensus was sixteen.

Nick's English teacher chose to read them *Goodnight Moon*, then have them ponder its profundity in silence. And Nick's social studies teacher, Mr. Brown, drank Jack Daniel's straight from the bottle, laughed a lot, and kept saying, "What are they gonna do, fire me?"

To Nick's chagrin, Caitlin wasn't in school. She was at home at her parents' request, and she had also turned off her phone at her parents' request, because they did not want their daughter to spend her last day on earth engaged in "inane conversation,"

223

as they called it. And so instead Caitlin busied herself with her own form of coping. She frantically scanned and uploaded artwork, photos, and other bits and pieces of her life to the Cloud, fixed on the irrational belief that even after the earth was gone, the Cloud would remain.

Mitch wasn't in school, either. He chose to spend the day in bed, and his mother let him. He didn't sleep, however. Instead he tried to live his entire life in a single day. He closed his eyes and imagined everything. He would graduate from Yale (why not?), get a law degree from Harvard (why not?), he would prosecute the creeps who put his father in jail, and get them the death penalty (why not?). He would also marry Petula Grabowski-Jones, who, once she grew out of her awkward phase, would become a top supermodel (admittedly, he was pushing it). In his fantasy, Mitch found and returned all those stolen virtual pennies—and the banks were so grateful they let him keep half of the money. With that $375 million he bought his own island, from which he launched spacecraft for fun and profit.

He could have died a very old, very happy man that day, except for one thing. The Shut Up 'n Listen, which he had brought back home with him from Nick's house, had begun acting weirder than usual. . . .

As for Vince, his quick and painless death had allowed him to avoid all the unpleasantness. Which was a shame really, because more than anyone, Vince would have enjoyed watching the world end.

His mother, no longer as cheerful as her house, yet still incapable of being as somber as her son had been, clipped every last award-winning flower from her garden and filled her home with wreaths of living color, saving a single rose, which she brought to the mortuary to lay on Vince's chest.

She chose the one with the most thorns, because she knew that's what he would have wanted.

One might argue the importance of the large, earth-shattering moments in history. Few people realize that destiny turns not on the large moments, but on the tiny ones that go unnoticed. The moment Captain E. J. Smith chose to leave the *Titanic*'s engines at full speed ahead before retiring for the night. The moment Albert Einstein decided enough was enough and quit his dead-end job at the patent office. The moment Sir Isaac Newton, tired of the sun in his eyes, said, "What the heck, I'll sit under this apple tree."

The small unobserved moment, which led to a final and literally earth-shattering event, was the moment Nick Slate decided to have a garage sale. It was obvious to Nick that the asteroid had been pulled here by his brother's mitt—because in spite of the revolution and rotation of the earth, its impact point was calculated to be the very same sports complex where Danny had wished upon stars. Had Nick left the attic alone, his brother would never have used that mitt.

Throughout the day, Nick couldn't keep himself from looking around and beating himself silly with the inescapable fact that all this would be gone . . . because of him. Could things have been any worse if the Accelerati possessed all of Tesla's inventions?

Long before the end of the school day, most parents had gotten over their initial denial and came to pick their kids up. Nick's father was no exception. He, Danny, and Nick spent the afternoon together.

At four thirty—less than an hour before the end—Mr. Slate was barbecuing steaks he had been saving for next weekend. Inside, the TV was tuned to an impromptu *Twilight Zone* marathon, rather than the news, which seemed preoccupied with various celebrity end-of-the-world parties.

Nick considered his brother, who sat at the patio table looking somewhat bored by this whole end-of-the-world business.

Does he know? wondered Nick. *Has he figured out that his mitt brought all this about?*

"Danny?" he asked.

His brother lifted his head. Nick opened his mouth to say something, but then he realized there was nothing he could say. If his brother knew, there was no way to comfort him, and if he didn't know, there was no reason to burden him.

"What? Are you going to tell me you love me, like Dad's been doing all day?"

When Nick didn't answer, Danny looked down and made a fist. "You know what? I'm glad," he said. "Because it means we get to see Mom sooner."

Nick couldn't help going over to Danny to give him perhaps the biggest hug he'd ever given him.

"You got it right, Danny."

Danny shrugged. "If it was just me, I'd be afraid of dying. But since it's everybody, I'm not. Isn't that weird?"

Nick just grinned at him. "Why don't you help Dad with the steaks?"

Danny got up to join his father at the grill, and Nick went up to his bedroom to try to find at least some of the perspective that his little brother had. But he couldn't lie down in his happy place anymore, because there in the center of the attic were all the objects that he and Caitlin had collected. They were still arranged to form a partially completed contraption. Whatever it was, whatever it did, didn't matter now. Nick would never find out.

As he stared at it, a sense of anger built up inside of him. All that had happened, all that he had been through, everything he had sought to solve, was now meaningless. How could Tesla have been so foolish to leave these things for an unsuspecting world to find? Or perhaps that was his intention. A last cruel joke on a world that had refused to recognize and reward his brilliance.

Nick should have burned these things when he had the chance—but it wasn't too late to destroy them. Not with the force of an asteroid, but with the force of his own two hands.

He scanned the room and in the corner he spotted the baseball bat—the only object that he and Caitlin couldn't find a place for in the cluster of curious objects. He hefted the bat and looked at the stack in the center of room. *Here's for all the teams I'll never play on. Here's for the girl I'll never kiss. Here's for the man I'll never get to be. Here's for the stinking Accelerati. And here's for Vince.*

Then, with all the fury he could muster, he raised the bat, tensed his arms, and leaned back, ready to swing away.

When word made it through Petula's Nick-related misery that all human history was about to be history, she took it personally. How dare the universe end her existence at this most awful of moments?

Once she learned the precise day and time of the doomsday clock, she went out to her backyard exactly twenty-four hours before to snap a picture of the end of the world. Then she went to Ms. Planck's house to develop it. Ms. Planck was not home, so Petula had to force her way in through a basement window.

Upon developing the picture, it proved the truth of the inevitable. The image, taken in her own backyard, did not show a backyard. It showed flames and chunks of semimolten stone flying in all directions.

The camera did not lie. This was indeed the end of planet Earth. Until she saw the picture, it hadn't been real for Petula, but the truth drove through her heart in a way the golden spike had not.

At home, her parents were satisfied to yell at each other, trying to squeeze a life's worth of bickering into what little time they had left.

Now she would die without ever having Nick's affection. Her only consolation was that Nick would be dead, too.

To cheer herself up, Petula spent the rest of the evening making a list of all of the people she'd be happy were dead, from despicable dictators to all those annoying people who ride side by side in the bike lane like they own the road. Sequestered in her room, she had no way of knowing that Ms. Planck had come across her negative of the end of the world, and she had her own thoughts on the matter.

Petula did not attend school on Monday morning, because there was no one in particular she wanted to see or say a fond farewell to. The house was fairly quiet, since her parents were not talking to each other. Hemorrhoid, blissfully ignorant, was satisfied to gnaw on a rubber bone, which is probably what he would do in doggy heaven for all eternity.

Petula asked herself the question "If I had one day left to live, what would I do?" She had asked herself the question as a hypothetical many times before, and her hypothetical answers were always lofty and self-sacrificing, like feeding orphans or comforting the elderly. In reality, however, all she really wanted to do before the world ended was watch the original three *Star Wars* movies. She calculated that the asteroid would be merciful and end Life on Earth before she ever had to deal with Jar Jar Binks.

It was late afternoon, just before the second Death Star was blown to smithereens, and a few minutes until the earth would suffer the same fate, when Ms. Planck showed up at her door. . . .

Nick, in his attic, held the bat poised, his eyes fixed on Tesla's mysterious inventions stacked before him, and he stepped in to swing—

—then a voice behind him said, "Nick?"

He turned to see Mitch standing behind him, as always clinging to the Shut Up 'n Listen. He looked troubled, for obvious reasons.

"What are you doing here, Mitch?" Nick asked. "You should be home with your mom and sister."

"I was, but this thing—there's something *wrong* with it."

Nick found his frustration turning to Mitch. "Why should that matter now?"

Mitch shrugged awkwardly. He couldn't look Nick in the eye, and Nick realized that Mitch's presence here had little to do with the object in his hands.

"Why are you really here, Mitch?"

"Well . . . I was thinking. You know that Bonk thing is made mostly of copper ore. And my father stole three hundred and fifty truckloads of pennies. I mean, sure, they were virtual pennies—but don't you see the connection?"

Nick shook his head. "Not really."

"Both our lives were ruined by a whole bunch of copper.

There's got to be something to that. It's like . . . I don't know . . . God is winking at us."

Finally Nick smiled. "I get it, Mitch," he said. In these last minutes, Mitch didn't need his mom or sister—he needed a friend. Someone to connect with—identify with. "Pennies from heaven," Nick said.

"Yeah. Weird, huh?"

Nick glanced at the Shut Up 'n Listen. "So what's wrong with it?"

"Watch." Mitch pulled the string, and held it. "The asteroid headed to earth will—"

He let the string go, and the device said, *"Moooo!"*

He tried again. "The planet Earth is about to—"

"Oink! Oink!"

And a third time. "In less than twenty minutes, everyone on earth will—"

"Gobble gobble gobble!"

"See?" said Mitch. "It's broken. And at the worst possible time."

Nick considered it, and something tickled the back of his thoughts. Something he couldn't quite get at yet.

"Mitch . . ." he said uncertainly, ". . . what would happen if you let the machine speak first?"

Mitch shrugged and gave it a try. He pulled the string, and the machine said, *"The cow goes—"*

"Mooo!" said Mitch. He covered his mouth as if he had unexpectedly burped. "Sorry, he said, "that just came out."

"Do it again!" insisted Nick.

He pulled the string and the machine said, *"The pig goes—"*

"Oink! Oink!" Mitch said. "Hey, stop that!" As if Nick was making him do it. Could it be that Mitch had become so connected to the thing that he was finishing *its* thoughts? What if that connection went deeper? What if this device had given Mitch some sort of link above and beyond anything they could understand?

"Again," said Nick. "Keep on going!"

Mitch pulled the string over and over, letting it begin the sentences, then blurting out the conclusions himself.

"The chicken goes—"

"Cluck!"

"The dog goes—"

"Woof!"

"The farmer sells his corn—"

"—at five dollars and eighty-four cents per bushel as per today's commodities market." Mitch went wide-eyed at the words coming from his mouth. "How did I know that?"

"Keep going!" said Nick.

Mitch, feeling the power of the moment, had a sudden surge of adrenaline, pulled the string with all his might . . .

. . . and it broke.

The dial of the Shut Up 'n Listen spun itself silent.

"Well," said Mitch, "that's that."

But Nick wasn't so sure. "The amount of rainfall in Topeka, Kansas last month was—" he began.

And Mitch said, "—the highest of any city in Kansas."

"The Eiffel Tower—" began Nick.

"—has exactly three hundred and forty-seven pieces of used gum stuck to its girders," said Mitch.

"The end of the world will come—" began Nick.

"—in sixteen minutes and forty-three seconds, or in four-point-six billion years."

"Bingo!" said Nick.

"*N-42,*" responded Mitch. "The winning number on the highest bingo jackpot in history. How do I know these things?"

"You don't!" Nick told him. "Somehow you're channeling the universe! The Shut Up 'n Listen made you like one of those radio telescopes that can tune in the Big Bang."

Mitch nodded, in a kind of mental shell shock. "Right," he mumbled.

"And that whole thing about us being connected—maybe it's true. Maybe it's going to take the two of us to fix things."

"How?"

Nick tried to quickly wrap his mind around what he had just learned. There were two options now. Either the world would end in a few minutes, or it would end in a few billion years, like it was supposed to. Which meant the Felicity Bonk fiasco could be still be avoided. It all depended on the thought he started . . . and Mitch finished.

And so he said, "The answer to everything—"

And Mitch responded, "—is right in your hands."

"Aha! So there *is* an answer!" Nick shouted. "But what does it mean?"

"Well," asked Mitch, far more timidly than usual, "what's in your hands?"

Nick looked down at the baseball bat that he was, indeed, still holding. He had felt so compelled to swing it and smash Tesla's mad creations. Only now did he notice that it really didn't quite feel like any baseball bat he'd ever held. Its center of gravity was different, and it seemed to vibrate with some dormant resonance, like the wood of a guitar moments after the sound of the chord has faded.

Was there a place for this item in the incomplete machine before him? Or was its purpose separate? Still related, but separate. Like the way the glove drew Celestial Object Felicity Bonk toward its rendezvous with earth.

A glove and a bat. A baseball game would not be complete without both.

And lots of games are won in the bottom of the ninth.

24 PINCH HITTER

"**H**ey, Dad," said Nick, coming downstairs with Mitch. "How about a little baseball before we go?"

Nick's father had given up on the steaks and was sitting on the sofa with Danny, his arm around the boy. No music, no TV, no video games. The two were appreciating the mere act of living, the sounds of birds from outside, the dusty smell of the old house. In the end, Nick supposed, everyone would truly come to believe that the best things in life are free.

His father looked at him blank-eyed for a moment, then smiled.

"Before we go . . ." he repeated. "Yes, Nick. I think that's exactly what we should do."

And even Danny, who had not been near a baseball since his ill-fated cosmic encounter, agreed.

They didn't go to the sports complex. There was no time. Instead they went to the park just a block away. A grassy field with no baselines and a cheap roll-away backstop. They were the only ones there, of course.

Nick looked up to where the asteroid was coming in from high in the eastern sky. Then he checked his watch. Four minutes to impact, and the thing still appeared smaller than the moon in the sky.

"You'd think it would look bigger," Mitch said.

"It's only fifty miles wide," Nick pointed out. He supposed it would grow immense and swallow the sky only in the last seconds before striking.

In the field, Nick positioned himself on the pitcher's mound with the looming asteroid behind him. He held the ball signed by every member of the Tampa Bay Rays.

"Play deep center field," he told Danny and Mitch.

"But we don't have gloves," Danny said.

"It doesn't matter, Danny," Mitch told him, and the two ran out to center field.

At home plate, Nick's father brandished the bat on his shoulder, and then he said, "I love you, Nick."

Nick tried to keep his eyes clear, but he found it difficult. "I love you, too, Dad."

And with that, Nick wound up and threw the most important pitch of his life.

Newton's Third Law states that for every action there is an equal and opposite reaction. When a baseball is hit by a powerful force, its reaction is to fly out of the ballpark. It's simple physics that makes any ball game possible.

"Whiffin' Wayne" Slate knew this was to be the last at-bat of his life. His one chance to redeem himself. To get a piece of the ball. He eyed the asteroid in the sky, above his son's head. In defiance of fate, he would swing away and blast that baseball right toward that killer chunk of rock.

The determination with which he swung at his son's pitch was unparalleled by any swing of his life. This was his moment. He could feel his entire soul in that swing. And as the bat came around, he waited for the glorious feel of stitched leather against wood—that moment when the bat would connect with the ball.

Nick, however, had thrown a curveball—and a good one. The ball headed straight toward his father, then veered right, missing the end of the swinging bat by half an inch. The ball hit the backstop with a rattle, and fell to the ground, leaving Whiffin' Wayne Slate, sadly, unredeemed . . .

. . . but the force of that swing, magnified by the curious nature of that antique bat, had to go somewhere. . . .

A shock wave spread out from home plate like a sonic boom, blowing Nick, Danny, and Mitch off their feet. Beyond the park, it shattered windows, but the vast majority of its energy headed skyward. . . .

"I thought we might have a little chat, you and me, on this lovely afternoon," said Ms. Planck as she stood in Petula's doorway.

Petula glared at her. "What could there possibly be to talk about"—she glanced at her watch—"with four minutes left to the world?"

"This!" Ms. Planck held up a three-foot-long cardboard mailing tube.

"I'm sorry to tell you this," Petula said, "but I think you missed the FedEx cutoff time."

"Maybe not. May I come in?"

Petula's parents, at some point during the day, had made up and were now making goo-goo eyes at each other at the kitchen table. Not an image Petula wanted to take with her to oblivion. So she closed the door to the kitchen.

Ms. Planck sat on the sofa where Mitch had kissed Petula a few days earlier. On the coffee table she rolled out a print of the very picture Petula had taken yesterday—only this one was four feet across and three feet high. As with the smaller image, this poster-size one clearly showed the utter destruction that was just a few minutes away.

"I took the liberty of enlarging your excellent photograph—and look how clear it still is. You can see every texture of flaming rock—every speck of spewing lava. That box camera of yours is quite—shall we say—ahead of its time."

Petula crossed his arms. "So you figured it out. A big lot of good that does now."

Ms. Planck ignored Petula's fatalistic attitude. "Tell me, Petula, where did you take this picture?"

"My backyard."

Ms. Planck nodded. "Show me."

Petula led her out to the yard, full of crabgrass that would never be pulled and dandelions that would never go to seed.

"Show me where you were standing," Ms. Planck said calmly.

"Why?" Petula demanded.

"Humor me."

Petula moved to the spot where she took the picture the day before, and Ms. Planck stood about six feet in front of her. Then she unrolled the large image of Armageddon, which stretched the full width of her reach.

"I would bet," Ms. Planck said, "that at precisely five nineteen, this will reflect the scene that your camera is destined to capture."

"Yeah. So?"

"Look at your watch, Petula."

Petula glanced at her watch to reveal that the time was five nineteen.

"Wait . . . but . . . I don't understand," Petula stammered.

But then she saw Ms. Planck's smiling eyes above the oversize image, and the truth hit her with the force of a meteor.

"I didn't take a picture of the end of the world!" Petula said. "I took a picture *of a picture* of the end of the world."

Petula held up her fingers in a square shape like a viewfinder, to see the image that a camera would see. The old box camera had, indeed, taken a picture of this exact moment in time.

"When you know the future," Ms. Planck said, echoing a thought Petula already had, "you can either let that future happen to you, or be the one to create it."

And at that moment a shock wave hit them with such power that it knocked them off their feet and tore the large photograph from Ms. Planck's hands. The photo flew off into the sky like a lost kite.

At home plate, Nick's dad looked morosely down at the ball he had missed. He picked it up and sighed. "I guess it's true, then. Now and forever I'll always be Whiffin' Wayne Slate."

Nick came running to him from the pitcher's mound, wearing a huge grin. Mr. Slate marveled at his son's ability to smile at a time like this.

Danny ran over a moment later, bewildered, with Mitch close behind. "What was that?" Danny said. "I thought it was the asteroid."

"If it was, we wouldn't be here," Mitch pointed out.

"That," said Nick, "was a grand slam."

"In case you didn't notice, I missed the ball," his father said.

But the grin didn't leave Nick's face. "Then how come the bat is cracked?"

Mr. Slate looked down, and sure enough, the bat had split lengthwise down the middle.

"Son of a gun. You're right."

The truth didn't quite fall into place until he looked up and saw that the asteroid was no longer growing larger. In fact, it seemed slightly smaller, and to be slipping sideways across the sky. None of them was willing to speak aloud the thought that something had changed—as if saying it would jinx it.

The four of them watched Celestial Object Felicity Bonk for five minutes, then ten minutes, then twenty—long after it was supposed to have struck Colorado Springs.

Mr. Slate picked up the cracked bat. Sometimes bats had illegal cork cores to give them greater hitting power. He had no idea what was in the core of this particular bat, and he suspected he would never know—but in the end it didn't matter. All that mattered was the result. He thought about the events of the past few weeks. The baseball glove that pulled things from the heavens, and now a bat that sent them back. And he marveled.

25 THINGS WE DON'T FULLY UNDERSTAND

When it was clear that the earth was still here, and would remain here indefinitely, people got pissed off. Across the globe, valuable possessions had been given away, and guilty consciences had been purged by shocking confessions, all in the belief that no one would live to regret it.

But the astronomers were wrong, and Felicity Bonk turned out to be a fickle lover. For although she had brazenly courted the planet, something had knocked her off her intended path, leaving her in a harmless, platonic orbit that barely even affected the tides.

The following morning a national holiday was declared, and a parade was established, with the real Felicity Bonk herself riding and waving from the lead float, as if she had done anything more than pay ten bucks for a big rock. By noon, people were already arguing about what to call the day, and whether or not it should be shifted to a Monday in future years to create a three-day weekend. Regardless, "Bonk Tuesday," as it was currently called, was sure to be celebrated in one form or another for years to come.

Petula, in spite of resolving not to, called Mitch that morning. "I told myself that the world would have to end before I accepted your invitation to the movies," she said. "Close enough." Then she gave him the time, place, and movie of her choosing, and suggested that a corsage would not be inappropriate.

Mitch, however, had other plans. "Actually, I'm going to visit my father today," he told her. "After what happened yesterday, I've really come to appreciate what little time I get with him."

"What?!" said Petula, suitably disgusted. "Is your father more important than a date with me?"

"Well . . . yes," he told her reluctantly, "but you're important, too."

"Fine. You will not get another chance. How about Saturday?"

He agreed, and she hung up on him, feeling frustrated by her own happiness over the matter.

That afternoon, Petula joined Ms. Planck for a stroll in Acacia Park, where they had first bonded over photography.

"The thing to keep in mind," Ms. Planck said, "is that you and I saved the world."

"How do you figure?"

"Simple," Ms. Planck explained. "If we hadn't intervened, with me holding up the enlargement at the precise time and place for you to catch it with the box camera, then your picture of the end of the world would have been the real thing. Thanks to us, it wasn't."

"I still don't get it," Petula confessed. "If the camera took a picture of a picture, where did the original image come from?"

Ms. Planck smiled. "Ah, I love a good paradox. Don't you?" They walked on a bit. "Think about it when you go to bed," she told Petula. "It's better than counting sheep."

That made Petula smile.

It was late afternoon. The sound of children in the playground became distant as they neared Ms. Planck's town house. In this quiet part of the park, they were very much alone. That's when Ms. Planck knelt down in front of Petula. Smiling warmly, she said, "I have a gift for you. Something very special to commemorate your noble actions."

She opened a small jewelry box, revealing a shiny gold pin in the shape of the letter *A*, but with the symbol for infinity through its center.

"Wear this close to your heart, Petula," Ms. Planck told her, "but don't let anyone see it."

"What is it?"

"It's a sign that you belong to a very special organization."

Petula turned the small pin over in her hands, watching it catch the light. No one had ever given her a gift of jewelry before, unless you count the friendship ring she wore on her pinkie. But she had bought that for herself.

"This organization . . . is it secret?"

"Very much so. A group of people wise beyond words, shrewd beyond measure, and destined to steer the course of all mankind."

Petula liked the sound of that, so she fastened the pin beneath the collar of her blouse, hidden from view.

"Thank you, Ms. Planck," Petula said. "But if you're part of this group, why do you serve us lunch?"

"We're in all walks of life, honey," Ms. Planck told her with the slightest of grins. "That's how we spot those who belong among us . . . and how we monitor certain persons of interest."

"So," said Petula, "you're undercover."

Ms. Planck stood up and continued walking beside her. "I prefer to call it hiding in plain sight."

Petula could relate. In a sense she felt like she'd been hiding in plain sight all her life, but now it would be with a purpose.

She thought about how Nick Slate had humiliated her, when all she had tried to do was save him. An icy vein of anger coursed through her.

"What are you thinking?" asked Ms. Planck.

"I was thinking that success is the best revenge."

"No, dear," Ms. Planck corrected. "Revenge is the best revenge. But we'll have plenty of time to discuss such things."

"Will I meet other members of this club," Petula asked, "and find out more about what you do?"

"You will," Ms. Planck said, "you will. And you can't imagine how thrilling your life is about to become."

Only now that the crisis had been averted did Nick's and Caitlin's attention turn to their fallen friend. They sat in Nick's room, Caitlin tearful and Nick nearly so, as they lamented how poor Vince was caught squarely in the wrong place at the wrong time. Although Nick knew that it had been the Accelerati's doing, he couldn't get past the fact that it was his hand that had aimed and fired the weapon that killed him.

"You can't think that way," Caitlin said, her voice soothing. "If you do, then they win." But Nick just shook his head. "It could have been any of us," Caitlin continued. "Your father. Your brother."

"Am I supposed to be happy it was Vince instead of them? Or you? It shouldn't have been anyone."

Caitlin dropped her shoulders and sighed. "I'm sorry. I'm just trying to help."

Nick gently touched her knee, a gesture that would have felt terribly awkward a week ago. "I know," he said. "Thanks."

They sat in silence for a moment, pondering Tesla's incomplete device before them.

"Without all the pieces," Caitlin said, "we'll never get it to work. In fact, we'll probably never even know exactly what it does."

"I'm not so sure of that," said Nick. He stood up and approached the odd-looking device, taking it in from all angles, as he had done since yesterday. "Did you know that the asteroid is made mostly of copper ore?" he asked. "NASA's already talking about sending up a mining probe."

"Great," said Caitlin. "So what?"

"The thing is," said Nick slowly, "I've been thinking. The core of the earth is mostly iron, right? That's why we have a humongous magnetic field. And you know what happens when you send a bunch of copper spinning around a magnetic field?"

Caitlin thought for a moment and gasped. "It's a generator."

"One so big it could power the entire world. For free . . . or for *F.R.E.E.* . . ."

"The 'Far Range Energy Emitter,'" Caitlin said.

"Exactly. The only device that can harness that energy." Nick glanced at Tesla's incomplete electronic puzzle, standing in the sweet spot of his room right beneath the pyramidal skylight, waiting for the rest of its wayward parts. Yet even incomplete, the machine gave off a sort of electric anticipation. It was as if somehow Tesla had planned for all of this—the garage sale, the asteroid, Nick's father's triumphant baseball swing.

"I know this sounds weird," Nick told Caitlin, "but it's like we're all a part of this machine. The things we've done—the things we still have to do—they're all connected."

He thought Caitlin might think he was nuts, but instead she said, "I know exactly what you mean."

The ramifications made them both light-headed. Nick had to sit down on his bed. And when he did, he felt something crinkle beneath the covers.

Caitlin smirked. "Eating chips in bed?"

"That wasn't a chip."

Nick threw back the covers to find a picture. Not of someone, but something. A starscape.

"I know what that is," said Caitlin. "It's the Horsehead Nebula."

Nick went slightly pale. "The Accelerati." There was no other explanation. They had been here, and they had left the Horsehead in his bed as a warning.

He turned it over. On the back was a paraphrase of a quote attributed to the Accelerati's founder, Thomas Edison. *We never do anything by accident.*

Nick took a deep breath and said to Caitlin, "Well, neither did Tesla. And neither do I." He crumpled up the photo in his hand.

Then he went to the device and made a decision. No outcome is certain, even when it seems so. Fates can change with the swing of a bat, or the flip of a switch, or the closing of a circuit. The somewhat mad genius who had orchestrated the world's potential end, its potential salvation, and all the potential energy it might ever need, knew that better than anyone.

It all came down to how far you dared to go to accomplish what the world thinks can't be done.

And so, taking a lesson from Tesla, Nick knelt down and pulled the wet cell out from the heart of the device, because currently it was needed elsewhere.

As he tugged it out, the toaster, perched slightly higher, fell, once again hitting him on the head.

"Ow," he said, putting his hand to his forehead. Caitlin hurried over to him. "Great," Nick said, "just what I need; another trip to the emergency room."

"Let me see," Caitlin said, taking his hand and moving it

away. "Well, it's not bleeding, although you may have a nasty bump." Then she took his head in his hands, leaned forward, and kissed it. "There. All better."

For a few seconds Nick felt like he had been knocked off his feet by Tesla's cosmic bat, but he only smiled. "That's much better medicine than stitches," he told her. Then he stood up and headed for the ladder. "Come on."

"Where are we going?" Caitlin asked, standing up.

"Where do you think?" he said. "To find Vince."

Caitlin glanced at the wet cell in his hands and understood. "You can't be serious."

"Why not?"

Caitlin stuttered. "I mean, it's not like we can keep that thing hooked to him twenty-four/seven. . . ."

Nick shrugged. "Why not?"

And since Caitlin could not find any reason why not, she shrugged back and said, "Okay."

"Besides, it's what Vince always wanted, isn't it? To be undead. He was already something of a zombie. Now it will be official."

"Shouldn't it bother us?" Caitlin asked as they clattered down the ladder. "Messing with life and death and things we don't fully understand?"

"If we fully understood them," said Nick, "what would be the point of messing with them?"

And together Nick and Caitlin set out into the bright afternoon, their hearts filled with a rare and special joy, as they went to reanimate their dead friend.

Camera

Battery

Ball Glove

Toaster

Reel-to-Reel

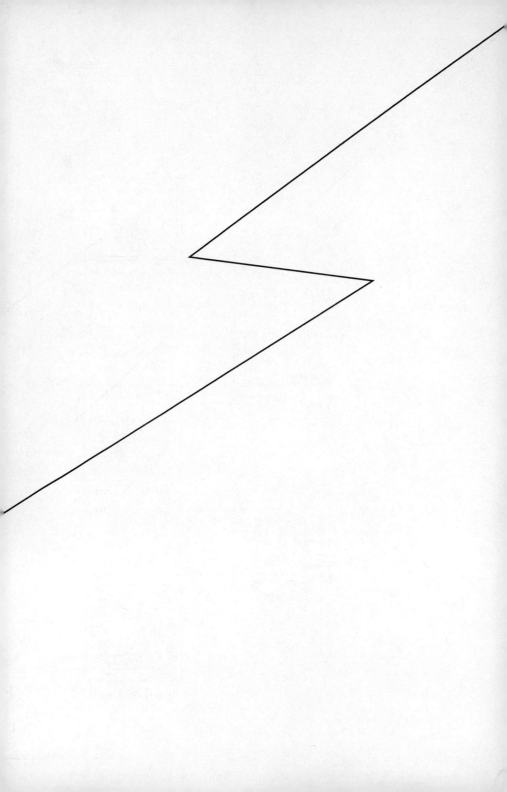